Books by Lani Diane Rich

Maybe Baby
Time Off for Good Behavior

Maybe Baby

Lani Diane Rich

WARNER

FOREVER

NEW YORK   BOSTON

Copyright © 2005 by Lani Diane Rich
Excerpts from *Ex and The Single Girl* copyright © 2005 by Lani Diane Rich.
All rights reserved. No part of this book may be reproduced in any form or by any electronic or mechanical means, including information storage and retrieval systems, without permission in writing from the publisher, except by a reviewer who may quote brief passages in a review.

Cover design by Diane Luger
Cover illustration by Robert Wagt
Book design by Stratford Publishing Services, Inc.

Warner Books

Time Warner Book Group
1271 Avenue of the Americas
New York, NY 10020
Visit our Web site at www.twbookmark.com

Printed in the United States of America

First Paperback Printing: June 2005

10 9 8 7 6 5 4 3 2 1

To the Kakapo, a beautiful, unique, and fascinating bird that takes a lot of hits in the course of this book. You are not a fat, ugly, smelly, obnoxious green chicken. I take it all back.

Acknowledgments

Thanks are always inadequate for the love and support it takes from friends, family, and colleagues to see a writer through a book. However, I'm gonna do the best I can, extending my heartfelt thanks to . . .

. . . my husband Fish and my daughters Sweetness and Light, for allowing me to spend six months writing furiously in the closet without calling for a psych eval.

. . . the Cherries, for their tireless support as I learned how to write a romance, learned how to *re*write a romance, and suffered through SOICO. Special Cherry love to Jenny Crusie and Judith Ivory, whose encouragement in the early days kept me going, and to Robin La Fevers, for her saintly patience through many frantic e-mails and panicked phone calls. Your halo's in the mail, babe.

. . . my fellow Literary Chicks, Alesia Holliday and Michelle Cunnah, for providing sympathy for my artistic angst while at the same time not letting me take myself too seriously.

. . . Eileen Connell, Cate Diede and Rebecca Rohan, for their critiques and cheerleading; my mother, Joyce Rich, for the stuffed parrot mascot; the New York State Wineries, for the wine that gave me the most wonderful "research" experience of my career; and Paul Jansen, of New Zealand's Kakapo Recovery Programme, for his willingness to answer questions that began with, "Let's say I smuggled a Kakapo into New York City . . ."

To my editor Beth de Guzman, for her faith in me. To my agent Stephanie Kip Rostan, for restoring my faith in myself. You're the dream team, girls.

And, always, to the readers; thanks for reading my book. I hope you love it as much as I do.

Maybe Baby

One

"I, Dana Elizabeth Wiley, take you, Nick . . ."

Her groom blinked. "Um, who?"

A fly zipped past her eyes, and Dana swatted at it with her bouquet, then puffed up a breath of air, fluffing her bangs away from where they tickled her forehead. It was another moment before she realized everyone in the rec room at the Rosemont Home of Central New York was watching her expectantly. She blinked.

"Hmm? Sorry? What?"

Her groom, a seventeen-year-old kid from Laundry with the longest and skinniest neck she'd ever seen, leaned forward. "Who's Nick?"

Dana felt her heart take a tumble at the mention of the name.

"What? Nick's no one. No one's Nick. Why? Did I say Nick?"

The groom gave her a small smile. "Yeah. Kinda."

She turned and looked at Milo, her boss and daily tor-mentor. The Bible he was holding was upside down.

"Did I say Nick?" she asked him.

"Doesn't matter," Milo singsonged through clenched teeth and a plastic smile as he nodded toward the guests. "There's a cross-stitch event at eleven. Let's move it along, people."

A cross-stitch event. *Ah, Milo.*

Dana glanced around. Two dozen aged, happy faces stared back at her, none of whom knew who she was or would even remember by dinnertime that they'd been to a wedding. According to Milo, gatherings such as weddings, graduations, and baptisms—even pretend ones—raised the morale of the Alzheimer's residents by 53 percent. Of course, it was patently ridiculous to quantify morale, but who was she to question? As Milo liked to remind her, she was just a secretary with a wedding dress that still fit. Nothing more.

She blew another noisy puff of air toward her forehead and looked at the groom, who had been recruited at the last minute when her usual groom, Mark from Accounts, called in with a bad case of I-really-don't-feel-like-it. The Laundry Kid was heavily freckled and looked a little out of his element in Mark's faded tux, which was two sizes too big, ruffled at the neck, and powder blue. Poor kid. She pulled on a smile and leaned toward him. "I'm sorry. What's your name again?"

He tugged at his collar. "Um, Chad."

Dana leaned back. "I, Dana Wiley, take you, Chad . . ." She paused, waiting for Chad to cue her with his last name. He stared at her blankly. She improvised. ". . . O'Laundry-guy . . ."

"Oh, sorry!" he said, realizing his omission. "Actually, it's McCamish."

"Doesn't matter," Milo admonished through a false and overly toothy smile. Dana exchanged a look with Chad. *Ah, Milo.*

"To be my lawfully wedded husband," Milo prompted.

"To be my lawfully wedded husband," Dana recited. She felt a tension pain in her shoulder, followed by a roiling in her stomach.

Had she really said *Nick*?

Why would she say *Nick*? Not that it mattered much, except that if her subconscious was trying to get a point across, having her say her ex-fiancé's name in the middle of a fake wedding was a really rude way to do it, far as she was concerned.

"For richer, for poorer . . . ," Milo read.

"For richer, for poorer . . ." She ran one satin-gloved hand over her hip, smoothing the skirt of her dress. It was a lovely dress; a clean, sleeveless A-line, no lace or decorative hoo-hah sewn in to clutter things up. She always imagined that she looked a bit like Audrey Hepburn in it, with its ten-foot train and satin gloves that didn't give up until they reached her upper arm. And she would be Hepburnish, if she was taller and less curvy and could pull off the short hair thing without looking like a boy.

Regardless, the dress was lovely. Damn shame it was cursed. On the first day she wore it, she got into a fender-bender with a cop, accidentally set a priest on fire, and ran out of the church, leaving a stunned Nicholas James Maybe in her wake.

And yet I put it on twice a week to get out of filing, she thought. *I'm so cheap.*

"Dana."

She blinked. "Hmm?"

Milo gave her the death glare and enunciated his words carefully. "In sickness and in health . . ."

Oh. Yes. "In sickness and in health . . ."

Although really, if she looked at things practically and analyzed all events with an unemotional, objective eye, Dana would have to admit that the problem was probably not the dress.

It was her. She had a tendency to be in the wrong place at the wrong time, dress or no dress. Take the night of her would-be wedding, for instance, when she'd come back to the house she shared with Nick on the edge of the family vineyard. After an afternoon of self-loathing and excessive drinking among the lonely reception trappings at the Wiley Wines bar-slash-gift shop, she ran to the house to tell Nick that she'd made a horrible mistake, and found him in the embrace of a half-naked woman. And not just *any* woman, either. Melanie Biggs, Dana's nemesis since high school, and quite possibly the third Antichrist of which Nostradamus spoke.

Yeah. That had been bad. And Dana had changed into a nice little sweater-and-jeans ensemble by that point, so . . . probably not the dress.

Milo cleared his throat with obvious irritation, and Dana snapped back to the moment. She'd missed another cue. Ah, well. What did it matter anyway?

"Love, honor, and obey," she rattled out, "from this day forward till death do us part, yadda yadda yadda." She smiled at Chad. "Your turn."

Milo's face tightened with irritation, but he just gave a martyr's sigh and moved on. "I, Chad McCamish . . ."

The first couple of times she'd done the fake weddings, she really played it up, the blushing bride and all. Now, pfffft, morale-schmorale, no one cared. She could show up in a T-shirt and jeans singing "La Cucaracha" and residents would be just as happy. The cynic in her believed the buffet was the actual culprit behind the 53 percent jump in morale—Gladys from the kitchen made a killer Waldorf salad—but it didn't matter. The residents were happy, Milo got his funding, and Dana got out of filing.

Everybody plays, everybody wins.

". . . take you, Dana Wiley, to be my lawfully wedded wife . . ."

Had she really said *Nick*? Why would she do that? She hadn't even thought about Nick in . . . well, okay, not since last night, but that was just because she'd caught a glimpse of Dennis Franz having wine in an *NYPD Blue* rerun and . . . well, Nick managed a wine bar in Manhattan. But before that it had been a while. Days, even. Weeks probably. And since she'd actually seen him, it had been longer. Much longer.

Six years as a matter of fact.

Wait.

Six years?

Dana gasped and put one daintily gloved hand to her mouth.

"What's today's date?" she blurted.

"In sickness and in . . . what?" Chad said, then glanced awkwardly at his watch. "Uh . . . the fifteenth."

Her heart sank. "October fifteenth?"

Milo cleared his throat. "May we continue?"

Dana nodded and swallowed hard. It wasn't just six

years since she'd seen Nick. It was six years *to the day.* Six years since what was supposed to be the best day of her life had turned into the worst day of her life. She felt heat rise up the back of her neck, soon to be followed by the cold sweat. How had she forgotten?

Well, actually, she *hadn't* forgotten. She'd said *Nick.*

Stupid subconscious.

She closed her eyes, and time slowed as the memory of that day hit her in one powerful wave. Suddenly, she was back in St. Christopher's, at her own wedding, pulling Nick aside while Father Michael doused the fire out of his robes with the holy water.

I can't do this.

'Course you can, Diz, he'd said, using his pet name for her—a play on her first and middle names.

No, she'd said, feeling all her breath go out of her body as she took a step backward. *I can't.*

Nick's eyebrows knit together. *What are you talking about?*

What I've been talking about for the past year, Nick.

Understanding washed over his face, and he sighed. *Come on, Dana. We've been through this. We're not your parents.*

No, she said. *We'll find our own special way to destroy each other. But it'll still happen.*

Nick put his hands, warm and strong, on either side of her face. He leaned his face down toward hers and smiled, his eyes sparkling at the edges the way they did whenever he looked at her. That was when it occurred to her that he'd probably never touch her that way again, and she started to cry.

It won't happen, he said. *I promise you. You're just*

panicked. It'll pass, and when it does, I'll be right there with you.

She swiped at her face and glanced at Father Michael, who was patting a towel on the singed, wet sleeve of his robe.

But I set the priest on fire. It's a sign.

Nick smiled, brushed her bangs away from her forehead. *Don't read anything into that. It was an accident.*

No. It's an omen. Don't you see that? I can't do this, Nick.

His eyes stopped sparkling, and his smile disappeared. *Dana. I won't let it happen. Just trust me.*

For a moment, she'd considered just sucking it up and getting through the ceremony, but the very idea made her chest constrict, and she couldn't breathe. She touched Nick's face and knew in that moment that her heart would never beat right again.

She opened her mouth to tell him she loved him, that it wasn't him she didn't trust, it was marriage, but it was all too pathetic to say out loud. Sure, she loved him, so much it made her soul hurt, but that wasn't going to keep her from running, so what was the point in saying it? She wheeled around and ran down the aisle, the wrong way, the faces of the stunned guests flowing together as she rushed past them, the only sound in her head that of her elegant, Hepburnish, cursed dress swishing behind her as she negotiated the church steps two at a time.

She opened her eyes, crashing down back in the rec room of the Rosemont Home. Panic gripped her as the knowledge she'd been fighting for six years suddenly descended on her in a heart-stopping moment of razor-sharp clarity.

Dana Maybe. That's who I should have been.

"Oh my God," she whispered.

"Are you okay?" Chad whispered, a concerned look on his face. "You kinda look like you're gonna hurl."

Dana nodded and let out a squeak that might have passed for "Fine," if she could have gotten some breath in her lungs.

No, no, no, she thought. *I've made my peace with this. I did the right thing. It was best for both of us. It was . . .*

. . . a mistake.

Dana put her hand to her chest. Her heart pounded out a lopsided rhythm as she fought the clarity washing over her.

Dana Maybe.

"Oh, crap," she breathed.

"Till death do us part." Milo slammed the Bible shut and shot a look of stern disapproval at Dana. "You may kiss the bride."

Chad leaned forward awkwardly, he and Dana exchanged a lightning-quick half-lips, half-cheek smooch. She wanted to grab him by the shoulders and shake him, tell him to take his youth and run, that adulthood was for the birds, and that once you hit the age of consent one bad choice could effectively ruin your whole life, but Milo clapped his hands together and broke the moment.

"Buffet time!"

The residents shuffled over to the buffet table, and even the random choruses of "Wasn't she just lovely?" and et cetera didn't do much to allay the panic that was winding its way through Dana's gut. She stood, riveted to her spot. Tears crowded behind her eyes, and she blinked hard, reminding herself of the morning after the wedding that wasn't, when Melanie Biggs had found Dana at the winery to tell Dana not to worry, she'd been there to comfort Nick.

All night long.

She swallowed again. Somehow—despite Melanie, despite the deaf ear Nick had turned to Dana's concerns about marriage as an institution—the certainty that she'd made a mammoth, life-destroying mistake lodged itself in her gut and showed no signs of leaving.

And there she was, in the rec room of an old-age home, where she was doomed to repeat forever the one thing she hadn't been able to get right when it mattered.

Chad approached her, holding a plate with a piece of cake on it.

"You'd better get over there," he said, motioning toward the buffet table with his plastic fork. "You wait any longer, there will be nothing left."

Dana swallowed hard against the panic rising in her throat, and the clarity faded away, leaving a hollow coldness in its wake.

"You know what?" she said, gathering her train in one arm and whipping the veil off her head with the other. "I have a headache. Cramps. I think I'm coming down with something. A flu. Tell Milo for me, will you?"

Chad blinked. "Um. Okay. You gonna be all right?"

"Anything's possible." She grabbed her bag from behind the altar and hurried out of the room, oddly comforted by the familiarity of the swishing sound the dress made when she ran.

Two

Nick Maybe drummed his fingers against the bar at Murphy's, the sound echoing across the polished wooden surfaces in the empty room. Despite having managed the place—and having lived in the apartment directly above it—for six years, he couldn't get used to it in the daytime. At night, it was full of trendy Manhattanites who came for the wine tasting, the food, and the opportunity to show everyone that they were both willing and able to drop fifty bucks on a glass of wine. But at least then it was alive. During the day, it was just . . .

. . . lonely.

He tossed a disgruntled glance at the clock on the wall. Eleven wasn't early for people with regular jobs, but considering his day didn't start until 5 P.M. and often didn't end until 4 A.M., eleven might as well be the crack of dawn. Most people knew better than to call him before one.

Babs Wiley McGregor, however, wasn't most people. She called whenever she felt like it, and when she did, it was usually for the same reason. Well, this time, Nick decided, it would be different. This time, he'd just say no and go back to bed. Then he'd do his last shift at Murphy's, spend the next five days packing, hop his flight on Saturday, and that would be that.

This phase of his life would finally be over.

Nick pushed himself up from the bar and walked over to the espresso machine. Dealing with Babs at this time of day definitely called for him to be on his toes. He felt a twinge in his neck as he tamped the fine coffee grounds into the metal porta-filter and craned his head to the side to work out the kink. It was way past time to get out of New York, way past time to get away from Babs Wiley McGregor and everything she represented.

Like, for instance, her daughter.

Dana. A flash of her face shot through his memory. Chestnut curls catching fire in the sun. Freckles scattered across her nose and cheeks. Crisp blue eyes, somehow hot and cold at the same time. Full lips, smiling to reveal a wicked sense of humor and slightly crooked teeth.

And, of course, there was the view from the back, as she ran down the aisle of St. Christopher's, leaving him holding a set of meaningless rings in front of 150 of their closest.

Nick shook his head.

"Way past time," he muttered.

There was a tap on the door. Nick glanced through the window and saw the outline of a woman he knew was Babs. Tall, thin, graceful. Clad in a white outfit with clean lines and wearing, if he wasn't mistaken, a tremendous white hat with some sort of pink fluff sticking out of the top.

He situated two espresso cups beneath the filter and headed for the door.

"Morning, Babs," he said. "Nice hat."

"There was a man on the street outside who just told me I was a hottie," she said, lifting up on her toes to kiss him on the cheek as she entered the bar. "He was buck-ass naked, so I didn't respond, but I was flattered just the same. When you get to be my age, you take your compliments where you can get them."

Nick laughed and shut the door behind her as she floated into the bar. She was skating over the back end of her fifties, and still she moved like a girl. Maybe not as quickly as she used to; she'd definitely slowed down some. But there was a weightlessness to her step, as though there wasn't a worry in the world that could hold her down.

Unlike Dana, who worried about everything, who never took a risk, who held to the status quo like it was a damn life raft.

Let it go already, Maybe, Nick thought. *Life's too damn short.*

"Whatever you're here for, Babs," Nick said as he rounded the bar and tended to the espresso, "the answer is no."

She put her purse on one stool and settled herself on another. "Well, that's rude."

"Sorry. No time to be polite. Espresso?"

"Please," she said. "And how do you know I was coming here to ask for something? Maybe I was just stopping by to spend some time with you before you abandon me for California."

Nick chuckled as he placed the espresso in front of her. "And she comes out swinging."

"I mean, is it so unreasonable that I would simply want to have a nice visit before you hop a flight and leave me forever?"

"I'm going to San Diego," Nick said for what felt like the zillionth time, "not Siberia."

"Oh, pooh." Babs waved her hand dismissively and pouted. "I can't imagine anything you can get in California that you can't get right here in Manhattan."

"Oh, I don't know. Clean air. Ocean breezes. Personal space." He shot her a grim smile. "How much time you got?"

Babs held her hand up. "No need. It's all a bunch of poppycock, anyway."

Nick raised an eyebrow. "Poppy-what?"

She placed her elbows on the bar and leaned forward, her face full of knowing accusation. "You can spout off all you want about clean ocean personal space blah blah blah. I know why you're really going to California, and I don't mind telling you, I think it's just foolish."

Nick rolled his eyes. *Here we go.* "I can put that espresso in a to-go cup, you know."

"I still can't believe you took a job working for Melanie Biggs," she said, pointedly ignoring him. "The woman is the Antichrist, you know. That's why she never wears her hair up."

"What?"

Babs motioned toward the back of her head. "Mark of the beast, right there at the nape of her neck. I've seen it."

"That's a birthmark," Nick said.

"In the shape of the three sixes?"

Nick heaved a rough sigh, knowing where the conversation was going and knowing also that once Babs got on a riff about Melanie Biggs, there was no stopping her.

"You know she just wants to take you from Dana."

"Kinda hard to take me from someone I haven't spoken to in six years."

"She's always had it in for Dana, ever since you all were in high school together. You're the one thing she could never take away, and she's obsessed. She always has been."

"Is my hearing going, or did you just bring up high school?"

"A woman can hold a grudge for a very long time."

"You don't say," Nick responded flatly.

"You can't trust her to keep up her end of this bargain," Babs continued. "We don't know if that nonsense about taking over Dana's winery is even true. It's not exactly like Melanie has a history of telling the truth."

"Drop it, Babs."

"Remember when she told Dana you two had slept together after the wedding? Big fat lie."

Nick grabbed a bar towel and clenched it in his fist. "Which Dana was quick to believe, as I recall."

"Only because you let her believe it."

"I was already out of town," Nick said. "I didn't even know what Melanie said until you told me about it. And why exactly are we having this conversation again?"

Babs tossed one arm up in the air dramatically. "Because apparently we need to. You seem to have entirely blotted out the Antichrist portion of the program."

Nick started wiping down the bar, even though it was clean. "No, I got it. Hair down. Mark of the beast."

"Did I mention the toads that fall out of the sky when she walks down the sidewalk?"

He tossed the towel over his shoulder. "Not today."

"And this latest manipulation about taking over Dana's winery is just nonsense. Dana hasn't said anything to me about being in trouble."

"Dana hasn't said much to you about anything."

Babs picked up her espresso cup and balanced it between the fingertips of each hand, but didn't drink. Nick instantly regretted what he'd said. This was one of many reasons he didn't like talking about Dana with Babs. Too many land mines, for both of them.

"I'm sorry," he said. "I didn't mean that the way it sounded."

Babs sighed and put the cup down. "Not your fault. I know Dana and I aren't exactly close. But still, if it were true—"

"It doesn't matter if it's true," Nick said, cutting her off. "I didn't accept the job just to keep Melanie away from Dana."

Babs narrowed her eyes at him. "Then why?"

"It's just time for me to move on," he said abruptly, leaning back against the wall as the all-too-familiar guilt washed over him. He'd had enough of the guilt. Guilt over not listening to Dana closely enough before the wedding, not fully understanding her qualms about marriage, not giving her more time, not waiting for her to really be ready. Guilt over being so angry that he'd let Dana believe he'd slept with Melanie that night. Guilt that by the time he'd gotten over the anger, he'd been too much of a coward to go see her and tell her the truth. It was guilt that prompted him to spend six years looking after Babs in some subconscious attempt to make it up to Dana, and now that he knew it wasn't ever going to be right, he had guilt over abandoning Babs. Now, he was so desperate to get it all behind him that he'd made a flimsy deal with Melanie Biggs just to get out. As noble as it might have seemed on the surface to accept the job in exchange for Melanie's solemn vow to keep her mitts off Dana's winery, the reality was, he wasn't doing it to save Dana.

He was doing it to save himself.

"Well, of all the people to move on with," Babs said after a thick silence, "I don't see why it has to be *her.*"

"It doesn't have to be. It just is," Nick said, suddenly operating under a strong desire to change the subject. "So, you gonna tell me why you called me or what?"

Babs's mouth screwed up to the side in a small smile. "Like I said, I wanted to have a quality visit before you run off and—"

"Babs," Nick said in a warning tone.

"Oh, fine," Babs huffed. "I don't mind telling you, Nick, you're not as much fun as you used to be."

"Probably because I'm not as stupid as I used to be," Nick said, relieved finally to be moving the topic away from Melanie Biggs, although he was wary of what was coming next. "Now, out with it, lady."

Babs opened her purse and began digging inside. "It's my friend Vivian—"

Nick sighed. He knew it. "Another favor?"

Babs pulled out a piece of paper and smiled up at Nick. "She needs her bird picked up."

"Then she can pick it up."

"She needs you to get it at midnight, at this address." She stuffed the paper into his hands. He glanced at the scribble, which indicated a ritzy neighborhood on the Upper East Side. He pushed the paper back at her.

"Can't. Stuff to do. Thanks for stopping by. Don't let the door hit you in your big fluffy hat on the way out."

Babs ignored him with a bravado he had to respect, even if it drove him nuts.

"You'll need to damage the windows," she said. "Make a bit of a mess. It should look like a robbery."

Nick watched her for a moment. "Christ, Babs. Where do you find these people?"

"They find me. They need me. I help them, and you help me."

Nick shook his head. "Not anymore. I'm out of the favor game. I already told you. Whatever sticky situation your little society friends get into is not your problem, and it's sure as hell not mine."

"Come on, Nick," she said, leaning forward and giving him puppy dog eyes. "It'll be fun. You'll be helping someone too crazy to help herself, and I'll have something to do. I'm bored, Nick."

"Take up knitting."

"Oh, please. Old ladies knit." She took a sip of her espresso, then daintily set the tiny cup back on the saucer and smiled up at Nick. "So, midnight then?"

"I said no, Babs. I have stuff to do."

"Like what?"

"Like . . ." He searched his mind for an excuse. "Work. I have my shift tonight."

"It's your last day. Surely you can leave early. That nice Grady is all trained and ready to take over for you."

"I have to pack."

"You have five days to pack."

"Babs," he said, leaning over the bar and looking her direct in the face so she'd know he meant it. "No."

"How can you say no?"

"Easy. I think it, then I say it. *No*. See? Like that."

"Oh, fine. Killjoy." She picked up the piece of paper and glanced at it. "I'll just have to do it myself then."

Nick eyed her as she played innocent, reading the information on the paper.

"I know what you're doing, Babs," Nick said, "and it's not going to work."

"Oh?" She blinked at him innocently. "What am I doing?"

"Trying to manipulate me into stealing that bird."

"Not *steal*. Pick *up*."

"Semantics. And I revisit my *no*." Nick watched her for a moment suspiciously. "Why are you so insistent about this, anyway?"

"Because I'm so bored I could spit. Do you know I spent an entire evening last night watching reality television? It's insupportable. And that stupid bachelor chose the absolute wrong girl." Babs looked at him and sighed. "They're fun, these favors. I like helping people solve their problems."

"Babs . . ." Nick began, but she held up her hand.

"Nick, there are only so many charity benefit luncheons one can organize before one wants to chop off one's own hand and stick it in the punch fountain. Now I came up with a solution for Vivian, but I need your help. It'll just be this one last time." She reached over and patted his hand.

"Vivian is going to make a substantial donation to St. Jude's for this."

Nick closed his eyes. *Here it comes.*

"All those sick little children," Babs said, her voice plaintive. "This donation will get them teddy bears, and Nintendos, and crucial medication—"

"Enough," Nick said, holding up his hand. He tapped his fingers roughly on the bar. Babs had been suckering him into doing these wacked-out favors for years, and he always caved when she brought up the sick kids. The woman had absolutely no shame. He let out a rough exhale.

"What kind of bird is it?"

Babs straightened up in her seat. "I'm sorry?"

"Is it big? Little? What color is it?"

"It's a Kakapo," she said, her words flowing fast in her excitement, "that's all I know, and I don't know exactly what that means. It's from New Zealand, I think. But it'll be the only bird in the room."

"Fine." He nodded toward the paper in her hand. "One more, but that's it. Saturday I get on that plane, and it's over. I mean it."

He held his hand out. She happily tucked the piece of paper into his palm. He opened it and stared at the address, then turned back to face Babs.

"So, that's it? I just get the bird and . . . what?"

Babs's motioned vaguely. "Vivian will give you the check for St. Jude's, you bring it to me in the morning, then you can do whatever you want with the bird. It might be nice for you to have a pet, don't you think? I don't think it's good for you to live alone. It makes you cranky."

"I don't need a pet," Nick said. "You take the bird."

"I can't bring a pet into that building without jumping through hoops that would make a tiger at the *Cirque de Soleil* shudder in abject horror."

Nick shot her a look. "You need to move out of that place."

Babs lowered her eyes. "Bryson's partners at the firm let me stay there for free. It would be an insult to their generosity."

Nick sighed. Babs's second husband, real estate mogul Bryson McGregor, had died practically penniless almost ten years ago. Bryson's partners had purchased most of his assets in an attempt to help him get back on his feet. Six months later, he dropped dead of a heart attack. Babs had been taken by surprise, though, and the partners had worked hard to protect her from the public eye; as far as Nick knew, Bryson's lack of solvency was still a secret. Nick hadn't even known until a couple of years ago. McGregor's life insurance doled out a monthly stipend that covered everything Babs wanted for, which wasn't much, but the entire subject was still a sore one for Babs.

She looked up at him. "Please, Nick. You'll only have to keep it for a little while until I figure something out."

"By Saturday?"

She blinked innocence at him. "Why? What's Saturday?"

"When I get on the plane," Nick said, leaning forward and giving her the I-mean-it stare. "And I won't be staying because of a bird."

"Of course not," Babs said, smiling triumphantly. "Don't worry. I will have a solution by Saturday."

"Fine." Nick tucked the paper in his pocket, hoping the bird would be small, quiet, and sleep a lot. Chances were slim, but a guy could hope.

Three

Hand shaking, Dana plunged her key into the lock at Wiley Wines. She'd spent the entire forty-minute drive home from Syracuse reasoning with herself, trying to shake the nagging conviction that she'd ruined her life. Nothing made her feel better, and by the time she got out of her car, she was teetering on the ragged edge of despair.

Stupid moment of clarity.

She pushed the door open, walking into the combination gift shop and tasting bar. The old wood floor creaked beneath her feet as it had creaked under the feet of three generations of Wileys. It was a beautiful place, open and bright with floors of smooth golden wood and log walls with large windows to let in all the light they could squeeze out of the upstate New York skies, which were traditionally stingy with the sunshine. The family home on the other side of the vineyard was built in the same style, and usually when Dana walked in either place she felt calm, at peace.

Now, she felt like she really needed a glass of wine. She tossed her garment bag on the end of the tasting bar as she ducked behind it, searching for something to match her mood.

"What goes with despair and blind panic?" she muttered to herself, pulling out a dusty bottle. "Perhaps a cabernet."

"You're here."

Dana glanced up and saw Silla coming out of the office, her strawberry blond hair held precariously off her neck with two pencils and a letter opener. Of all the college-aged bookkeepers who'd answered Dana's ad promising irregular hours at crappy pay, Silla had been the most intriguing to Dana. She'd brought an umbrella to the interview on the sunniest day in the summer. Just 'cause you never know. Dana'd hired her on the spot.

"I'm here," Dana said, popping open the bottle of wine. "Thought I'd celebrate. Whatcha working on?"

"Accounts payable," Silla said. "I hate accounts payable. Have I told you that?"

"That's what makes you such a great bookkeeper, your openness about despising what you do." Dana held up the bottle. "Want some?"

Silla's eyebrows knit, and she glanced at her watch. "It's not even noon."

Dana shrugged as she poured herself a glass. "It's five o'clock somewhere." She stared toward the ceiling, doing the time zone math in her head. "Moscow, you think?"

Silla shook her head. "No, I mean, shouldn't you be at work?"

Dana swirled the wine in the glass, then took a sip. She leaned her head back and closed her eyes as the glorious liquid slid down her throat, warming her belly. "Got out early. Time off for good behavior."

"Oh, no," Silla said, her eyes watching Dana warily. "Did that Milo fire you?"

"No. *That Milo* enjoys threatening to fire me too much to actually fire me," Dana said, leaning her elbows on the bar. "Sil, have you ever had a sudden moment of clarity?"

"A sudden moment of clarity?" Silla thought on it for a moment. "No. Can't say that I have. Why?"

"No reason. I just was wondering, you know, if other people have these sudden moments of clarity, like when they suddenly just know something."

"Just know something?"

"Yeah." Dana shrugged. "Like when they *just know* they're in love. Or when they *just know* that something awful has happened to a loved one." She took a sip of her wine. "Or, you know, when they *just know* they've made a monumental mistake and screwed up their entire lives. Stuff like that."

Silla stared at Dana for a moment. "Are you okay?"

Dana waved her hand dismissively. "Yeah. I'm fine." She let out an overexuberant laugh. "Fine. Better than fine. Great, as a matter of fact." She took another sip of her wine to shut herself up. She had crappy poker face. Time to change the subject. "Tell me about those accounts payable."

Silla slipped her glasses off her face and rubbed her eyes. "The bank people called."

Dana's stomach turned, and she fought to maintain her smile. "Yeah? When are they signing over that big fat check so we can open up again?"

Silla went quiet. Dana took another gulp of her wine.

"Can't blame a girl for being optimistic," she said finally.

"I'm sorry, Dana," Silla said. "They don't think it's a sound investment, given the state of things."

Dana groaned. "Did you tell them what the grape doctor guy said?"

Silla raised one eyebrow. "You mean the botanist?"

"Did you tell them that the crops were fine, all disease-free, clean bill of health?"

Silla sighed. "They don't care. All they want to look at is the numbers, and the numbers weren't that great before the grapes got sick. I'm sorry."

Dana raised her head and looked out the tiny window above the bar, remembering how her father used to push his open mouth up against the glass and inflate his cheeks as she walked back from the bus stop when she was a kid. Sure, as an adult, she thought it was kinda gross, but at the age of nine she'd never been more charmed.

"So," she said, still staring through the window, "what are our options?"

"Well," Silla said slowly, "there's the thing we discussed about asking your mother to cosign a loan . . ."

"Or," Dana said, snapping her fingers, "I could turn the gift shop into a brothel and sell myself for money all winter until I've raised enough money to open again in the spring."

Silla smiled supportively. "That's a thought."

"And, you know, any excuse to use the word *brothel*."

"It's a great word."

"Honestly, though, I don't think I'd be any good with the professional sex. I'm barely an amateur. Been so long

I'd probably stick the condom on the guy's ear. Can virginity grow back?"

"Not that I'm aware of," Silla said. "Back to the cosigning—"

"Or," Dana said, "I could join a traveling circus for the winter. I hear they pay well if you're willing to be shot out of a cannon. Even better if you're willing to be shot out of a cannon naked while holding a porcupine."

"Or," Silla countered, "you could talk to your mother . . ."

"Is it bad that I'd rather take my chances with the porcupine?"

Silla shrugged. Dana sighed.

"Is there anything else? Any other way?"

"Well"—Silla started, looking warily at Dana—"you could always reconsider the offer you got from Melanie Biggs."

"Did you just say her name? You said her name." Dana wagged her finger at Silla. "You know the rules. Five bucks in the kitty."

"I'm serious."

"So am I."

Silla let out a sharp exhale, looking pained as she spoke. "She said she'd keep you on staff. Nothing would have to change. And then you could hire everyone else back in the spring."

"Yeah, so we could all work for the unholy demon spawn of Dolly Parton and Donald Trump? No. Thank. You. I will find another way." Dana pointed at the ceramic Cheshire cat that sat on a shelf behind the bar, watching them with a vacuous smile. "You know the rules. You say her name, you pay up."

Silla hesitated, then spoke. "She's going to be in town this week, checking on her other properties here."

"No," Dana said firmly. "Now put the money in the kitty and let's get back to watching my family business crash and burn, shall we?"

Silla pulled a five-dollar bill out of her pocket and handed it to Dana. Dana turned, stuffed it into the ceramic cat, then pulled a five out of her own pocket and handed it to Silla.

"Congratulations. You got a raise."

Silla smiled and took the money. "Thanks."

"Hey, I may be a brothel-owning, porcupine-loving, naked piece of cannon fodder, but I only take money from people I dislike."

"Which brings us back to your mother," Silla began.

"I like my mother," Dana said. Silla nodded, sweetly pretending to believe it, but Dana could tell it was a charade. She stared down into her wineglass. She'd been right—Cabernet did go great with panic and despair. "It's just that I don't understand her. And every time I talk to her there are these weird awkward silences that stretch on forever. Seriously. You could bury Jimmy Hoffa in those silences. Matter of fact, I think that might be where he is."

"Well, I'm out of ideas," Silla said, "unless you think you might have a hundred thousand dollars or so in spare change stuck in your sofa cushions. I'd be happy to help you look."

"Boy, you are just the most dedicated bookkeeper ever to escort a business into Chapter Eleven, you know that?" Dana pulled down another wineglass, filled it, and slid it across the bar to Silla. "You've earned it."

Silla took a sip. Dana leaned her elbows on the bar and

put her face in her hands. "My father was four when Grampa Wiley built this place. Did I ever tell you that?"

Silla shook her head. Dana straightened up and pointed through the window. "My parents were married in the gazebo out back."

She motioned toward the east side of the vineyard. "I lost my virginity in Nick's pickup at the edge of the vineyard." She pulled her head up and cringed at Silla. "Too much information?"

Silla laughed lightly. "Little bit."

"I can't lose this place," she said, as much to herself as to Silla. Silla said nothing, just watched her quietly with that penetrating gaze that only severely sincere bookkeeper types can muster.

"So," Dana said quietly, "what do you think is the proper outfit for running to your estranged mother and asking for money? Should I go hobo-chic, with my holey jeans and worn flannel top, or should I do straightforward abject penitence and just wear the hair shirt all the way down?"

Silla blinked. "You have a hair shirt?"

Dana lifted her glass.

"Hobo-chic it is." She smiled at Silla. "Why don't you get going? I'll lock up when I'm done with my self-pity bender."

Silla hesitated. "Are you sure? I could stay with you for a while?"

Dana shook her head. "You go on. Thanks."

After Silla escaped, Dana pulled the garment bag toward her and unzipped it, revealing the white satin wedding dress inside.

Then she stared at it as she took another drink.

One good thing about the impending doom of selling the business that had been in her family for three generations—it put her moment of clarity in perspective. The whole freak-out had probably just been misplaced anxiety over the winery anyway, she told herself. It wasn't a huge stretch to imagine—she'd known Silla was talking to the bank people today, and while she'd been hopeful, she knew they might not give her the loan. She was simply misplacing her emotions, as she often did. She knew she'd made the right decision with Nick, and anyway, a man she hadn't seen in six years was the least of her problems.

Losing the family business, land, and home all in one fell swoop—that was a problem so tremendous and breathtaking in scope that it could easily eclipse a stupid little moment of clarity. No doubt about it.

She leaned back against the wall, her head resting on the cool window her father used to watch her through every morning. She stared up at the rough log ceiling, wondering if her father was watching her from above.

Then she quickly looked at the floor. It was equally possible Frank Wiley was watching her from a more southern perspective.

Either way, he was probably not impressed. He'd managed to keep Wiley Wines above water through an untold number of bad seasons, and even through the initial post-divorce years when he'd been so drunk that half of the time he'd forgotten little details, like opening the shop or paying taxes. And yet Dana, predominantly sober, couldn't keep it running through the aftereffects of one stupid little diseased crop.

Except she could. All she had to do was swallow her

pride, go see her mother, and ask for money. The thought sent acid spiking through her stomach.

It's not really asking for money, Dana thought. *It's asking for ink, a little ink in the form of signature that will make her responsible for the loan if I fail to breathe life back into Wiley Wines.*

Oh, hell. Who was she kidding? She was asking her mother for money. Her mother. The woman who didn't get her Christmas call from Dana until March. The woman who repeatedly extended invitations for Dana to visit her in Manhattan only to receive lame excuses like *Can't, having a root canal.*

But there was the flip side of the coin. She was also the woman who had left Dana's dad after twenty-five years of marriage to run off with a wealthy Manhattan real-estate magnate. The woman who'd attended fabulous charity functions on the French Riviera while Dana helped her drunken father make it up the steps and into his bedroom before passing out. The woman who had left Dana behind to clean up her mess and watch Frank Wiley wither away and die of a broken heart.

Dana lifted herself up off the bar and put her empty wineglass in the sink. After she'd buried her dad, she'd sworn to herself she'd never touch a dime of Babs's money. It felt tainted, somehow disloyal to her father, as Babs's money was Bryson McGregor's money, no matter how dead both men were. And Dana really didn't want the money, anyway. As long as she had a roof, three squares a day, and clothes and shoes with patchable holes, she was happy. Money just didn't mean that much to her.

But this place did. It meant everything.

And, although she barely wanted to admit it to herself,

not letting Melanie Biggs get her stinking Antichrist claws on Wiley Wines meant more.

"You have to understand, Dad," she said, pulling the garment bag off the bar, "I'm out of options. I wouldn't do this if I had a choice."

She dug into her pocket for her keys.

"As much as I sympathize with you hating Bryson, and as much as I know you're rolling over in your grave like a rotisserie chicken at the thought of his money saving this place . . . there's no way in hell I'm letting that bitch get her skanky little hands on my winery."

She pulled open the front door and stepped outside into the crisp fall air.

Garment bag bumping lazily over her shoulder, she started down the long gravel path toward her house at the edge of the vineyard. Her credit card would creak and complain, but it would get her one round-trip ticket to New York City, where she would ask her estranged mother for money and officially become the lowest form of life in the world.

It was a plan.

Four

Dana rolled her head from side to side, trying to work out the stiffness the trip had put in her neck as she watched the floor numbers tick by in bright red on the elevator panel.

5 . . . 6 . . . 7 . . .

She checked her watch—10:30. Late, but not by Babs's standards; Dana was pretty sure her mother would still be up. Edgar the doorman had smiled brightly when he saw her and didn't bother calling up. Apparently Babs had put Dana on the short list of people who didn't require being announced, which had surprised Dana. She half expected to be on the blacklist, wedged between vacuum salesmen and door-to-door evangelists. Instead, Edgar had led her to the elevators, keying in the penthouse floor and making polite chitchat by saying he was sure Babs would be thrilled to see her daughter.

If only Dana could be so sure. Three hours in standby

mode at the airport, two hours on the plane, then forty minutes of a death-defying cab ride had done little to lower the anxiety she'd been working up all day. The closer she'd gotten to Babs's place, the more certain she was that she was heading into disaster, that Babs would have her thrown out as soon as she walked in. Which would be easier, honestly. If Babs was awful about it, Dana could at least feel better about her own part in the tension in their relationship. But Dana knew exactly what to expect from her mother.

Graciousness, humor, and a big fat *Where do I sign?*

Dana's sense of self-worth plummeted as the elevator lifted her closer to her mother. Only thoughts of Wiley Wines falling into the hands of Melanie Biggs kept her from hitting the emergency button and stopping the elevator altogether.

18 . . . 19 . . . 20 . . .

Dana wrung her hands together. They were starting to sweat. She should have called first. Maybe it would have been better if she'd written a letter. Hired the Goodyear Blimp to do a flyby over the penthouse. Sent smoke signals or a telegram.

Mom. Stop. In big trouble. Stop. Need lots of money. Stop. Please save me as I am pathetic and useless. Stop.

"Oh, crap," Dana grunted and glanced up at the numbers again.

28 . . . 29 . . . P.

Ding. The elevator doors opened, and Dana forced her shaky legs to carry her out into her mother's penthouse. The living room, all white leather and gleaming glass, was empty. Dana glanced to her left, where an open archway showed her an equally sparkling, and equally empty, kitchen. She heard flamenco music coming faintly from outside and glanced toward the window over the sofa that looked out on the terrace. Light shone through, and Dana guessed her mother was outside enjoying a little autumn night air and likely drinking something with an umbrella in it.

"Well," she muttered to herself, "time to get this show on the road."

She tossed her bag below the coatrack and moved down the hallway to the sliding-glass terrace door. She could see Babs stretched out on a lounge chair, dressed in white and wearing some sort of fluffy pink monster on her head. Dana smiled; she'd been right about everything, except the umbrella. Babs was drinking a scotch and soda.

Dana slid the door open, walked over to the portable stereo and lowered the volume, then turned to face Babs as her mother pulled the hat off her head and squinted up at Dana.

"Hi," she said weakly. "Nice hat."

Her mother blinked twice in silence. Dana could feel Babs looking her up and down, probably deciding that the red in her hair was done badly. Which it probably was. It was out of a box and Dana was no hairdresser but damned if she was going to pay seventy-five bucks for someone to damage her hair with poisonous chemicals when she could do it herself for ten. She ran a hand over her head and waited for Babs to say something.

After the initial moment of shock passed, Babs smiled and stood up, drawing Dana into a hug in which they both put their faces to the same side, then each moved, then finally fit chins to shoulders briefly before they each backed off and just looked at each other.

"Dana, darling," Babs said, her smile a little too bright. "What a surprise."

"Yeah," Dana said, scuffing one sneakered foot against the terrace's polished concrete floor. "Sorry. I should have called first."

"No," Babs said. "It's fine. I'm so glad you're here."

"Me too."

They stared at each other for a long moment.

"Drink?" Babs said.

"Please."

Dana followed Babs back into the penthouse to the fully stocked bar at the edge of the living room. Dana settled on a barstool and watched as her mother fixed a gin and tonic, complete with fresh lime, and slid it across the bar.

"Thank you," Dana said, and took a large sip, feeling a wash of conflicting emotions. Happiness at seeing her mother. Guilt. Love. A touch of anger, a sprinkle of disappointment, all topped off with a healthy helping of self-loathing.

She took another drink.

"I'm sorry I didn't call you back after you left that message on my birthday . . ." she began.

Babs waved a hand dismissively and scoffed at her. "Oh, not at all. I know you're busy."

"It's just that work . . ."

Babs smiled. "Of course."

"I had to take a second job."

Babs's smile faded a touch. "Why? Are things okay at the winery?"

Dana shook her head and let out a strained laugh. It was a perfect segue into the reason she'd come by, but she faltered right over it. "Oh, no. Fine. I just . . . you know . . . extra . . . miscellaneous . . . car payments."

She tried not to roll her eyes at herself. She still drove the same crappy Ford Escort she'd bought used after college graduation. She was such a pathetic liar.

Babs grinned. "You got a new car? What kind? Something fast and stylish, I hope. Please don't tell me it's something sensible like a pickup truck or a minivan."

Dana felt her brow crinkle under the stress of both lying and trying to understand her mother.

"I didn't get a car."

"You didn't?"

"No." Dana stared down at her feet. "I have a second job because I had to close the winery."

Babs's drink paused in midair. "What happened?"

Dana felt the tension rising up her back, settling on her shoulders. She played nervously with the mixer straw in her drink. "Diseased grapes. I don't know how it happened. I mean, it's not like they're out there on the vine, having indiscriminate sex and sharing dirty needles."

Dana let loose with a nervous giggle. Babs stared at her, unsmiling.

Oh. Hell.

"So, anyway, they all got diseased and I wasn't gonna have enough yield to justify the expense of the summer hires, so I closed the place down for the season. It's really no big deal." Dana took a gulp of her drink and forced a tight smile. "So, what have you been up to?"

Babs shrugged. "Oh, you know. Lots of indiscriminate sex and sharing dirty needles. The usual." Her expression grew more serious. "What are you going to do?"

Dana lifted her glass. "Finish this. Have another."

"I meant about the winery, Dana." Babs paused, took a breath. "You're not going to have to sell it, are you?"

"No," Dana said quickly. "No, no. I went to the bank. You know, for a loan."

"Oh. Good. How did that go?"

"Well, it was uncomfortable at first, you know, what with the crawling up my nether regions with a microscope, but . . . they're thinking real hard about it. Of course, I'm going to have to jump through some hoops first."

"Hoops?"

"Yeah. You know. Sacrifice a chicken, promise them my firstborn . . ." Dana took another sip of her drink and kept her eyes on the bar as she blurted out the last, painful bit. ". . . get a cosigner."

Silence. Dreadful, horrible silence. Dana waited for the *Where do I sign?* she'd been expecting, but it didn't come. She glanced up at her mother, who was watching her. Dana cleared her throat.

"Which . . . ," she stammered, ". . . is kinda why I'm here."

Babs nodded. "I see."

More silence. "But you don't have to do it. There are other options. I think I saw something about the blood of a virgin in the paperwork."

Babs tilted her head. "Will they want to crawl up my nether regions as well?"

Dana took a breath to answer but was saved by the elevator bell. It wasn't until she heard Nick's voice coming from the front hall that she realized it was very much a frying pan–fire situation.

"Babs, hey," he said as he stepped in. "Did you forget

to charge your cell phone? I've been calling for the last hour, and your landline is going straight to . . ."

He stopped. His eyes narrowed slightly as they landed on Dana, flashing disbelief at first, then slowly cooling. Dana's stomach did a flip, and she prayed her gin and tonic wouldn't make an encore appearance.

". . . voice mail," he said finally, his voice flat, his eyes still on Dana. "And it's not accepting new messages. Must be full."

Babs shot out from behind the bar to intercept Nick. "Sorry, Nick. I, uh . . . I must have put the phone on DO NOT DISTURB and just forgotten about it. Is there something you"—she glanced at Dana, then back at Nick—"you needed?"

"Hmmm?" Nick pulled his eyes away from Dana and turned to Babs. "Yeah. I was on my way to this bird thing, but I couldn't read your handwriting here." He pulled a piece of paper out of his pocket and handed it to her. "That a five or a nine?"

Oh, God, oh God, Dana thought, glancing around, looking for escape. She could dart behind the big treeish plant in the corner next to the bar. Or she could toss herself over the bar and duck behind it, with any luck hitting her head on the minifridge and knocking herself out cold.

Would have been a decent plan, if she could move, but she couldn't. She was frozen in her spot, staring at Nick. Her Nick. Nicholas James Maybe, who even after six years still seemed as familiar to her as her own skin. He looked broader across the shoulders, although the straight-lined black leather coat could have been responsible for that impression. His dark blue jeans clung tightly to muscles she remembered too well. His hair was still the same chocolate brown, still kept short to keep the waves in check. His face was the same, all sharp edges that went soft when he smiled. Same deep blue eyes, only without the sparkle at the edges when he looked at her.

She kinda missed the sparkle.

He turned his head again and looked at her. She swallowed tightly, wiped her shaking hands on her jeans, and slowly lowered herself off the barstool. Part of her wished desperately that this was all a big nightmare, but since she wasn't standing naked in Lincoln Center while being expected to conduct the Philharmonic through *Carmina Burana*, she knew the chances were slim. She wrapped her arms around herself and felt the worn-out spot on the elbow of her flannel shirt, and wondered what kind of God would allow her to go hobo-chic on the day she just happened to bump into her ex-fiancé.

"Hey, Nick," she said, her voice barely loud enough to register over the deafening silence.

He continued to stare at her. Just when Dana thought she was going to break down if someone didn't say something soon, he spoke.

"You changed your hair," he said. It seemed less a point of interest and more the only thing he could think of to say, but it was a start.

"Yeah," Dana said, her stomach flopping like a fish on dry land. Panic gripped her, and before she knew it, she added lamely, "It's not natural."

"Yeah." The slightest hint of a smile tinged the edges of his eyes, then they went hard again. "I remember."

She tried not to cringe at the sheer social pain of it all and glanced at the window. People had certainly thrown themselves from buildings for less than this. Who would blame her, really?

Another long moment passed, then Nick turned his eyes to Babs.

"So," he said, his voice tight as he motioned toward the slip of paper he'd handed her. "Five or nine?"

Babs glanced at the paper, then handed it back to Nick. "Five."

Nick nodded, folded the paper into exact quadrants, and shoved it into the inside pocket of his coat. Dana could see the muscles working in his jaw and knew he was as painfully conscious of her presence as she was of his.

"I'll call you in the morning," Nick said tightly, "to coordinate the other stuff."

Not-so-hidden message: Make sure Dana isn't here the next time I am. It had been a long time since Dana had seen Nick, but she could still read him like a kindergarten primer.

Babs gave him a little smile. "Sure. Tomorrow."

Nick turned his face toward Dana, and with obvious effort raised his eyes to hers. "Dana."

She swallowed. "Nick."

He turned and walked purposefully into the still-open elevator. Dana didn't release her breath until she heard the *clunk* of the doors closing, at which point the question her brain had been too frozen to form suddenly hit her.

What the hell was Nick doing there in the first place?

"I'm sorry," Babs said. "Darling, you have to believe me, I would have warned you if I'd had any idea he was going to show up here like that."

"Of course you would."

"Are you okay?"

"Never better," Dana said. "But, hey, here's a thing. What was he doing here?"

Babs glanced back at the elevator door, then looked to Dana. "Nick and I are still in touch. You knew that."

"I knew you'd seen him. At that wine bar where he works. Monkey's."

"Murphy's, dear."

"Whatever," Dana said, swiping her glass off the bar and taking a swift drink. "And I knew you weren't being actively mean to him. Like, you weren't egging his door or anything, but I didn't realize you guys were—you're friends?"

"Well . . ." Babs took a breath, then continued. "We sort of work together."

"You work together."

"It's kind of a freelance thing. For charity."

Dana blinked. "A freelance thing. For charity."

Babs gave her a bright smile. "Yes. Understand?"

"Sure," Dana said. Of course she didn't understand, but she was sure her heart would stop that skipping nonsense eventually, and probably faster if she just focused on the reason why she was here.

To beg her estranged mother to rescue her failing winery.

Dana lifted her empty glass. "I could really use another one of these."

"Of course," Babs said, shuffling behind the bar.

Dana settled on a barstool and leaned her elbows on the bar. "You know those moments when you think things can't possibly get any worse, and then they do? They should have a word for that."

"They do," Babs said as she splashed the gin over the ice in Dana's glass. "It's called life."

Dana let out a laugh. "I'll drink to that," she said.

Babs reached under the bar and pulled out the bottle of scotch.

"Not without me, you won't," Babs said. She poured her glass and lifted it in the air for a toast.

"To life," Babs said. "May we die before it kills us."

Five

Nick made his way down Seventy-third Street and checked his watch: 11:48. He casually glanced up at the East Side town house and checked the number: 245 E. Seventy-third Street.

Right place. Almost right time. Twelve more minutes to kill. One more stroll around the block, and he could get the stupid bird, and move on with his life. Until then, he would circle the block again and think.

About Dana.

Some more.

He'd been able to think of little else since he'd seen her. She was just as beautiful as always, the red in her curls making those blue eyes and freckled cheeks jump out and grab him with more intensity than he would have ever thought possible. He had imagined seeing her a thousand times over the years, and in none of the scenarios had he ever frozen up as he did. In his imagination, he'd always been cool, always unfazed. In reality, he'd been thunderstruck. For a moment, when their eyes first locked, he literally thought his heart had stopped.

What the hell was wrong with him? He crumpled the paper with the address on it and stuffed it angrily into his pocket. Better question—what was wrong with *her*? What was she doing at Babs's place, lying in wait to tear his gut into pieces with her presence? It wasn't right, one person having that kind of effect on him. And why did she have to visit tonight? He would be gone in less than a week. She couldn't have waited a few days? What the hell was wrong with her, anyway?

Even as he had the thoughts, he knew they didn't make any sense. How would Dana have known he'd be there? Babs didn't even know he'd be stopping by, and it wasn't like Babs and Dana were exactly gushing to each other with personal details, but still. He was pissed off about it, and he might as well just be pissed off with Dana.

Old habits die hard.

He reached the town house again, checked his watch: 11:54.

Screw it. He'd rather be a little early than think about Dana Elizabeth Wiley for one more minute. He pushed open the alley gate, which had been left unlocked as promised, and headed into the alley. His eyes took a moment to adjust to the muted darkness, but his hearing was just fine, and based on the ragged breathing that didn't match his, he figured he wasn't alone.

And . . . what was that *smell*?

"Umph," he said, as something big smashed into his shoulder.

"Sorry, mate," he heard a man grumble as he rushed

past him. Nick watched as the man, carrying a large cardboard box, walked out into the Manhattan street. Nick caught only the glow of a shaved white head and a flash of a denim jacket before the man was gone.

Weird, but not his problem. He pulled a flashlight out of his back pocket and used it to illuminate the rest of the alley. Nobody. Nothing. He negotiated his way to the back, and there was the ladder, also as promised. It was hitched right up against the wall, leading, Nick could only presume, to the window he wanted.

He looked down the alley in the direction the bald man had gone as a bad feeling rumbled in his gut. Babs's friends were all pretty much nuts, so this kind of strangeness wasn't exactly unusual, but something was off about this one.

He tucked the flashlight into his breast pocket, put on his leather gloves, and started up the ladder. When he got to the window, it was slightly ajar.

Hmmm. Didn't Babs say Vivian wanted him to break glass? Maybe she'd changed her mind. It wasn't unusual for Babs's friends to do that. Nick climbed into the room and was hit instantly by the same aroma he'd smelled in the alley, sweet and earthy and strong as hell.

Well, crap, he thought. *Looks like I got to this party a little late.*

He moved back toward the window to inhale some fresh air and think. Before he got a chance to do either, the door burst open and a woman—blond, late thirties, braless in a flowing satin negligee—hurried in. Nick blinked. He thought women only wore lingerie like that in the movies.

"Oh, thank God!" she said, shutting the door quietly behind her. In the moonlight, Nick could see the large room, accented with the random feather, and the empty birdcage, door wide-open, behind her.

"Ow!" she said, then stepped back and leaned down to pick up a tiny syringe on the floor. She glanced at it for a minute, then smiled.

"Oh, that's how you kept it quiet, huh? You drugged it. Clever." She walked over to the window. "But we don't want the police to track you, now do we?"

She tossed the syringe out the window. Nick recoiled.

"Hey," he said. "You don't know what's in that needle. You can't just—"

"Oh, hell," she said, looking at the window. "I thought I told you to break the glass." She sighed, put her hands on her hips, looking around the room. She grabbed a poker from the set of fireplace tools and smashed it into the glass. Nick jumped back. She calmly put the poker back and smiled up at him.

"So, where is it?"

Nick glanced at the window and back at her, not sure how to respond. Her smile widened and her eyes lit up.

"You threw it out the window?" She laughed, then stopped. "You do know it's flightless, right?" She glanced over the edge of the window down into the yard below, then pulled her head back in and sighed. "Drugged it and threw it out the window. Sick bastard. I just wish I had been here to see it."

A man's voice called from another area of the house. "Vivian?"

"Argh!" she grunted. "Six vodka tonics, you'd think the man would sleep through a little breaking glass!"

She put her hands on Nick's shoulders, nudging him toward the window as she prattled on at him. "If there are any remains, clean it up. It's a valuable bird; no real bird thief would throw that thing out the window when he can get a quarter mil for it on the street."

Nick's gut dropped. *A quarter mil?* What the hell kind of bird was this, anyway?

"Oh, and tell Babs I'm a little strapped for cash right now, but I'll give her the money in a couple of weeks."

"What?" Nick asked. "Wait—"

"Vivian!" The man's voice was getting closer.

"Just go!" Vivian said, practically pushing him over the window's edge. Nick shook his head and started negotiating his way down the ladder. A moment later Vivian's head poked out of the window above him.

"And don't forget to take the ladder down."

She disappeared again. Nick's feet hit the ground, and he pulled the extension ladder away from the house and condensed it down to its original length. He glanced around, saw a small shed, and leaned the ladder against it, then headed down the alley.

At least tonight was weird enough to get my mind off Dana, he thought, then paused.

"Shit," he grunted, irritated with himself. He might as well just pass her a note in study hall and get it over with. *NM Loves DW 4-Ever, Even If She Yanks His Heart Out Of His Chest And Does A River Dance On It.* Pathetic.

He'd reached the gate when something on the ground caught his eye. He turned on his flashlight, knelt, and picked up two pieces of paper crumpled together. One, a yellow sticky note, had bullet points on it.

- *Break in around 11:30–midnight.*
- *Bird will be in cage. Unlocked.*

- *Gate is open.*
- *Ladder is by the shed.*
- *Alarm is disabled.*

A sticky note. Presumably left out where any old some-one could find it.

Any old bald someone, maybe, he thought. He scoffed. He never understood how some people got so rich while being so unbelievably stupid. He uncrumpled the next piece of paper.

A receipt for an order of curly fries and two mugs of Guinness at Bleeker's Pub, a place in the middle of a bad neighborhood on the Lower East Side.

Nick stood up. By all accounts, everything seemed fine. Vivian got rid of her bird, St. Jude's got its donation, and the thief got away with something. Still, it didn't sit right with him. He tucked the papers into his pocket, just in case.

Then he made his way to the street and tried with mini-mal success to keep Dana Wiley out of his head as he started the long trek home.

Babs fired up the computer, its blue light giving her office a dull glow. It was two in the morning, but it wasn't like she was going to sleep, anyway.

Dana needed her. For the first time since she could re-member, her daughter actually needed her, and Babs would be damned if she was going to let Dana down. Again. She had to find a way to save that winery. Cosigning a loan didn't seem like a good idea, considering the whole microscope-up-the-nether-regions thing. That sounded very uncomfortable, and Babs's finances, such as they were, would never make the cut.

After tossing and turning for hours, the solution had finally struck her. She went into the office to see if it might work.

She clicked on a search page and typed in *Kakapo*. She leaned forward, her face closer and closer to the screen as she clicked on the links before her.

There were only eighty-six Kakapos known to be in existence, making them extremely rare.

They were illegal outside of the conservation habitats in New Zealand.

Her heartbeat quickened. She went back to the search engine and typed in *bird black market*. That wasn't nearly as helpful, mostly articles written about the black market. Perhaps the Internet wasn't the place to find out how much she could get for the bird.

But it was a plan. She could call Nick tomorrow and have him drop off the bird (it would only be a few days, and what the board didn't know wouldn't hurt them), then connect with this black market (and really, she was in Manhattan, black markets were everywhere, how hard could it be?) and find a buyer.

Easy as pie.

She smiled, turned off the computer, and went back to bed, where she fell quickly into a deep sleep.

Six

Dana pulled her robe on over her T-shirt and trudged into the kitchen. She'd given up the ghost of getting any sleep hours ago, but now that the sun was starting to come up, she figured she could get away with making the morning coffee and starting the day.

After finishing the drink with Babs, Dana had made her excuses and gone to bed. Before letting her go, Babs had wrestled a promise from Dana that they'd talk more about the winery in the morning, after they'd each had a good night's sleep.

Unfortunately, there'd been no good night's sleep for Dana. She tossed and turned in the guest room, unable to get Nick out of her head. Every thought she had—of the winery, of Babs—brought her back to Nick, and the hollowness in her chest expanded with every breath she took. By the time the sun started molding the darkness into blue shadows, she thought there'd be nothing of her left.

How could one man affect her like that? she wondered as she padded into the kitchen. It was just rude, is what it was. The one night in the year when she was at Babs's, and he had to barge in unannounced. Dana didn't care what kind of freelance charity work they were doing—and since when is volunteer work considered freelancing?—it simply wasn't right.

At the same time, she knew it wasn't his fault. He would have had no way of knowing she'd be there. She rarely was. And, based on the look on his face, she'd taken just as large a chunk out of him as he had out of her. She knew she didn't have any right to be angry with him.

Not that a little thing like reason was going to stop her from doing just that.

She opened the freezer and smiled as she pulled out the pound of Dunkin' Donuts coffee. No matter that Babs could probably afford to buy her own personal coffee plantation, she still knew there was only one acceptable brand of coffee for the discriminating palate. Dana spooned the beans into the grinder, pushed the button down, and inhaled the magnificent smell. She stopped grinding and perked her ears up for sounds of Babs stirring. On a typical morning, it would take a nuclear bomb to wake Babs before ten, so Dana doubted the coffee grinder, loud as it was, would do it. When she heard nothing, she poured the grinds into the filtered basket and turned the machine on.

"Dana."

She screamed and spun around. She knew the voice, of course, but the unexpectedness of hearing it from behind her sent her heart careening around in her chest, bouncing around her rib cage like a gerbil on amphetamines.

"Jesus!" she yelled, her hand on her chest. "Don't you ever call first?"

Nick glanced down at an envelope he had in his hand. "I didn't think you would be awake yet. I didn't want to disturb you. I just . . . I wanted Babs to get this as soon as she woke up. I'm going to be busy later, and something unexpected happened when I ran the errand for her last night. I thought she should know about it."

Dana's eyebrows knit. What was he talking about? Didn't he know babbling was her thing?

"I would have called," he continued, "but her phone is still . . ."

Dana nodded. "DO NOT DISTURB. Yeah. I'll talk to her about that."

His jaw muscles tightened. "This just explains what happened. Not a big deal, but, like I said . . ."

"You'll be busy." *Avoiding me,* she added silently.

"Yeah." He held her eyes for a moment, then stepped past her to put the envelope on the kitchen table. He kept the tips of his fingers on it for a few moments as if he wasn't sure what to do next. Dana used this time to pull her robe closed around her and cross her arms over her stomach.

"I'll make sure that she gets it," she said.

Nick looked at her. "Sure. Thanks."

He just stood there, watching her. It was as though he couldn't move, which Dana kinda understood, as she kept telling her feet to carry her somewhere else, and yet there she still was. Ignoring her internal pleas, her legs kept her cemented to the spot and staring up into the sweet blue eyes of the biggest mistake she ever made.

Nick swallowed and tried to move away, but he couldn't. She was still so beautiful. Even with her auburn curls sticking up on one side of her head. Even with that old flannel robe tied clumsily around her, stopping at the knee to reveal smooth legs he remembered too well. Even with her oversized gym socks, the right one clinging to her calf, the other scrunched around her left ankle. It shouldn't have been a beguiling image. He should have been able to walk away, easily. After all, this was the woman who had ruined his life, kinda. Ruined him for other women, anyway. He should have been able to walk away.

But he couldn't.

Nor was he able to say anything. What could he say? Last night, he'd pretty much proven himself unable to engage in small talk with the "You changed your hair" comment. He cringed at the thought of it.

"You okay?" she asked, her voice soft and quiet, reminding him of the hundreds of mornings he'd woken up to it, taking for granted that he'd wake up to the sound and smell of her for the rest of his life.

"No," he answered honestly. He could lie, tell her he was great, but it wouldn't do any good. Dana had known him since the tenth grade. She'd detect a lie from him before he could even get the words out.

She gave a little nervous giggle. "Well, I'm great. Never been greater. My life is perfect, pretty much."

"Good," Nick said stiffly. "Glad to hear it. See you later."

But he didn't move. Just stood there, staring at her in that robe, with the messy hair and the . . . legs.

Oh. God. The. Legs.

He needed to get out of there. Now.

Without a word, he turned and walked toward the elevator.

"Wait," he heard her say behind him. "Nick."

He'd almost made it to the elevator when she caught his arm, stopping him. The heat from her fingers zapped him, even through his jacket.

"I'm sorry," she said. "I don't know why I said that. I'm just . . . seeing you is difficult."

He nodded. "Yeah."

"I mean, not that you're hard to look at," she said. She was starting to babble, as she always did when she was nervous. "I mean, definitely easy on the eyes. Especially with the . . ." She motioned vaguely toward his chest. "I like the leather."

He raised his eyes to hers, and they locked on to each other. In that moment, a thousand memories came rushing back at him. The prom, graduation, long drives to and from SUNY Potsdam, where they'd both gone to school. Having sex for the first time in his truck at the edge of the vineyard. Proposing to her in a small hotel room in Niagara Falls.

The view from the back as she ran out of St. Christopher's. The look on her face when she walked in and found him with Melanie Biggs.

And then, he was back to the robe and the smooth legs.

"You're looking at me funny," she said. "It's the hair, isn't it? I get horrible bed hair and—"

His restraint ran out at that moment and he reached for her, stunning her into silence as his hand slid under her robe and around her waist. It was like instinct, so natural as he maneuvered his palm against that special place in the small of her back and pressed her against him, remembering what that used to do to her.

Based on the look on her face, some things hadn't changed.

"So the hair's okay, then?" she whispered. The sound of her voice, all breathless and soft, broke down the final wall. He kissed her, although not to shut her up. He kissed her because all the forces in God's green earth couldn't have stopped him, he wanted her so bad. There was barely a pause before she responded in kind, her arms wrapping around his neck, her hands in his hair, on his face, their tongues writhing against each other as their bodies did the same.

He pulled back and looked at her, breathless. Her lips were reddened with the force of the kiss, and she exhaled slowly, showing him a bit of those slightly crooked teeth that nearly sent him over the edge. He knew this was the point where his reason should return, where he should let her go, apologize, disappear. But he couldn't. Neither could he lose himself in her the way he wanted to. *That way lies madness,* he thought.

Not that he wasn't already plenty mad. That was fairly obvious right now.

He put one hand on her face, ran his fingers down her cheek, his thumb tracing her bottom lip.

"Dana," he whispered.

Her chest heaved as her breath caught, and he looked in her eyes. There were tears there, not enough to spill down her cheeks, but enough for him to know that she was as deeply affected by him as he was by her.

At that moment everything changed. He let her go

quickly, as though he suddenly realized he was holding a blazing coal, and he stepped back. Her lower lip trembled.

"Nick?" she asked.

He swallowed hard against the pain rising in his chest and walked into the elevator.

"Nick?" she said again, stepping up to the elevator door, but staying inside the penthouse. Nick avoided her eyes as he hit the button. The doors closed. He released his breath and leaned back against the elevator wall as it descended. It was one thing to feel crazy with lust, or even to be slapped in the face with the reality that he still did, and probably always would, love her. He could deal with that. He had been dealing with it with varying degrees of success for six years.

What he didn't want, what he didn't need, what chewed holes in his gut was that, for a brief moment, he'd felt the one thing he never wanted to feel again.

He felt hope.

And it scared the hell out of him.

Dana put her fingers to her lips, which were still tingling from Nick's kiss. She stood in front of the elevator door, staring at it, stunned.

"Well," she said to herself after a moment, "that was interesting."

Although *interesting* might not have been the word. *Surprising* would have worked. *Hot* definitely applied. *Disconcerting* was appropriate; her hands were still shaking. The rest of her body, however, was revved up and ready to go, and very desperately wanted Nick to come back through those doors and press her up against the wall and do things to her that would make the coat rack clutch its pearls.

"Oh, this isn't good," she said, and rubbed her hands over her face. Slowly, she stepped away from the door. Nick was gone, and based on the look (of what? Disgust? Terror? Indigestion? Why didn't she ever have a pocket thesaurus when she needed one?) on his face when the elevators closed, she'd bet the farm he wasn't coming back.

Ever.

She shuffled numbly over to the kitchen table and sat down. It had just never occurred to her, not for a second, that he might still have feelings for her, but that kiss told a different story.

Then again, it could have just been the hair. Nick had always been partial to the disheveled look.

She took in a deep breath, trying to calm the hopped-up gerbil in her chest. None of this made sense. In the world as she knew it, she had a few things she could always put her back up against. The sun came up every morning. The Democrats always took New York in the presidential elections.

And Nick Maybe hated her.

That was just the way it was.

She stared at the envelope on the table, Babs's name written in Nick's firm hand on the floor. She smiled, remembering the letters he used to write her, putting them in the mail and sending them from his dorm to hers, which were less than fifty yards apart. He'd deliberately written the hokiest love letters he could manage, filled with tongue-in-cheek passages of blatantly absurd crap. Her favorite passage: "Your lovely face is emblazoned on my eyelids, as though an evil elf snuck into my room at night and embroidered it there." But he always ended them with the same simple, "Yours. Always. Nick."

And she still had them, in a shoe box in her closet. For a moment, she wanted nothing more than to go home and read them, but then she remembered there really was no point.

She ran her hands through her hair. None of this made sense. Not the moment of clarity, not the cosmic coincidence of their running into each other now after six years of successful avoidance, not the inability to go five minutes in a room alone together without throwing themselves on each other like a couple of teenagers on prom night.

The kissing had been good, though. A little too good. She was going to have to change her underwear.

Dana sighed and shook her head. There was no point in obsessing over Nick all morning. That wasn't why she was there. This trip was about having to run to Mommy to get bailed out of trouble. It was important she focus on one failure at a time. The disaster that was her and Nick was not on the agenda.

She glanced at the clock: 6:30. If history served, Babs wouldn't be up until nearly eleven, and if she sat around the penthouse all morning, she'd go nuts first from trying not to think about Nick, and later from thinking about him.

"Okay," she said to herself, getting up. "Cold shower, long walk on the city streets, enough caffeine to revive the dead, and Nick Maybe will be out of my system before noon."

And she padded toward the bathroom, trying to ignore the voice in her head that mocked, *Fat chance.*

Seven

Dermot Finnegan pulled his PDA out of his jacket pocket and flicked it on. Except for the ridiculously overpriced items *Chez Animaux* stocked for people who were too rich to realize animals were not people, the place was empty. It was a loser job, selling fur-lined cat boxes, diamond-studded dog collars, and books on how to psychically communicate with your cockatiel, but it was a means to an end. In six months there, he'd gotten more leads than he had in the two years he'd been working birds previously. He figured three, maybe four more jobs, and he could get out of it entirely. Although he had to admit that every job was kinda fun—the adrenaline rush as he picked locks, disabled security systems, and worked the sale—he'd grown over time to hate birds with the white-hot passion of a thousand suns. He hated the way they smelled, the way they chirped and squawked, the way they molted all over his apartment until he was finding feathers and fluff in his toothpaste. He was twenty-seven years old and just now realizing that life was too short to waste on stealing birds.

He tapped the stylus to the screen and started to play solitaire. He was halfway through the game when the front door jingled and an older, well-dressed woman in a dark blue suit and an expensive-looking coat walked in. Finn tucked his PDA back into the pocket of his jacket and smiled.

"Good morning, ma'am."

She grinned at him. "Call me Babs."

Finn tried to conceal his surprise. Most of *Chez Animaux*'s clientele preferred he walk ten feet behind them and never make direct eye contact. He liked this woman already.

"Okay, Babs," he said. "Can I help you with anything this morning, or will you just be browsing today?"

She pulled off her sunglasses and smiled at him. "Actually, I'm hoping you can help me. I need supplies for a bird."

A bird. Hmmm. "We have a wide selection of bird supplies. What kind of bird is it?"

"It's from New Zealand."

Finn started checking off the possibilities of valuable New Zealand birds in his head. Not that he was going to steal from her. She seemed like a nice lady, and he tried to steal only from the assholes. But still. Habit is habit.

"New Zealand. Nice place. Do you know exactly what kind of bird it is?"

"It's a parrot," she said.

A parrot. From New Zealand. And she was being cryptic about it. People didn't tend to hide things unless there was something to hide. All signs pointed toward a job worth doing, which would be one job closer to getting away from birds forever.

Too bad he wasn't going to steal from her.

"Where'd you get it?" he asked. "Just curious."

"Gift. From a friend."

Finn smiled. Again with the cryptic. "I see."

"I'll need a cage, too, I think. Something I can carry it around in."

"We have an excellent selection of cages. How big is the bird?"

"Big. Chicken-sized."

Something clicked at the back of his head. He eyed her for a moment. "Flightless?"

"Yes."

Big. Flightless. New Zealand parrot. Finn scanned his memory for something specific, but came up dry. He was sure he knew what this bird was, though.

"So, what do you think? Regular parrot food or . . . Oh!" She made a face. "You don't think it's one of those birds that eats living things like mice and smaller birds, do you? Because I don't think I could do that. I have difficulty killing spiders. I've been known to carry fleas outside and release them. Not that I don't believe in the food chain, I do, I'm just all soft inside."

"It's the rare parrot that's actually carnivorous," Finn said, leaning forward amiably. "For future reference, though, you'll want to avoid owls and hawks."

She smiled at him. "Great. Do you think you can help me?"

"Absolutely." *Big. Flightless. New Zealand. Dammit.* "Let's take a look at what we've got."

Finn hopped out from behind the counter and directed her through the store, writing up the order on a receipt as they chose a cage, some parrot food, and various chew toys, all the while trying to figure out what the bird was.

"I'd like it all delivered to this address," Babs said, after they'd returned to the counter. She grabbed a sticky note from a pad by the register and scribbled down her address. "Today, if at all possible."

Finn glanced at the Beekman address, which promised swank digs with beaucoup security. Too bad he wasn't going to steal that bird. He sure loved a challenge.

"That should be just fine," Finn said. He punched the numbers into the register. "That'll be $362.08."

"Great." Babs pulled out her card.

Finn grinned, swiped the card, and handed it back. He drummed his fingers on the counter and waited for the transaction to approve.

Big. Flightless. New Zealand.

And, suddenly, it hit him. A Kakapo.

This woman had a quarter million dollars of bird sitting up in her penthouse. It was like a gift from heaven, dropped right in his lap.

Forget three jobs. This one would be it. The last bird job he'd ever have to work.

Ever.

He pulled the slip out and handed it to Babs to sign.

"Thank you so much for your help," she said as she scribbled her signature.

"We'll get that delivered for you this afternoon," Finn said.

Babs smiled and handed him back the slip. "I'll let my doorman know to expect you."

"Excellent." He separated the slip and handed her the receipt. "Have a nice day."

Finn watched her as she picked up her bag and headed out the door. Sure she was nice, but not nice enough for him to pass up a quarter million dollars.

No one was that nice.

Babs slipped on her sunglasses as she walked down the street. She couldn't help but smile. It was a beautiful October day in the city. The sun was shining. The air was crisp.

And life was very, very good.

She'd woken up to find that Dana had gone, and had been disappointed at first, until she saw the envelope from Nick on the kitchen table, and her heart had soared. Perhaps Dana had been awake when Nick stopped by, and the two of them had a nice conversation, perhaps gone out to breakfast together. Which could lead, perhaps, to some mended fences, which could lead, perhaps, to a few dates. By the time Babs finished her coffee, she was planning their second wedding, including superadhesive to keep the bride's feet in place.

Just in case.

She'd gotten showered, dressed, stuffed the envelope from Nick—which she assumed contained Vivian's check—into her purse and headed out to run her errands. The first thing on her list was getting supplies for the bird, which had been extremely pleasant—especially since that clerk had been so nice. And young and handsome, with light green eyes and spiky red hair. If she were thirty years younger, she'd have asked him out to dinner. *That's* how good she was feeling.

Now, it was off to St. Jude's, then she'd go back home and call Nick—maybe Dana would even answer his phone—and have him drop off the bird. The matter of finding a way to sell it on the black market would be tricky, but she'd navigated rougher waters than that before. She could do it again.

Bach's *Minuet in G Minor* played from her bag. Maybe it was Dana; she was glad she'd remembered to charge her cell phone last night. She pulled it out and flipped it open. "Hello?"

"Babs. Vivian Bellefleur. Is the bird alive?"

Babs stopped walking. "What?"

"I need the bird back," Vivian said. "Can you have your guy bring it over? Like now?"

"Well, no, Vivian," Babs said. "You can't have it back."

"I'm sorry," Vivian said, not sounding the least bit sorry. "Perhaps you didn't hear me. I said I need the bird."

Vivian's voice was laced with desperation and just a touch of hysteria, and a thought occurred to Babs.

"Well, maybe," she said slowly. "How much is it worth to you?"

"Worth?" Vivian screeched. "It's my bird."

"Not anymore," Babs said. "It'll cost you."

"You bitch," Vivian snapped, then followed it almost immediately with, "How much?"

"A hundred thousand." That should be enough to get the winery opened again. And now no birdie black market to deal with.

The day just couldn't get any more perfect.

"Fine," Vivian said. "We'll add it to my tab. But I need that bird."

"Your tab?" Babs reached into her purse and pulled out the envelope she'd found on the table that morning.

"I need that bird, Babs, unharmed," Vivian ranted on as Babs opened the envelope and began to read the letter tucked inside. "The psycho you hired drugged it and tossed it out the window and I need it."

Babs looked up from the letter. "What?"

"I don't know what kind of people you work with, Babs, but he was crazy. I bumped into him. I was afraid for my life."

Babs glanced down at the letter. "What did he look like? The guy who drugged it and tossed it out the window?"

"Tall. Dark. Cheekbones that could cut glass."

"Yeah, that's my guy." Babs skimmed the last of Nick's report, her heart sinking as she read.

Well. If I've ever wondered how quickly a day can go downhill, now I know.

"Look, Viv," she said with a sigh as she folded the letter and tucked it back into her purse. "We don't have the bird."

There was a long pause, then, "What?"

"We don't have it. Someone else stole your bird."

"But I *saw* him," Vivian said. "I saw him drug it and throw it out the window. And you just said that was your guy."

"The guy you saw was my guy. The guy who took your bird was another guy."

There was a slight pause, then a dramatic, "Oh. My. God."

Babs put her hand to her head to ward off the headache that was forming. "Viv? You okay?"

"No," Vivian said. "We have a problem."

"Viv," she said loudly into the phone. "You're breaking up, sweetie. Look, stay there. I'll be right over."

Babs pulled her phone away from her face and stared at it before flipping it closed and stuffing it back in her purse. She stood out in the street and raised her arm to hail a cab. Whatever Vivian's problem was, she was sure she could solve it.

After all, that's what she did.

Eight

⌐

Dana stood out in front of Murphy's Wine Bar, staring up at the building to the windows on the third floor.

Nick's windows.

She hadn't planned on coming here. Well, obviously she'd thought about it—she'd looked up the address for Murphy's in the phone book before she left. But she hadn't definitively *planned* on it. She was just going to walk around Manhattan, maybe get a cup of coffee. It was purely coincidence that she'd ended up in front of Murphy's.

Or something like that.

She played absently with the empty coffee cup in her hand as she stared up at the building, her heart beating faster with every second. She could walk away, play it safe, go on with her life as planned, and just let it go.

Or, she could take the chance. It had to be a sign that Nick popped back into her life right after her moment of

clarity. And that kiss. That kiss had nea_____
both over. It had to mean something.

Didn't it?

She exhaled. Three hours she'd been _____
Manhattan, thinking of signs and coinc_____ and what
might be meant to be. Her winery was the only one in the
Finger Lakes to have diseased grapes. If that hadn't happened, she never would have come down to see Babs last
night. What were the chances that on the one night she was
at her mother's, Nick would just happen to show up? On the
very day she'd had a moment of clarity? What if her
moment of clarity wasn't misplaced anxiety, but a message?
What if the kiss this morning—which was still tingling on
her lips no matter how much lip gloss she applied—actually
meant something? What if all this convergence pointed to
her one chance to make it right, and she blew it?

That would be bad. Then again, what if she went up
there to talk to him and he told her to get lost, that he was
over her, that he wanted no part of her?

That would be infinitely worse.

Better safe than sorry.

Nothing ventured, nothing gained.

"They're closed."

She turned around to look at the source of the gruff
voice, and saw a hot dog vendor about three yards away.
She took a few steps toward him, tossing her coffee cup in
the garbage pail next to his cart.

"Yeah. I know. I'm just . . . I know the guy—"

"Who?" he said. "Nick?"

"Yeah," she said. "Nick."

The hot dog vendor whistled and shook his head. "All
the ladies want Nick."

na blinked. "What do you mean, all the ladies? at ladies? Who ladies?"

"Dana?"

She spun around to see Nick standing right there, holding a cardboard box in his arms.

Oh, Jesus, he looks good.

"Hey," she said. Her throat went dry.

"Hey," he said.

"Hey, Nick," the hot dog vendor said. "Who's your friend?"

Nick smiled. "Out of your league, Oscar."

Dana tugged on Nick's jacket. "The hot dog guy's name is Oscar?"

Nick looked back at Dana, and his smile faded a touch. "Yeah. Why?"

She giggled nervously. "Is his last name Mayer?"

"Gee, never heard that one before," Oscar said flatly from behind her.

"Sorry." Dana turned back to Nick and motioned toward Murphy's. "Can we go inside for a minute?"

Nick nodded. "Sure." He shifted the box onto one hip and dug into his pockets, pulling out the keys. Dana waited behind him as he unlocked the front door, giving a quick wave to Oscar before following him inside. It was a gorgeous place, a big fireplace in the back, wine racks lining the sage green walls, and hardwood floors so golden they practically glowed.

"Wow, Nick," she said, her voice echoing in the empty space as she stepped inside. "This place is incredible. How many varieties do you serve?"

"About fifteen hundred," he said, setting the box down on a table close to the front. He leaned against it and crossed his arms over his chest, watching her with almost no expression. She took in a deep breath and motioned toward the box.

"Shipping some stuff?"

"Yeah." Something flashed in his eyes. "Babs didn't tell you?"

Dana blinked. "Tell me what?"

"Nothing. It's . . . not important." They stared at each other in silence for a moment. Nick shifted his weight. "Did you need something?"

"Yeah," she said, feeling her throat constrict as she watched him. Somewhere in the back of her mind, a voice was telling her that she wasn't off to a stellar start, but the din from the blind panic kind of drowned that voice out.

"Dana?" he prompted. "Are you all right?"

"Have you ever had a sudden moment of clarity?" she blurted.

Nick's eyebrows knit. "What?"

"A sudden moment of clarity," she repeated, feeling almost as stupid as she sounded. Still, she pushed on. "You know, like when people just know something."

He blinked. "Just know something?"

"Yeah, like when they just know that they're in love, or that something bad has happened to a family member, or"— she looked down—"that they're going to throw up all over glowing hardwood floors." She took in a deep breath and forced herself to meet his eye. "Have you ever had one?"

He watched her for a moment, then shook his head. "Don't think so."

"Well I have," she said. "I had it yesterday, and then I came to see Mom—not about the moment of clarity, about something totally different—but then when I saw you last night I kinda thought . . ." She stopped and tilted her head as she looked up at him. "You've really never had one?"

Nick shook his head, watching her with those eyes that cut right through her. How did he do that with just his eyes? Not that it mattered. He did it, and he was the only one who ever had.

"It was about you," she said finally.

He met her eyes, his face expressionless. "What was about me?"

"The moment of clarity." She exhaled, took in a deep breath. "I think I made a mistake."

Nick released a long breath before responding. "You think you made a mistake?"

"Yeah. When I left you. At the wedding. You remember the running?"

He nodded. "I remember the running."

"Yeah. That. It was a mistake." She swallowed hard and searched his face for some sign that he wasn't going to yell at her and tell her to get the hell out, but she couldn't read him.

"You don't have to say anything," she said quickly. "I mean, I don't expect that it matters. Much. I mean, it matters to me, but to you. . . . it shouldn't. Really. I just thought you should know that . . . um . . ."

He continued to stare at her.

"So," she went on, "that's why I came by. Just to, you know, tell you that I was wrong, and I know I was wrong, and I'm sorry."

Her voice cracked on the "sorry," and Nick's face finally softened. He pushed up off the edge of the table and took a step toward her. Dana took a step back.

"You really don't have to say anything," she said. "I mean, if you had something to say, you would have already said it, so anything you say now is really going to just be something to say, and who needs that, right? I just wanted you to know, that's all."

Nick shook his head. "You're not the only one who's made mistakes, Dana."

Dana stared up at him. "Melanie."

"Yeah." He dropped his eyes. "Actually, about that—"

"You don't have to explain anything," Dana said, laughing nervously and waving her hand in the air, her stomach turning at the thought of hearing about his night with Melanie. "I don't care that you slept with her."

Confusion flashed over his face. "You don't?"

"Oh, don't get me wrong. At first I did. For a while there, it was my most sincere wish that her little cloven feet would gouge your shins out." She laughed too loud and cringed, then went on. "I mean, it's not exactly a pleasant thought, you two together, but after what I did, who could blame you?"

"You don't blame me?"

She shook her head. "No."

He huffed out a small laugh, tinged with sadness. "You should. I screwed everything up as much as you did. I should have listened to you. I should have paid more attention."

"Ah, shoulda, woulda, coulda." Dana waved her hand dismissively in the air and smiled up at him. "There's no point. I'm sorry, you're sorry, yadda yadda yadda, right?"

He smiled back. "Right."

And suddenly there it was, that little sparkle at the

edge of his eyes, the one that was only for her, and her heart soared. For the first time since that damned moment of clarity, she thought maybe . . .

"I'm moving to California," he said, his smile fading.

Or, you know, maybe not.

"Whoa," she said, trying to catch her breath. "California. Big move."

He nodded. "Yeah."

"Where in California?" she asked, pulling on a forced smile.

"San Diego."

"Nice place. Pretty beaches."

"So I hear."

"New job?"

"Yeah."

"Doing what?"

Nick hesitated, then shrugged. "Nothing interesting."

"Great," she said, overpunching the enthusiasm. "Congratulations. Good for you. That's wonderful."

Shut up, she thought. *Just shut up and get out.*

"Thank you." He gestured with his shoulder at the box on the table behind him. "I was just . . . shipping some stuff."

"Wow," she said. Her fingertips were tingly, going numb. She guessed all the blood was flowing to the gaping psychic wound in her gut. "Well, then. I'm glad we had this little talk. Clear the air so we can both gain closure, move on, follow our bliss. Just like Oprah says. You know, she's really smart. Oprah."

Nick nodded. "Yeah."

"Yeah. So. Great. Well . . ." She looked up at him and tried not to read into what she thought she saw in his eyes. It didn't matter, anyway.

Stupid California.

"'Bye."

She moved clumsily past him. Her legs felt like tree trunks, they were so heavy. He touched her arm lightly, and she froze where she was, staring at the floor.

"I'm sorry," he said quietly. "About this morning. I shouldn't have . . ."

"Oh, no," she said, her eyes filling with tears. She clenched her teeth and tried to blink them away, thinking *Not now, oh please, not now.* "It was a good-bye kiss. Just a good-bye. It was time to, you know, say good-bye."

She shot up on her tiptoes and kissed his cheek, mostly so he wouldn't see the tear that was tracking down hers.

"Good-bye, Nick," she whispered, then darted out the front door. She thought she heard it open behind her, and someone's footsteps going out to the sidewalk, but she didn't turn around to look.

There really wasn't any point.

Nine

Babs sat on Vivian and Gary Bellefleur's leather sofa. Vivian, a tall thin blonde in her late thirties, with a patrician nose and an overdeveloped sense of drama, stood to Babs's left, her arms crossed over her stomach as her fingers tapped nervously over her elbow. Gary, a short balding guy with an unusual and disturbing fondness for golf clothes, stood to Babs's right. She felt like a little kid being scolded by her parents, and the sensation didn't sit well with her.

"A bald guy?" Vivian asked, staring at Babs in disbelief.

"You hired someone to steal Mr. Saunders?" Gary asked, staring at Vivian with a similar stunned expression. Vivian waved her hand at him dismissively.

"Well, you wouldn't let me have him killed—"

"With good reason!" Gary shouted.

"Zip it, Skippy," Vivian hissed.

Babs leaned forward. "Who's Mr. Saunders?"

Vivian rolled her eyes. "The stupid bird."

Babs leaned back. "Oh. Okay."

Gary sat in the chair next to the sofa. "My father loved that bird."

"Your father was a vicious nutcase."

Gary leveled his finger at Vivian. "Don't speak ill of the dead."

"Oh, pffft," Vivian huffed. "That bastard should have kicked it ages ago." She situated herself on the sofa next to Babs. "Fifteen years, Babs. Fifteen years of *Baby, fetch my meds* and *I dropped my remote, bend over, and pick it up, would ya?* and *Hey, Sweetcheeks, it's time to change my bedpan* and I did it. I did all of it. Took care of him. Took care of his stupid, smelly, stinky bird. So when the guy finally kicked off, I got rid of it. Yes." She put her hands on Babs's arm. "I mean, really, Babs. You would have done the same, wouldn't you?"

Gary flew up off the chair. "Not if it meant losing $25 million!"

Vivian hopped up off the sofa, her hands on her hips as she leaned into her yell. "How was I supposed to know the rotten old coot would leave everything to the stupid bird? You'd better hope crazy skips a generation, buddy, or you're screwed."

Babs stood up. "All right, both of you. Enough. Sit down. Please."

She pointed to the chairs on either side of the sofa. Vivian threw herself down. Gary scuffed one toe against the floor in protest and also sat down. Once they were seated and quiet, Babs settled back on the sofa.

"Explain to me"—she held her hand up as Vivian opened her mouth—"*calmly* what happened this morning."

"Albert came by," Gary said.

Babs looked to Vivian. "Who's Albert?"

Vivian rolled her eyes. "Family lawyer."

Babs looked to Gary. "Okay. And?"

"And he said that my father left his entire estate to the bird. We have to bring it in to the office on Friday so they can verify Mr. Saunders's good health before they can release the funds."

"And if you don't bring the bird?"

Vivian slumped into the chair. "Then we'll just have to find the most stylish lines for government cheese."

"Okay," Babs said, keeping her voice soft and calm. "We're adults. We'll find a solution."

"Here's a solution," Vivian said, sounding like a bratty teenager. "Send Cheekbones out to find the guy who stole my bird!"

Gary looked appalled. "*Cheekbones?* Is that a mob name?"

Babs tried not to roll her eyes. "His name is Nick, and he's not available."

"He was available last night," Vivian said.

Babs turned hard eyes on Vivian. "Last night was his last favor for me."

Vivian let out an exasperated sigh. "Then we'll throw some money at him."

"With what, Vivian? Government cheese?" Babs shook her head. "Besides, he doesn't do it for money."

"Then why does he do it?" asked Gary. "There has to be some way to convince him to do this for us. He's the one who saw the guy who took Mr. Saunders, and I think we're all agreed that none of us are exactly detective types."

Babs pinched the bridge of her nose between her fingers to ward off the migraine that Gary's high-pitched voice was bringing on.

"Look," she said, pulling her hand away from her face, "he's like a son to me. The things he did, he did because I asked him. He worked to help me, and I can't ask him to do anything else."

"There has to be something we can offer—" Gary started.

Babs shot an iron look at Gary. "I said *no, Gary.*"

Gary bristled a bit, but he shut up.

Babs turned to Vivian. "Tell me again why we can't call the police?"

"Because the bird is kinda illegal," Vivian said. "They'd have to turn it over to the conservation people in New Zealand. There are only, like, eighty of these birds left on the planet, and everyone's all freaking out about it."

"Wait. If the bird is illegal, why didn't you just call the conservation folks and have them come and take it?"

"I did!" Vivian huffed, slamming her arm down in frustration. "I called, and I said, 'Hey, let's say hypothetically someone had an illegal Kakapo, what would you do?' and the guy went on and on about this authority and that authority and blah blah frickin' blah. It would have taken them *weeks* to cut through all the bureaucracy and get their little Kiwi asses out here."

"And you couldn't wait a couple of weeks to do it right?" Babs asked.

Vivian gave her a dark look. "You've obviously never smelled a Kakapo."

Babs rolled her eyes. Fine. No police, no Nick, and the conservationists were now the enemy. She should have just gotten up and left, but getting this bird for Vivian and

Gary was very possibly the only way she'd be able to help Dana, and that was important enough to put up with Vivian and Gary for a little while longer.

"It'll be okay," Babs said to Vivian. "We just have to think up a plan and execute it, that's all."

Gary, fresh off his sulk, stood up from his chair.

"Actually," he said, walking across the room, "I think I might have a plan."

Babs pulled on a patient smile and watched as Gary removed a painting from the wall and turned the combination lock on the safe behind it. It wasn't until he turned around and she saw the gun in his hand that Babs let her smile drop.

"Gary?" she asked. "Exactly what are you thinking of doing with that?"

He lifted it, the barrel pointed unmistakably at Babs's chest.

"If this Nick helps you," he said, "make a call. Tell him you *really* need his help now."

Babs let out a light scoff, unable to believe that soft little Gary was actually threatening her. She turned to Vivian.

"Vivian? You want to handle this for me?"

"Oh my God, Gary," Vivian said, standing up and walking over to him. "I can't believe you. This is really good!"

"What?" Babs said.

"It's perfect!" Vivian said. "If Cheekbones won't do it for money, certainly he'll do it to save your life, you know, since you guys have that whole mother-son thing going on."

Babs stared at them. What a couple of idiots. She didn't

care anymore how much money she might be able to get from these two by getting that bird back. She'd find some other way to save the winery. This was over the line.

"That's it," she said, standing up. "I'm leaving, and you two can figure out on your own how to get your stupid bird back."

She took a step but stopped when a pop sounded and a piece of abstract artwork flew off the end table and crashed against the wall, leaving behind a smoking bullet wedged in the woodwork. Slowly, clutching her purse tightly in her hands, Babs turned her eyes to Gary.

"I went to a very well rounded prep school," Gary said. "Skeet shooting. I'm really good. If I miss you, it's because I intend to miss."

Babs's eyes narrowed. Skeet shooting? Was he *kidding*?

Gary's voice was dead serious. "That bird is worth $25 million, Babs. I've lived under my father's tyranny for forty years to get that money. I'm sorry, but if I have to threaten to kill you to get it, then I'll do that."

Babs slammed her purse against her thigh, the edges of her anger turning to fear as she looked at Vivian's face, smiling brightly a head above Gary's.

She couldn't believe it. She was being kidnapped by Boris and Natasha.

"Make the call," Gary said. "Use your cell. We'll tell you what to say. As soon as we get access to the money on Friday, you go home safe."

"How do I know you won't kill me once you've got the money so I won't go to the police?"

Gary's face pinched. "I hadn't thought that far ahead."

"We'll figure that stuff out later." Vivian turned to Babs. "Got your cell, sweetie?"

Babs grunted something rude and reached into her bag for her phone.

Nick sat on his sofa, staring at the box he'd carried back up after Dana left. He'd stood on the sidewalk watching her until she'd disappeared into the subway. He must have looked pretty pathetic; even Oscar didn't say anything. By the time he was done standing and staring, the thought of making a post office run was beyond him. He simply picked up the box, carried it back upstairs, and sat, running their conversation over and over in his mind.

What had she actually said? That she was sorry. That it was a mistake. But she didn't say she wanted him back, she didn't say she still loved him.

Gain closure. Follow our bliss. Like Oprah says.

What did that mean? Did it matter? He was finally about to put Dana behind him, get a fresh start, a clean slate. That was what he wanted.

Wasn't it?

No. What he wanted was to find Dana and kiss her until neither of them could see straight. He was fooling himself to think he was over her. He'd never be over her; he knew that. No matter what he told himself, no matter what he tried to be, the simple and ugly truth was that a part of him would always be hers. That's just the way it was.

So what were they going to do? Do you just get back together after six years? And what would happen when he told her that he hadn't slept with Melanie, that he'd let her believe that out of bitterness and spite? Would she still think she'd made a mistake then? And what about when she found out that he was going to California to work for Melanie? He couldn't play the hero on that one and pretend he'd done it to keep Melanie away from Dana. He couldn't lie to her even if he'd wanted to. But the truth—that he'd used saving her winery from Melanie as an excuse to accept the job—didn't shine very brightly on him, either.

Dana might think she made a mistake now; there was no guarantee she would once she knew the whole truth. Chances were good she'd want nothing to do with him.

He let out a bitter laugh. The irony was so tight it was almost poetic. He'd managed to screw up his second chance before he even knew he might get one.

His cell phone rang. His hand flew to it, and he had it open and to his ear before the first ring ended.

"Dana?" he said.

"Nick?"

Babs. Oh. Hell. He sat forward. "Yeah, Babs, what's up?"

Babs sighed. She sounded irritated, and Nick remembered about the flubbed job the night before.

"Look, sorry about the bird thing," he said, "but I think it'll probably be okay. Your friend just seemed happy the bird was gone and—"

"Get it back," a man's voice said. Nick blinked.

"Hello?"

"Get it back, or she dies," the voice said. It sounded like a teenage kid disguising his voice to be deeper, and it grated on Nick.

"Put Babs back on the phone," he said.

"You have until tomorrow at . . ." There was a sound, like the guy was muffling the phone with his hand, and Nick could hear him say in a higher, more effeminate voice, "What do you think? Ten?" Nick rolled his eyes. He heard the guy move his hand away from the phone and clear his throat before saying in a deep voice, "Tomorrow at ten. Bring us the bird."

"Put Babs on the phone."

"No police, or she dies," the voice said, then added, "Oh. And no conservationists."

No conservationists? What the hell was this guy talking about?

"Put Babs on the phone, or when I find that bird I'll fry it up for dinner."

There was a pause, then Babs got on the phone.

"I'm so sorry, Nick," she said.

"What's going on, Babs? Are you okay?"

Babs's voice faded, like she was holding the phone away from her face, as she said, "What?"

"Babs?" Nick said. The back of his neck was going cold. Whatever was going on here, even if Babs was being held by a psychotic fifteen-year-old as it sounded, he didn't like it. He heard Babs sigh into the phone.

"He says to tell you he'll kill me," she said flatly. She sounded more annoyed than scared.

"Who?" Nick asked. "And does he realize that I'm gonna rip his throat out when I find him?"

"Nick, I'm sorry. I really am. But I need your help. Please . . . do you think you can locate the bird?"

Nick remembered the receipt he'd found with the sticky note instructions. He knew he was looking for a bald guy with some sort of accent, possibly staying in the Lower East Side. Of course, there were probably over a million people in the Lower East Side alone. Forget the 9 million in the rest of the city.

"I don't know," he said. "Maybe. But I can definitely come over there and beat the hell out of this guy. Just tell me where you are."

"I can't," Babs said. "He's got a gun pointed at my head."

Nick felt his gut take a tumble. "What?"

"I think it'll be okay, Nick," Babs said, "but the easiest way out of this is just to get the bird. Can you do that for me?"

"Yes," he said, injecting more certainty in his voice than he actually felt. "Now put him on the phone."

There was a shuffle, and the guy came on with the fake-deep voice. "Yes?"

"Listen, asshole," Nick said. "I'm getting your bird because Babs asked me to. But if you touch a hair on her head, I will kill you. Do you understand me?"

The voice cracked slightly. "Yes."

"Now, where are we meeting tomorrow?"

There was another shuffle, the sound of the guy asking a question in his real voice, and a woman, not Babs, answering. Nick raised his eyes to the ceiling.

This is fucking ridiculous.

"South Street Seaport," the guy said.

"You want to trade out a ransom at the South Street Seaport at ten o'clock on a Thursday morning?" Nick said. Good God. Leave it to Babs to get kidnapped by Boris and Natasha.

"Rockefeller Center?" the guy said in his regular voice, which was high-pitched and a bit nasal. Nick didn't recognize it, but it didn't sound like the voice of a killer. It sounded like the voice of an accountant.

Nick rattled the address of an empty business property

on Fifth Street that Murphy had talked to him about the week before. "We'll meet you there at five Thursday morning."

There was a pause, a phone shuffle, more muffled consulting, and something from the guy that sounded like, "But that's so early."

Nick gritted his teeth.

The guy came back on the phone. "Okay. Fine. Bring the bird."

And he hung up. Nick pulled his phone away from his ear and checked the Caller ID. Babs's cell phone. Well, it looked like Boris and Natasha weren't quite as stupid as they seemed. He disconnected and dialed Babs's home number, which went straight to voice mail.

Of course.

He sat for a minute and thought about what he should do, but he already knew. He grabbed his coat and headed out the door, hoping he got to tell Dana the news before the kidnappers did.

He owed her that much.

Ten

Dana leaned forward on Babs's couch and reached for another tissue.

"Okay," she said out loud as she wiped the newest tears from her cheeks. "This is just stupid."

She'd started crying on the subway back from Nick's place and had yet to stop. Most people had ignored her, but then this woman with a tremendous bag full of knitting needles—no yarn, just the needles—sat next to her. The woman began knitting an imaginary sweater and said she was making it just for Dana to cheer her up. *It's a special brand of pathetic, when the crazies take pity on you,* Dana had thought as she gratefully accepted the imaginary sweater before getting off two stops early. As nice as Imaginary Sweater Lady had been, there was only so much humiliation Dana could stomach in one day.

What had she been thinking? That Nick's life would be on hold, waiting for her to come back, just because hers had been? That was stupid. He was going to California. Better, he'd been planning on going without even telling her. That's how over they were. O-Ver.

That was it. As soon as Babs got back, they were going to the bank, cosigning the loan, and she was getting the hell out of Dodge. She'd go home, get the winery on track, and start her life over again. No more waiting for men to seek her out. She was going to get out there, start her life, lose her second virginity. Hell, she might even have a one-night stand. She might have a few. Little Ricky from the Blockbuster had been making eyes at her lately, and there were worse prospects out there.

She sighed. Even if Little Ricky from the Blockbuster was a dynamo in the sack—which she kinda doubted—no one's touch would ever do to her what Nick's had. She knew that, as sure as she knew anything. She'd had her chance, she'd blown it big-time, and she was just going to have to settle for . . . whatever was left.

"Well," she said as a fresh well of tears sprung from her eyes. "I hope Little Ricky likes Italian."

She reached for another tissue as the elevator dinged. She sniffed and swiped at her face, hoping her mother wouldn't notice. One glance in the mirror over the sofa shot those hopes to hell, though. Her face was red and streaked. She looked like the Sta-Puff Marshmallow Man's suicidal housewife.

Well. Maybe Mom won't say anything. Dana smoothed her hands over her orange turtleneck sweater and jeans— the best going-to-the-bank outfit she could muster from what she packed—and started toward the elevator to meet her mother.

"I'm really glad you're here," she sniffed, picking a

fuzzy off the bottom of her sweater. "I think we should run right to the bank and get the paperwork started because I really have to get back to the—"

She glanced up and froze in her tracks. It wasn't Babs. It was Nick.

And the hits keep on coming, she thought.

"Dana," he said, moving into the penthouse, stopping when he saw her face. He exhaled and looked almost as torn up as she felt. "Oh, hell, Diz."

He walked over to her and pulled her into his arms. Stunned, she let him, although a small voice in the back of her head was protesting the use of the pet name for her and railing against the mixed signals and the unfair play and . . .

And then he kissed the top of her head, his breath falling warm over her scalp and down her neck to her shoulders, and she didn't give a crap about pet names or fair play or California or her future with Little Ricky from the Blockbuster. It felt too good to have Nick hold her. She wrapped her arms around his waist and pulled him tight to her.

"Don't worry," he said. "We'll get her back. She's gonna be just fine."

"Mmmm," Dana said, snuggling her face into his chest. Then her brain processed what he'd said. She opened her eyes. "What?"

Confusion flashed on Nick's face, and he stepped back, putting his hands on her shoulders and looking into her eyes. "Didn't Babs call you? You looked so upset, I thought . . ."

Dana shook her head. "No. Mom has been gone all morning. I was just . . ." She motioned vaguely toward the couch, where she'd wept away much of the past hour. She sighed and turned back to Nick. "It doesn't matter. What's up with Mom?"

Nick ran his hand through his hair, watching her warily. She could see the wheels turning in his brain as he took in the crumpled tissues sprinkled on the floor by the couch.

"Diz . . ." he said softly, shifting back to her in all her Sta-Puff glory.

"I'm fine," Dana said, her anger rising anew at the mixed signals and the unfair play and the nerve of him even pretending to care if he'd ripped her heart out. "What's going on with Mom?"

Nick's jaw muscles clenched. "Maybe we should sit down."

Ice crawled up Dana's spine, and she felt nauseated. Whatever Nick had come here to say, it wasn't good. She could see the tension in his eyes, and his fists were clenched.

Something was very wrong.

Something with her mother.

"I don't want to sit down," she said. "Something's wrong, and you're going to tell me what it is. Right now."

Nick started to say something, then stopped and sighed. Dana's lips started to tremble, and she could feel the tears fixing to make an encore appearance.

"Is she okay?" she asked, trying to keep her voice even.

"Yeah, she's fine," Nick said. "She's just been . . . well . . . kidnapped. I think."

Dana blinked. "Kidnapped? You think?"

Nick nodded. Dana stood motionless, trying to take it in. Babs was kidnapped? Who got kidnapped anymore? Didn't that go out of style in the seventies?

"By who?"

Nick shook his head. "Not sure."

Okay. Babs was kidnapped.

"What do they want?"

"A bird."

A bird. She squinted up at him, sure she'd heard him wrong. "A what?"

Nick put one hand gently on her arm. "Why don't we sit down, and I'll tell you everything I know, okay?"

Dana nodded and allowed him to guide her to the kitchen table. She sat and stared at her hands as he made tea and told her the story of apparently inept kidnappers and Babs's plea that they find some bird. At the end, Nick was sitting across from her at the table, his fingers running absently over the mug of tea he hadn't touched.

"So . . . let me get this straight. She's been kidnapped by Boris and Natasha? From *Rocky and Bullwinkle*?"

Nick shook his head. "I don't know who they are. But they sounded like Boris and Natasha."

Dana blinked. "Russian?"

"No. Stupid. Which works in our favor, although I don't want to take any chances. Babs said the guy had a gun, and I have no reason not to believe it."

A gun. Great. Super. "So we have until tomorrow morning to find a bald British guy living in the Lower East Side with a smelly bird?"

"He might be from Australia. Maybe New Zealand. One of those countries where men call each other 'mate'," he said.

"So, Irish, possibly?" Dana felt her breath catch in her throat. "Do they say 'mate' in Ireland?"

Nick put his hand on her lower arm, leaning closer to

her. She stared at his hand, amazed at how strongly she felt it through the general numbness.

"Hey," he said. She raised her eyes to his. He gave her a soft smile. "I can find this guy. I can get that bird. It's all going to be fine."

Dana's vision blurred under the tears as emotion found its way through the fog.

Her mother was kidnapped. With a gun to her head. Possibly scared, but Nick said she was pissed off, but how could she not be scared?

"Diz," Nick said, one thumb rising to her face to wipe away a tear. "She's gonna be fine. We'll get her back. I promise you."

"Okay," Dana said, nodding. Nick gave her arm a squeeze and leaned back. Dana wiped her face and stared into her tea. A question presented itself in her mind, and she voiced it on autopilot.

"What exactly do you do for my mother, anyway?"

Nick watched Dana, not sure what to say. They'd been having a nice moment, a connected moment. After she'd run out of Murphy's, he didn't think they'd ever have another one of those. He knew it was only temporary, but it was nice, and the last thing he wanted to do was ruin it by talking about what he did for Babs. He got up and walked over to the kitchen phone, cycling through the Caller ID list.

"What are you doing?" Dana asked.

His cell phone and two unknown numbers were all that had called today. No good. He stared down at the number pad.

"Do you know how to take this thing off DO NOT DISTURB?"

"No. You're avoiding my question. Mom said you free-lanced for charity."

He put the handset back on the cradle and leaned against the island in the middle of the kitchen. "Free-lanced for charity? Since when is volunteer work called freelancing?"

"That's just what I thought," Dana said. "So, what, she lied to me?"

"No," Nick said. "It's just hard to explain. I do favors for her, kinda."

"Favors?"

"Kinda."

"Like what? Like changing lightbulbs or fixing the occasional sink?"

Nick let out a light laugh at the thought. "Babs knows more about sinks than I do, and that's not saying much."

"Okay, fine, so if it's not sinky stuff . . . what is it?" Her face crinkled in suspicion, and she leaned back away from him. "You two . . . you aren't . . . ?"

It took a moment for Nick to get what Dana was implying.

"No! God, no! Dana, Jesus, how could you even think—?"

"I don't know," she said, focusing on her tea mug. "I rarely talk to her and I never talk to you and any-thing's . . . possible."

"Not with your mother, it's not," he said.

"Why?" Dana said, and he could see that he'd offended her. "What's wrong with my mother? She's still a very beautiful woman, and she's smart and fun and lively."

Nick couldn't help but laugh. "What, you *want* me to date her?"

"No, but . . . ," Dana stammered, "she's a beautiful, smart, lively woman."

"No argument, but she's *your* mother," he said. He waited until she looked up and met his eye before continuing. "There are a million reasons why that would never happen, not the least of which being that she's like a mother to me. But at the top of the list, Diz, is you."

She gave him a slight smile, and he returned it, holding her gaze for a moment before looking away. He leaned forward, grabbed his mug off the table, and brought it to the sink.

"She has a lot of rich friends, and they have . . ." He paused as he poured the tea into the sink, trying to think of the right word. ". . . errands they need run. I run them."

"So you're an errand boy?"

He shrugged. "More or less. Usually the things they need done are a bit unorthodox."

The left side of her lips quirked in a semismile, and her eyes brightened with amusement. For the first time, he noticed that she'd aged a bit about the eyes, just slight creases indicating she still smiled as much as she used to. This buoyed and saddened him at the same time; he was glad she was still smiling and sad he'd missed whatever had been making her laugh.

"So," she said, "you're an unorthodox errand boy?"

Nick realized he was staring at her and turned back to washing the mug.

"Yeah. For instance, once, one of Babs's little friends wanted a new necklace worth the gross national product of a small country, but her husband refused on the grounds that she already had too much jewelry, so she put a handful of things she didn't want in a box and hired me to break in and steal it."

Dana's smile dropped, and her eyebrows knit together. "What? You broke in? You know how to break in to places?"

Nick shrugged. "Sure." He felt a bit uncomfortable under her gaze and cleared his throat. "I mean, no. I mean, it wasn't really breaking in, since she asked me to do it."

"But her husband didn't," Dana said.

Nick watched her in silence as she stared at him, her expression one part stunned and two parts . . . what? Disappointed? Probably. Maybe she wasn't regretting her mistake so much anymore, which he guessed was a good thing.

For her, anyway. He dried the mug and put it back in the cabinet.

"Look, we should start concentrating on this bald guy."

Dana stood up, bringing her mug to the sink. "I wasn't judging you."

"Yeah, you were," he said, moving away as she came toward him. "But it doesn't matter. We've got other things to think about right now."

She sighed and turned to face him. "Why do you do that?"

He crossed his arms over his chest. "What?"

"You never want to talk about things," she said. "You just change the subject, shuffle it under the carpet."

"I talk about things when it might make a difference. I don't see the point in beating a horse that's still gonna be dead when we're done."

"Well, sometimes the horses aren't dead. Sometimes

they just want you to listen and talk and . . ." She trailed off, threw her hands up in the air. "You can't just proclaim a horse dead because you want it to be."

Nick stared at her for a moment. "What?"

"Nothing." She let out a big sigh. "Look, I can tell I offended you, and I'm sorry. I was just trying to understand what you do, which I still don't, but now, I just don't care. Okay?"

She turned to face him, and he felt it again, that wringing in his gut that happened when she got close. One more motivation to get Babs home safe as quickly as possible.

"Okay," he said.

"Thank you." She turned to wash out her mug. Nick leaned back on the counter behind her, keeping his eyes on anything but the curves of her backside.

"So," he said, after giving her a moment to calm down, "I figure I'll start with this bar in the Lower East Side. A guy like that should be memorable to someone. I should be able to get some information pretty quickly—"

Dana tossed the dish towel on the counter and turned back to face him. "*You?* You mean *we.*"

"No," Nick said. Just the idea of spending any more time with Dana than absolutely necessary made his shoulders knot up like a Boy Scout's rope. "I mean *me.* You will stay here."

"And in what universe did you think that was going to fly?"

Nick let out an exasperated sigh. He should have known it wouldn't be that easy. "You're not going with me. What if Babs calls? Someone should be here—"

"If she calls, she'll call you. Like before. On your cell. And when she does call, I'm going to be there."

"Fine," he said, reaching into his pocket and pulling out his phone. "You keep this here, with you."

She pushed it back at him. "They'll want to talk to you. And anyway, I don't need your permission. It's my mother. I'm going."

She stomped out of the kitchen toward the front hallway. Nick ground his teeth and followed her.

"It'll be better for everyone involved if I do this alone, Dana."

"Sorry? What was that? All I heard was 'Blah blah blah I'm a macho jerk blah blah.' "

He grabbed her by the arm and pulled her around to face him, releasing her almost immediately as he did. "Maybe you should listen a little more carefully, then. I'm not taking you with me."

She stared up at him, her blue eyes piercing into his, and he felt it again. That same instinct—no, not instinct, need—to pull her to him and kiss her until neither of them could think straight. He took a step back. She grabbed her jacket off the rack and hit the call button for the elevator, staring at the doors, as though he weren't there.

"We don't know who this guy is or what he's willing to do to keep that bird, and I'm at a disadvantage if I have to worry about you."

Her face softened a bit, and he felt a ray of hope that he might be able to get her to stay. He put his hand on her arm.

"Look, Diz—"

Her face quirked, and she pulled her arm away from him.

"Please stop calling me that."

Nick felt as though he'd been slapped. When had he

started calling her "Diz" again? How had he slipped into the old familiarity without realizing it?

The elevator dinged, and the door opened. They watched each other for a moment, then Nick held out one arm.

"Ladies first," he said.

"Thank you." She stepped into the elevator and hit the button. Nick followed, and there was nothing but silence for the thirty-floor ride down to the lobby.

Eleven

Finn walked into the lobby of Babs McGregor's building, checking the place out as he moved. Marble columns. Oriental rugs. Exactly the swank digs he'd expected. He walked up to the reception desk and pulled on his brightest corn-fed smile.

"Hi," he said. "Delivery for McGregor from *Chez Animaux.*"

The doorman glanced up at him, then sat forward and checked his clipboard.

"Yeah, she called about you guys this morning. Birdcage, parrot food, box of toys," he read. He glanced at Finn. "All of it outside?"

Finn nodded. "You betcha. It's just me doing deliveries today, so I'll have to make two trips."

The doorman flipped the clipboard at him. "Says you can go on up. I just need you to sign here."

"Surely," Finn said, then scribbled "Big Bird" in unreadable man-scratch on the clipboard. The doorman took it back without looking at it. Good news—complacency in the door staff.

"Service elevator is out. You'll have to use the main. I'll call up so if anyone's there, they know to expect you."

Finn gave him a big smile. "Sounds great." He himself had called about ten seconds ago, and no one had answered. So far, so good. He returned to his double-parked van, pulled out the bulky birdcage, and walked back inside the lobby. A woman with a dog and a fur collar glanced at him. He gave a bright smile and a small wave.

"Howdy," he said. She looked away. Finn had learned a long time ago that the more friendly people in uniforms are to a certain segment of the population, the harder that certain segment works to make them invisible. If it ever came down to a police interrogation, it would be as if the interaction had never happened.

These people were just too easy.

The doorman waited for him by the elevators. One opened, and a pretty woman flew out, followed by a tall guy in a leather coat. They both looked upset about something. Finn moved out of their way and kept his head down.

"Ms. Wiley. Mr. Maybe," the doorman said as they stormed past without giving him so much as a nod.

He keyed in the penthouse floor, and Finn stepped inside. He checked his watch—12:38. Mrs. McGregor had said the bird would be arriving in the afternoon, so it might not be there yet. If it wasn't, he'd at least be able to get a good look at the security system. He knew the weaknesses of most of them, and the secret to jobs like this one was having a handle on the weaknesses. All he had to do was find one, exploit it, and come back later.

Easy, breezy, Japanesey.

A Kakapo. A friggin' Kakapo. His fingers tingled as he thought about it. He already had two buyers lined up at two hundred thousand each—pit them against each other, and he'd have an offer of a quarter million by tomorrow. Then it would be good-bye *Chez Animaux,* good-bye birds, and hello . . . something else. He didn't know what, exactly, but he knew that if it didn't involve birds, it would be good.

Very, very good.

Dana watched as Nick leaned over the bar to talk with the bartender. Bleeker's Pub was a dingy hole in the wall with peanut husks on the scuffed, dark wood floor. The place was predominantly belowground, so the only light from the sunny October day outside came through the grimy front window. Some brand of Irish drinking music piped out of the worn speaker system, and at two o-clock in the afternoon, business was slow. It was the perfect place to wallow in a depressed bender.

Dana decided she could get used to this place. Between Nick's moving to California, her mother's kidnapping, and the impending financial implosion of her winery, a depressed bender in a dank pub sounded like a damned good idea. She was kinda disappointed that she hadn't thought of it sooner.

The bartender said something to Nick that made him chuckle. Dana watched him and couldn't help smiling herself. When Nick smiled, even that small one that stayed mostly in his eyes, he lit up a room. Or at least, he lit it up for her.

Little Ricky at the Blockbuster didn't have a smile like that. He was very nice, though. Four feet tall if he was an inch, but he had a solid job. He knew all the best anime films and could probably snag her some nice movie posters to wallpaper the one-room studio she'd be moving into when she lost her winery, her home, and her sense of purpose in the world.

Oh, God. She really needed to get started on that bender.

Nick traded some cash for two beers and returned to their table.

"According to the receipt I found, our guy was here on Monday at seven," Nick said. "We got lucky. The waitress who works that shift comes on in two hours."

"Lucky?" Dana said. "How is that lucky?"

Nick raised his beer. "We get to sit here and drink until she shows up. Trust me, this is comfortable compared to other jobs I've done for Babs."

Dana sipped her beer, then took another. With each drink, she felt a little better. This wasn't bad at all. "Why does my mother get these jobs?"

"Because Babs is the person crazy rich people go to when they've got a problem."

Dana watched him, her heart suddenly stung by the fact that he knew more about her mother than she did. Not that it was anyone's fault but her own, really. "She helps people?"

Nick shrugged, smiled lightly. "Yeah. It makes her happy. I just do the stuff she can't do."

"Like breaking into people's homes and taking their birds," Dana said, smiling.

He raised an eyebrow. "With their permission. Yeah."

Dana lowered her eyes first. "So what's with the charity thing?"

"Oh." Nick took a sip of his beer and settled it carefully back on the table. "She coerces donations."

Dana chuckled. "Coerces donations?"

Nick smiled. "Yeah. You know Babs can't sit still, and organizing fund-raisers got boring pretty quick, I guess. So, she does these favors for her rich friends and in lieu of a fee, they make donations to one of her pet charities. Usually St. Jude's."

Dana felt a small surge of pride, an unusual feeling to be connected with her mother. "The children's hospital? Really?"

"Really."

"Wow," Dana said.

Nick smiled, that smile that sparkled at the edges of his eyes, and Dana felt dizzy and leaned back in her seat, for the first time noticing that half of her beer was gone. Whoa. How had that happened?

Nick noticed it, too. "Have you had anything to eat today?"

Dana blinked, then shook her head. "Didn't sleep much last night, either. But I feel fine." She grinned up at him. "Really fine."

"Stay here," he said, starting up from the table. "They've got a menu at the bar."

"No," she said, and put her hand on his. Wow. She must be drunk. If she were sober, she'd never have the nerve. She kept her hand there and looked up at him. "The beer took the edge off, and I've been way edgy. I'm okay. Really."

He gave a brief nod and settled back into his chair, nudging the bowl of peanuts on the table toward her with a soft smile.

"Compromise?"

She dipped her hand into the peanuts, pulling out a handful and settling them on the table in front of her and reaching for the beer.

"At least slow down on the beer," Nick said.

"I'm fine," Dana said. "I can hold my drink. Remember that time in the eleventh grade when Becky Doosey and I went to the elementary school playground and got drunk and she threw up all over the . . . the . . . the . . ." She snapped her fingers, trying to remember what they called that thing. "You know, the twirly thingie."

One side of his mouth quirked up. "The merry-go-round?"

"Oh, thank you, that would have bugged me all day." She sighed, took another sip of her beer, and giggled. "I think you're right. I'm getting drunk fast. I can't remember what I was talking about. What was I talking about?"

"Shhhh," he said.

Dana leaned forward and said in a stage whisper, "Oh, God. Am I at that point already? When I'm even whispering too loud? Oh, that's just pathetic."

He put his hand on hers, and she could see his eyes following something over her shoulder. Without looking at her, he talked coolly.

"Lucky break. Our guy just walked in," he said. "Glance

behind me, like you're looking at the TV. Do you see a large guy with a shaved head sitting at the bar?"

Dana tried to be casual as she let her eyes wander over to the television hanging above the bar. Instantly, she locked on to the back of a shaved bald head. The guy was big, broad across the shoulders. She couldn't see much of his face in the dirty bar mirror, but she'd have guessed his age at about thirty-five. He wore a denim jacket and jeans.

"Very eighties in the fashion sense," Dana said as she sat back. "What do we do now?"

He ran his fingers lightly over her hand. "We act casual, like we're just here for each other's company."

Dana tried to breathe normally as the tingle from his touch made its way up her arm. Nick leaned forward, smiled at her, but his eyes were serious. She glanced over his shoulder at the bald guy.

"Hey," Nick said. "Don't worry about him. I want you to keep your eyes on me."

She pulled her eyes off of the bald guy and looked at Nick, but the way he was holding her hand, gently rubbing his fingers over hers, felt really good, and she knew she didn't want it to feel good, but her head was going all woozy and all she really wanted to do was jump over the table and have her way with him right there, but that would be stupid.

Very, very good, but really, really stupid.

"Dana?"

She blinked at the sound of her name. "Hmmm?"

"Did you just hear a word I said?" he asked quietly, looking at her the way he used to before all the crap came down between them. She knew he was just playing a role to keep attention away from them, but man it felt good.

But. Oh. Wait. He'd asked her a question.

"Hmmm?"

He laughed and pushed her beer away. "We're switching you to water." His eyes lost the twinkle of amusement, and he leaned closer, speaking softly. "I said I'm gonna need you to do exactly what I say, no matter how strange it might seem."

Dana nodded, and it felt a bit like the room was nodding with her. "No matter how strange. Got it, cap'n."

"Remember we're here for Babs. So no matter what I ask, you have to do it without argument. Just trust me, okay?"

Dana held his eye. "I trust you."

Something flashed on his face, and he looked away for a moment as he leaned back, still holding on to her hand. When his eyes raised to hers again, they'd lost any trace of a smile.

"Does he have his drink yet?" he asked.

Dana glanced casually over Nick's shoulder as the bald guy took a sip of a dark, thick beer that looked like syrup. Yugh. She nodded and took a sip of her own amber lager.

He gave an exasperated sigh. "What do you think you're doing?"

"Being casual."

He nudged the beer away from her. "Water, remember?"

She rolled her eyes. "Fine. What now?"

He glanced around, even though there was no one in the bar besides them, the bald guy, and the bartender. He leaned forward and spoke quietly, his voice soft and his expression all smiles as if he was whispering sweet nothings, but his eyes were calculating.

"Pick a fight with me, and keep pushing me until you knock me into him."

Dana pulled her hand away. "What?"

He grabbed it back, pulled it to his face, kissed the palm.

"You said you trusted me," he said. "Did you mean it?"

"Uhnhuh," Dana garbled in the affirmative through her closing throat as she tried to ignore the tingling on her palm where his lips had just touched her.

"Then pick a fight with me," he whispered. "Now."

"What . . . what . . . what am I mad about?" she whispered, her heart rate climbing.

"Anything," he said. "Say whatever you want, just back me up into that guy."

She glanced at the guy. Holy crap. She wasn't ready for this. What would she say? What would she do? What if she screwed it up? She grabbed her beer.

"Um . . . Dana?" Nick said warily, as she downed the last of her drink.

"Liquid courage," she said, pulling her hand away and standing up, knocking her chair back. The bartender and the bald guy both turned to look, but she kept her eyes on Nick.

Showtime.

"You big stupid jerk!" she yelled.

He stood up, his face flashing with surprise. She stomped up to him and stabbed her index finger into his chest.

"California?" she shouted into his face. "What the hell is so great about California?"

She pushed him backward, and he stumbled. She knew the shock on his face, the stumbling, was all an act, but it felt kinda good. She advanced on him again, slammed her palms into his chest.

"California's stupid. Do you know how expensive it is to live out there? Property taxes are through the roof!" She huffed out some air, blowing her bangs off her forehead. "No pun intended."

"Dana," Nick said, staring at her with a confused look. "You expect me to believe you're pissed off about property taxes?"

She felt her eyes start to brim up and threw herself into the part. She was acting, after all. Why not play it up?

"No," she said. "But you could have told me. Maybe I didn't deserve to know, but I think I deserved to know. You know?"

His face softened a bit. "Dana . . ."

"It's just so far away," she said. The first tear had fallen, and her lower lip had begun to tremble. "Why does it have to be so far away?"

His breath caught. "Dana . . ."

She swiped at her face. He walked toward her, put his arms around her, drew her to him. She let him hold her for a moment, then braced her hands against his chest.

"No," she said, pulling back from him. "It's too late."

She used all her force to push him away from her. He played up her force with a stumble that looked real but wasn't, and he crashed into the bald guy, knocking the guy's beer all over him.

Dana swiped at her eyes and watched as everything played out in slow motion. Nick grabbing the guy's wallet out of his coat as he fell. The guy giving a shout and grabbing Nick by the collar. Nick feigning apologies, trying to dry the guy off with the napkin. The guy pushing him away and heading for the men's room. The bartender seeing them both out of the bar. A moment later, they were in the street, Nick raising his arm for a cab as Dana stood beside him and swiped calmly at her face, pushing away the last remnants of tears.

"You okay?" he asked.

She pulled on a smile. "Oh, yeah. That was fun."

He stared at her for a moment. "Fun? Really? So . . . you're okay, then."

She widened her smile, thinking, *No, I'm in a bottomless pit of hell, but I'm not going to let you see that, because it's just embarrassing.*

She said, "Oh, yeah, absolutely. I mean, it was just acting. Right?"

He nodded but didn't smile back. "Right."

"And acting is fun. I like it. I think I'll look into doing some community theater when I get back home."

"Yeah," he said, still seeming a little stunned. "You'd be great.

"I think I would. What's next?"

"Well," he said, pulling a hotel keycard out of his coat pocket, "this is for a room at the Fountain Street Arms. We start there." He eyed her for a moment. "Are you sure you're okay?"

"Never better," Dana lied. A cab stopped for them, and she walked over to it and opened the door. In truth, she'd meant every word she'd said and every tear was real and if she had her way, she'd be back in Bleeker's drowning her sorrows in something seriously alcoholic. But Babs needed saving and Nick needed getting over and she needed to move on to the next thing before she had time to think about a future full of depressed benders, imaginary sweaters, and late nights with Little Ricky from the Block-buster.

She turned to see Nick watching her, his eyes boring into her. Something was going on behind them, she knew, but now was not the time. Time to get cheery and make it through the rest of the day. She smiled brightly.

"Ready?"

"Yeah," he said, and hopped in after her, being careful to keep a good amount of space on the seat between them.

Which, she guessed, only made sense.

Twelve

In the cab ride over to the Fountain Street Arms, Nick discovered a few key pieces of information. The bald guy was named Simon Burke, he worked for the New Zealand Kakapo Wildlife Conservation, and he kept three thousand dollars in cash in his wallet. It was definitely some good starting material.

Dana chatted amiably with the cabdriver. Nick watched her and tried to recover from the scene in the bar. She'd seemed so sincere, so upset about his leaving, but then just minutes later she was all bouncy and happy like it was nothing. Maybe it was nothing. Maybe she really didn't care that he was leaving. In that moment in the bar, however, he'd been ready to cancel his plans and spend the rest of his life in that apartment over Murphy's if it would have made her smile again.

As it turned out, she didn't need him to. All it took was a short cab ride to a crappy hotel in a bad part of town.

Just went to show that Nick knew even less about women than he thought, and he'd never professed to understand them at all. Seventeen years of trying to figure out Dana Wiley, even with the six-year hiatus, had pretty much killed any delusions he had that he'd ever know what was coming next.

She leaned forward, arms on the back of the seat, and chatted with the cabdriver through the open bulletproof partition, making him laugh. It was the rare person who took the time to make a cabdriver laugh, Nick thought. As the cab pulled in front of the Fountain Street Arms, Dana glanced at Nick and caught him watching her. She mouthed, *What?*

Nothing, he mouthed back. He hopped out of the cab, paid the fare, and held his hand out to Dana to help her out of the backseat. He put his hand lightly on the small of her back to guide her into the tiny hotel. The lobby was small and dark, and the girl behind the desk was college age, chewing gum, and flipping apathetically through a magazine. Behind her on the wall were a series of boxes, each corresponding to a room.

The stars were aligned. He turned to Dana.

"Ready to play along?" he asked.

She smiled. "Sure."

He guided her to the front desk, then slid the hotel keycard and some of the cash he'd nicked from the wallet into his pocket before laying the wallet down on the counter.

"Hi," he said, grinning brightly at the girl. "We found this outside. Thought it might belong to one of your residents."

The girl cracked her gum, flicked the wallet open, and began typing in the computer. Nick draped one arm over

Dana's shoulders, pulling her so close he could smell the flowery fragrance of her shampoo, mixed with the spice that was only Dana. His body instantly reacted to her scent, and he pulled back a bit.

There was a job to do. He had to concentrate on the job.

The girl tossed the wallet into the slot for 319, then looked back up at Nick and Dana.

"Yeah. Thanks. You guys need anything else?"

"Actually, yeah." Nick slid sixty of Simon Burke's dollars across the desk with a bright smile. "We'd like a room. For about an hour. And we'd like to pay cash, if you know what I mean."

He could feel Dana's shoulders tense up for a moment, but when he looked at her, she'd pulled on a bright smile for the benefit of the desk clerk. The girl looked from Nick to Dana, then back to Nick. She raised one eyebrow.

"It'll cost you eighty."

Nick slid her another twenty. The girl sighed, slipped the money in her pocket, slid a keycard through the machine, and handed it to them.

"Room 405. And you got one hour."

Nick winked at her, took the card, and led Dana to the elevator. Silently, they got in and she hit 3. They smiled at each other and looked away, like a couple of kids on a first date.

"This is fun," she said.

"Really?" he said. "You think so?"

"Oh, yeah. You have to understand, I've been running a winery for ten years. And here I get to be all Remington Steele with you." She stared at the numbers blinking at the top of the elevator. "Takes my mind off worrying about Mom."

"We'll get her back," he said.

"Yeah." She gave him a brief smile. "I know."

The elevator doors opened, and Nick moved down the hall toward Room 319, with Dana following.

"So," she said, "what was I supposed to be back there?"

"What?"

"What was I?" she asked from behind him. "A prostitute? A secretary running out with her married boss for a nooner?"

He looked both ways down the hall, then reached into his back pocket for the keycard. "Either or. What does it matter?"

"I don't know," she said. "I guess I just want to know what I am to you."

Nick paused with the keycard in midair. "What?"

She shrugged and made a vague gesture with her hand. "I just think . . . you know . . . it'd be easier if I knew my role. You know . . ." She kept her eyes on his for a moment, then looked away. "To pretend."

Nick watched her for a moment. "I don't know. Be whatever you want."

"I think I wanna be a prostitute."

He raised one eyebrow and slid the keycard into the door. "Let's hope it doesn't come to that."

The door buzzed, and he pushed his way in, Dana following closely behind. The drapes were closed, and the room was dark, but Nick recognized the smell the moment he walked into the room. He remembered it from Vivian Bellefleur's house. Earthy, sweet, and very, very strong.

"Oh, my God," Dana said, her voice going nasal as she put her hand over her nose. "What is that smell?"

Nick reached over and flicked on the light and saw it, perched under the chair in the corner of the room. It had a body like a fat, graceless, green chicken. Its eyes were black, beady, too far apart, and set inside two round puffs of whitish feathers that gave its face an owlish appearance. Only, instead of having an owl's short beak, this thing had a long honker curving down the front of its face, giving it a slight resemblance to Horshack from *Welcome Back, Kotter.*

"We came all this way for a big, fat, smelly green chicken?" Dana whispered, huddling close enough behind him that Nick could feel her breath on his neck.

"It's a parrot," Nick said, grabbing the cardboard box lying next to the bed. He took a step toward the bird.

"Hey, Horshack," he said lightly. "Time to go, buddy."

Horshack, however, had other ideas. As soon as Nick moved toward the bird, he flapped his wings and let loose with a monstrous squawk reminiscent of an eighteen-wheeler screeching to a violent halt. Dana screamed and clutched at Nick's shoulder.

"What the hell is that thing?"

Before Nick could respond, there was a knock on the door.

"Housekeeping," a voice came through the door. Dana clutched harder at Nick's shoulder.

"What do we do?" she whispered.

Nick glanced around the room, then started to guide Dana toward the closet. The bird gave another squawk at their movement.

"You wait in here," he said to her. "I'll handle this."

There was another knock at the door. "Housekeeping. Is everything all right in there?"

Dana resisted. "But they'll see you. They'll know you're not him. He's bald. And from New Zealand."

Nick sighed. "You got a better idea?"

Dana's grip tightened on his shoulder, then suddenly released. She looked up at him, her eyes wide as a light-bulb went off over her head. "Oh! Yeah, I do!"

She began working the buttons of his shirt. He reached out and grabbed her wrist.

"Dana," he said, his heart rate quickening, "what are you . . . ?"

She met his eye. "Trust me."

Their eyes locked for a moment longer. Another knock at the door.

"Housekeeping," the woman said again. "I'm going to come in."

In a flash, she had his shirt off, and then pulled her own off, revealing a lacy, electric blue bra. Nick felt his breath catch in his chest.

"Dana," he said, trying to keep his voice even as his heart rate picked up, "why don't you tell me what you're doing?"

"Because you'll argue," she said, "and there's no time."

She pushed him back on the bed and placed a pillow over the top half of his head, covering his eyes and fore-head, then unbuttoned his jeans. He lifted himself up on his elbows as danger alarms went off in every area of his body.

"Dana—"

She put one hand to his chest and pushed him back down with a smile.

"Trust me," she said.

Nick sighed, lay back, and allowed her to settle the pillow back over his eyes. A moment later, he felt her straddle him and lean her body over his. It was warm and soft, just like he remembered.

Oh. God. This wasn't going to be good. He tried to think of England, think of kittens, think of anything but how good it felt to have Dana's nearly naked body on top of his.

"Dana," he said again, but was silenced by her lips on his. She tasted heady, like the beer she'd been drinking, and Nick felt the bed spin as she ran her hands down his chest, toward the waist of his jeans, nudging them down a bit lower on his hips. He reached for her, relishing in the feel of her bare, soft skin under his fingers. He slowly moved his hands down her back as their tongues danced hungrily, one over the other, and realized that at some point, she'd removed her jeans, leaving on something satiny and, he could only hope, electric blue.

He pulled her to him, arching up to meet her as they started to find a rhythm. He reached one hand up, tangling his fingers in her hair as he deepened their kiss. He had completely forgotten about the hotel room, the bird, and the maid outside until he heard the door open.

"Stay put," she whispered in his ear, then he was alone on the bed, her sudden absence almost physically painful.

"Oh!" he heard a woman say as the door closed shut. "I'm sorr . . . Is that a bird?"

"Yeah," Dana said, a giggle in her voice as she slid casually into a strong city accent. "It's mine. Some guys have a thing for birds. What are you gonna do, right?"

"Right. Sure."

Nick could feel the maid's eyes on him. Probably, on all of him. Some of which had become noticeably more noticeable as of late.

Gonna get you for this, Diz, he thought, but stayed still, as ordered.

"We don't . . . there are no birds allowed," the maid stammered.

"S'okay, sweetie," Dana said. "We'll be done in about fifteen minutes, and when I go, the bird goes. But I'm kinda running on the clock. Would you put the DO NOT DISTURB sign up for us, please?"

There was a moment of silence, then shuffling feet, then the sound of the door closing. Nick heard someone, he could only presume it was Dana, moving around the room.

"Can I get up now?" he asked.

"Sure," she said. He pulled the pillow off the top of his head and caught the slightest glimpse of Dana's electric blue bra as she pulled her turtleneck sweater back over her head. Her jeans were already on, leaving his curiosity about her underpants as unsatisfied as the rest of him. Nick hopped off the bed, turning his back to Dana as he arranged himself and zipped up.

"This is fun!" she said. Her face was bright and flushed, with no sign of any concern over what had happened between them just moments before. Maybe it had all been an act for her, just some quick thinking to divert the hotel staff. Nick, however, was still having trouble catching his breath.

"Don't thank me or anything," Dana said.

"For what?" Nick growled as he grabbed his shirt off

the bed, knowing his irritation resulted more from not being able to finish what they'd started than anything else.

"For saving us, you big dope."

She walked toward him to grab her jacket off the floor. Nick stopped buttoning his shirt to watch her.

"Yeah," he said softly. "You were good."

"I really thought on my feet, didn't I?" she said, walking back toward the bird and kneeling in front of it. "And I think little Horshack here kinda likes me."

She held out her hand to it. Horshack squawked, but it was admittedly a lesser squawk than the first. Dana shrugged and backed off.

"Well. Okay. Maybe not."

Dana got up, threw on her jacket, and grabbed a towel from the bathroom. Nick watched her as she moved lightly back across the room. She laid the towel down at the bottom of the box, then lifted the bird up and put it in. The bird flapped, but allowed her to maneuver it. She stood up and grinned at Nick.

"I'm good at this," she said, "aren't I?"

"A natural," he said flatly. He pulled on his jacket and headed toward the door. "Get the box."

She picked it up, a bright smile on her face, and followed him out. He could hear her unmistakable giggle behind him as they made their way down the hall, and he couldn't help but smile at the sound of it.

"Care to share your amusement with the rest of the class, Ms. Wiley?" he asked.

"I was just wondering," she said, filling her face with mock innocence as he tossed a look back at her, "why your shirt's untucked, Nick."

He allowed only a menacing chuckle in response.

"And you're walking kind of funny," she continued.

He held the door to the stairwell open for her. "You're really proud of yourself, aren't you?"

She tossed him a grin as she passed by him. "Sure you don't want to take a quick shower before we go?"

"No, thanks," he said.

"I'm pretty sure the cold water works," she added.

"Don't think you won't pay for this, Diz," he said, "because you will."

She giggled again. He closed the door and followed her as she bounded down the steps, the bird giving the occasional mild squawk of annoyance as they moved.

Babs lay back on the tremendous king-size bed in the Bellefleurs' guest room and stared into the canopy overhead. She'd been locked in there all afternoon with nothing but horrible daytime television to keep her company. She'd already scoured the place looking for things she might use to pick the lock, but there was nothing. The bathroom was stocked with the finest amenities— including an avocado facial that she'd done an hour earlier to fight the boredom—but not so much as a bobby pin anywhere. They'd taken her purse and jacket, so those resources were gone.

She huffed out a breath and sat up, flicking on the television. Ellen Degeneres was interviewing a chimpanzee. Well. It beat *Jerry Springer* by a mile.

There was a knock at the door. Babs hit mute on the television.

"Come in," she said. She heard the key move in the lock, then Vivian entered, carrying a large silver tray.

"Hey, Babsie," she said. "How ya doing?"

Babs stared at her. "I'm being held captive by two of the most irritating people in New York, which is saying quite a bit. How are you?"

Vivian settled the tray on the bed and sat down across from Babs, crossing her feet in front of her. "Oh, come on. Cheer up. You know it's nothing personal. Here. I brought you your favorite stuff." She pulled up the silver cover over the platter. "Cheeseburgers. Fries."

She walked to the front door and picked up two large drink cups from the hallway. "Chocolate milk shakes."

Babs stared at Vivian. "You brought me McDonald's?"

Vivian grabbed a burger and started unwrapping. "What? You love McDonald's."

"Not the point," Babs said. "I don't like being cooped up in here."

"It's just until tomorrow," Vivian said. "And I thought we could make it a girls' night." She grinned and pulled a DVD out from under the platter. "I rented *Moulin Rouge.*"

Babs stared at her. Vivian put her burger down and sighed.

"Look, this whole situation is less than ideal. I know. But we should just make the best of it. And—oh!—I'll double the fee. Two hundred thousand, just as soon as Gary and I get the money."

Babs crossed her arms over her stomach, hoping to mask the grumbling it was making in response to the smell of food. She was still too angry to respond to Vivian's attempts to buy back her friendship—and, obviously, her loyalty. She knew it was only so that Babs wouldn't go to the police after they returned her.

If they returned her. Crazy as they were, Babs couldn't take anything for granted. But Vivian's paper-thin overtures were just getting on her nerves, and all she wanted to do was smack the woman into next Tuesday.

But that wouldn't get her out of this room. Using Vivian's desperation against her, however, might. Babs uncrossed her arms and leaned forward, picking a fry off the tray and biting a bit off the end.

"*Moulin Rouge,* huh?" she said.

Vivian grinned. "Yeah. You wanna watch it?"

Babs shrugged. "Why not? What else am I going to do?"

Vivian patted her on the knee. "That's my girl. Make the best of it, right?"

Babs nodded. "Right."

She watched as Vivian made her way to the armoire and put the movie in the DVD player. Babs grabbed another fry and chewed thoughtfully as she watched Vivian bounce around like a teenage girl.

"Hey," Babs said after a moment, "why don't we really make it a girls' night? We can do manicures. And we can do each other's hair."

Vivian bounded back to the bed and sat down next to Babs. "Oh, great! I'm so happy you're going to enjoy staying with us."

Babs lowered the wattage on her smile. "Oh, I'm not staying with you, Vivian. I'm your hostage, and I haven't forgotten it."

The light in Vivian's eyes dimmed just a bit. Good. Babs's good feelings had to remain just out of Vivian's reach if the manipulations were going to work properly.

Babs leaned over and quickly patted Vivia
"But I recognize that I can sit here and be misera
can make the best of a bad situation." She reache
and grabbed her milk shake, taking a sip before ad
"There's this one hairstyle I've been dying to try. Do
have any bobby pins?"

Baby 121

n's knee.
ble, or I
d over
ding,
you

Thirteen

Nick and Dana returned to Babs's penthouse from the hotel to find that someone had delivered bird food and a cage; he figured Babs had set that up this morning, sometime before she got kidnapped. Nick got the bird settled on the terrace, which was no small feat. The second he opened the box, it hopped out and bit his hand. It was another ten minutes of chasing the damn thing around the terrace before Nick was able to capture it in the hotel towel and battle it into the cage. In the process, he discovered that the bird's smell got even nastier when it was pissed off.

Good to know. He guessed.

When he came back in, he found Dana sitting on the couch, staring at his cell phone, which she'd set out on the coffee table. Her eyes fluttered as she stared, and she looked exhausted.

"They're probably not gonna call," he said.

"They might."

"You should get some sleep."

"No."

"Well," he said, "I'm gonna go take a shower and throw these clothes in the wash."

"Yeah, you stink."

"Thanks a lot."

She grinned up at him. "That's one foul bird."

"Okay. Enough."

"Get it? Foul bird? *Fowl* bird? Come on. This is my best material."

"Get some sleep," he said over his shoulder as he headed to the laundry room. Since the hotel, something had shifted between them. Dana had seemed more comfortable, and they'd joked and laughed through most of the cab ride back to Babs's place.

It had been like old times.

It had been nice.

When he came out of the shower he found Dana passed out on the couch, her head leaning against the arm at an angle that was sure to hurt later. He tried to wake her up, but when it became obvious to him that she was down for the count, he gently lifted her and carried her into the guest bedroom. He took her shoes off and folded the quilt up and over her, then sat on the edge of the bed and watched her sleep until the dryer buzzed.

Later, he sat on the couch and stayed there for hours, he supposed, since it was now dark. Staring up at the vague city shadows playing on the ceiling, he thought about what he had to do next.

He had to tell her. Everything. It was time. Since they'd left the hotel he'd known that he was fooling himself thinking he could just leave and let it all go. The kiss that morning and the near sex in the hotel he could have chalked up to overwhelming physical chemistry, but it was the easy comfort they'd slipped into afterward that had made his heart ache for her. Sure, he wanted to find out if she was wearing electric blue underwear, but more than that, he wanted to wake up to her bad jokes every morning for the rest of his life.

He realized his chances were slim, but without coming clean to Dana about everything, he didn't have a prayer of keeping her. At least this way, if he ended up still going to California, he would know it was because Dana wouldn't have him and not because he never tried.

That might not be much, but it was something.

Dana opened her eyes and focused on the blazing red numerals on the bedside clock—10:23. Wow. She tried to put the day together, to distinguish what had been a dream and what had been real. It all seemed like a dream. Kissing Nick. Babs's being kidnapped. The fight in the dingy bar. The bald bird guy. The incredibly sexy interlude in the hotel, followed by a cab ride and the hottest up-against-the-wall sex of her life.

She blinked. Wait. She remembered the cab ride, then sitting on the couch staring at Nick's cell phone, but that was it. She must have fallen asleep on the couch, and Nick must have carried her into the bed in the guest room.

The hot wall sex was the only part that hadn't been real. She should have known, now that she thought about it, since the wall had been in her house back at the winery, but still.

"Oh, God," she thought, and put her hand to her forehead. What if she'd been having that dream while Nick was carrying her into the room? What if she'd done something or said something or worse—what if she'd . . . ?

She gasped and shot up in bed, the thought horrifying her as her face flamed.

"You okay?"

She looked up to see Nick silhouetted in the doorway, leaning against the doorframe. He was wearing his black T-shirt and jeans, and even with his back to the light she could tell by his voice he was smiling.

"Yeah," Dana said, moving her legs over the side of the bed. "Thanks for putting me in bed."

"You would have been in a world of hurt if I'd let you stay on the couch."

She nodded, looked up at him. "Did anyone call?"

Nick shook his head. "No. We probably won't be hearing anything until tomorrow morning."

"So, now we just . . . wait?"

"Yeah," he said. "Pretty much."

She couldn't see much of his face in the dark, but if he was feeling anything near what she was feeling, it was probably best to move it out of the bedroom. They'd managed, ever since the hotel, to get the friendly tone back in their relationship; but that was an easy boat to rock, and she needed something solid under her feet at the moment.

"Well, I don't know about you," she said, standing up and padding past him into the living room, "but I'm starving."

The hall light was the only one on in the whole place, leaving the penthouse washed in mostly the dull glow from the city outside.

"What's with the vampire ambience?" Dana asked as she headed to the kitchen. Nick followed her.

"Nothing, really," he said. "I've just been sitting. Thinking."

Dana pulled open the refrigerator door. "Thinking? About what?"

He cleared his throat. "Stuff."

"Well, at least it's nothing too vague." Dana inspected the contents of the fridge. Two containers of leftover Chinese food, some coffee creamer, and half a cannoli. She smiled and pulled out the Chinese. "There never has been a woman in my family who could cook worth a damn."

"No, there never has."

She glanced up to see Nick watching her, unsmiling. God. So serious. As soon as the Chinese food was in the microwave, they were definitely going to have to lighten things up. Starting with the lights.

"So," she said, holding out the two plastic take-out bowls, "Mongolian Beef or Szechuan Chicken?"

"I never slept with Melanie."

Dana stared up at him, her mind taking a moment to translate what he'd said. Had he just said he never slept with Melanie?

"So . . . the Mongolian Beef then?" she said weakly.

He kept his eyes on her, and in the glow from the still-open refrigerator, she could see the tension in his face. He took in a deep breath.

"I had actually planned that to come out a little smoother."

"I should hope to God so," Dana said, "because as far as jarring statements go, I'm still feeling that one buzzing in my teeth."

He met her eyes, and he looked nervous, which was definitely not like Nick. "She got to the house that night about five minutes before you did. I'd been drinking. She undressed and threw herself at me, then you walked in and I threw her out but I was too drunk to drive out after you so I passed out on the floor and left the next morning."

Dana blinked. "Are you babbling? Isn't babbling my thing? Am I still dreaming?"

He shook his head. "I didn't even know Melanie had told you we'd slept together until later and I didn't tell you the truth because I wanted you to hurt as much as I was hurting and by the time I got over myself it was too late."

Dana felt the left side of her body going cold, then she realized she was still standing in the half-open refrigerator. She put the Chinese food on the counter and shut the door.

"Gee. Get a load of that. I haven't eaten a bite, and I'm suddenly not hungry anymore."

"I know I should have told you . . ."

"You know, this could be a great diet. Every time I want to eat, you tell me about Melanie undressing for you. I'll be totally hot by bikini season."

He kept his eyes on the floor. "I'm sorry."

"You should be, you big ass," she said, not able to control the volume or stability of her voice. "I realize it's weird for me to be angrier about you not sleeping with Melanie than I was about you sleeping with her, because sleeping with her should be worse but . . ."

Nick's eyebrows twitched toward each other. "So . . . you're saying you're mad, then?"

"Yes, I'm mad!" she said. "I'm furious! I just don't know if I have the right to be, which is making me a little hysterical on top of it."

Nick ran his hand over his hair. "You have every right—"

"Don't do that!" she said. "Don't be all contrite and noble and 'I don't blame you' about it. It just makes my raving hysteria look worse, which makes me angrier, which then feeds the hysteria . . . Do you see how we're in a vicious cycle here?"

He finally met her eyes. "What do you want me to do?"

She stared up at him, her emotions jumbling in a mass of confusion at her center.

"You want to know what I want?"

"I want to know what I can do—"

"You can grow warts on your face and you . . . you . . . you can gain a lot of weight and go bald and smell odd so that every time I see you, I don't feel like this. You can be a horrible, petty, evil person, so that when I go to sleep at night alone—and it's always alone—I don't feel that cold hollowness in my gut because you're not there. You can . . . not be you, but you are you and I . . ."

She trailed off, having no idea where she was going to go with that last bit. The fact was, he was Nick, and he'd always be Nick, and nothing was ever going to change what he did to her.

He took a step toward her and touched her elbow, and it hurt. Everything about him hurt right now—the sincerity in his eyes, the honest contrition that radiated off him, making it really hard for her to feel justified in her anger. All she wanted was to not be around him for a while.

"I need some air," she said, pushing him lightly out of her way as she darted past him and out of the kitchen.

This time, she heard no sounds of his following her.

Fourteen

Finn spotted Toby as soon as he turned the corner onto Fifty-first Street. The guy was maybe five-foot-eight standing on a curb, unremarkable in every way, which made him the perfect accomplice. So innocent and ordinary that even when people remembered him at the scene of the crime—and that had happened once or twice—they never associated him with the bird theft.

Toby took a long drag off a cigarette as he leaned on one of *Chez Animaux* signature white vans, which had vague markings on the side that could either be a French poodle or the black mark of death, depending on which side of the Rorschach test you woke up on. Finn held out his hand for a smoke as he approached. Toby flicked his wrist, and a cigarette jumped out of the pack. Finn grabbed it, lit, and inhaled before speaking.

"What's the outlook?"

Toby jerked his chin indicating Mrs. McGregor's penthouse.

"Been dark since I got here, which was around ten, so I'm guessing no one's home. You want me to call up and see?"

"No," Finn said. If McGregor got the cops involved—slim chance, since his research informed him that Kakapos were illegal anywhere outside the conservation habitat, but still—Finn didn't want to have a call traceable to him at this time of night. This was the big job, the final score, the last time he'd ever have to deal with a bird for money. Fucking it up was not an option.

Toby opened the passenger-side door of the van and pulled out a blue jacket with CHEZ ANIMAUX embroidered on the front, tossing it at Finn. Finn peered into the van and saw a large bag of exotic bird food sitting on the front seat.

"You know the drill?" Finn asked.

Toby rolled his eyes. "Yeah. I go to the front door with the food. I make a distraction. You sneak in. Same as every other time." Toby pulled out a chunk of pink chewing gum and grinned. "I've got a new bit."

Finn put the cap on his head and gave Toby a dubious look. "Oh, Christ. Can't you just do a simple job without making a big production out of everything?"

"Look, man. You're the thief here. I'm an actor. You hired me to play a role, I'm gonna play it." Toby popped the gum in his mouth. "Epileptic Fit with a side of Choking on Bubble Gum. It's gonna be great. Too bad you'll miss it."

Finn shook his head, shrugged into the jacket. "Whatever, man."

"Why? What's the matter with Epileptic Fit?"

"Nothing."

"It's a good bit," Toby said.

"Whatever."

Toby smacked him on the shoulder. "I'm telling you, it's great. Check it out." He twitched from his shoulder, rolled his eyes back in his head, jerked his arms around a bit, made choking sounds, then smiled and cracked his gum. "See? Good, huh?"

Finn sucked down the last of his cigarette and stomped it out on the ground. "It's just a little obvious. That's all I'm saying."

"Hmmm." Toby blew a big bubble and popped it, sucking the gum back into his mouth. "Fuck it. I like it. I'm going with it."

"Look, man, I don't care if you do the first act of Hamlet, just get the doorman out that front door. Got it?"

Toby grinned. "Got it."

"Good. Give me the sack."

Toby reached into the van and pulled out a canvas bag, handing it to Finn. Finn held his hand out. Toby stared at him blankly.

"What?"

"Keys."

"But I signed the van out."

"Yeah, and I'm not gonna be taking the subway with the bird when the doorman calls the paramedics and has your epileptic ass hauled off to the hospital."

"Fine, just bring it back first thing in the morning. I don't want to get a call from Greeley chewing my ass out." Toby dug into his pocket and handed over the keys. Finn started to cross the street.

"Hey, asshole," Toby called.

"What?" Finn said.

"Actors Guild rules, man. I get paid up front."

Finn watched Toby for a minute, then dug in his pocket for his cash.

"You know, it's a shame how people can't trust each other anymore," he said, peeling five hundred-dollar bills off the small wad of cash in his hand. "Sign of a society in trouble."

Nick looked through the sliding glass door and watched as Dana leaned against the wrought-iron railing that lined the terrace. He clenched her white down jacket in his hands. She'd been out there for fifteen minutes in just a T-shirt and jeans. He knew he should give her more time, but the thought of her being cold was making him feel even worse than he already did. He slowly slid the door open and walked out to stand behind her.

"I thought you might be cold," he said, touching the jacket to her arm. She glanced at it, but didn't make a move to take it, just turned to look back down at the street. Nick moved closer and draped the coat over the terrace railing, internally debating whether he should go or stay when she finally spoke.

"Something's going on down there," she said.

Nick moved next to her and glanced down at the street. In the middle of a small crowd on the sidewalk, it looked like a guy was having some kind of a seizure.

"Think we should call 911?" Dana asked flatly.

Nick could see the doorman pushing his way into the crowd. "I'm sure someone already has."

Dana nodded. "I figured it out."

"Hmmm?" he said, for a moment thinking she was talking about the guy on the sidewalk.

"Why I'm so upset," she said. "I figured it out."

He felt his stomach tighten, but didn't say anything.

"That day," she went on, her eyes focused on some spot out in the distance, "when I went into that church and said what I said, I would have sawed off my right arm if it meant hurting you even a little bit less."

"I know," Nick said quietly.

She turned to look at him. "Hurting you has kept me up nights for six years. Not having you with me, not seeing you, not being able to run to you when my life is in the shitter—all of that was bad, but hurting you was the worst of it." She paused for a moment, shook her head, and looked back out over the city. "Apparently, hurting me wasn't a problem for you. Seems more like the endgame."

"At first, yeah," he said, resting one elbow on the railing as he leaned closer to her. "But it's not like that now. I need you to know that. I'd give anything to be able to go back and do it differently."

She glanced up at him. "Yeah? What would you do?"

"I don't know. I would have told you about Melanie right away. I would have talked to you more, tried to get you to trust me."

"Trust you?" she said, turning to face him. "I trusted you."

He met her eye. "Then why did you run out?"

She shook her head. "Didn't you hear me? At all? Any of those nights I woke up crying, panicked over marriage—"

Nick pushed up off the railing. "Yeah, because you thought I'd let you down, that I couldn't be . . . I don't know. Marriage material."

"No, Nick . . ." She closed her eyes and sighed, then opened them again and looked up at Nick, her expression tired. "It's all six years old, and I don't want to fight about it. It's over. It's done. We both screwed up, and there's nothing either of us can do to change that. Can we just let it go? It was so nice before when we were friends again. I really need that right now."

Nick smiled and brushed some curls away from her shoulder.

"You got it," he said, then waited a few moments before speaking again. "So . . . are we okay?"

"Well, I'm not likely to kill you in your sleep. That's an improvement over five minutes ago." She sighed. "I just want to get Mom home safely and worry about the rest of it later. Do you think we can do that?"

"Yeah. We can." He grabbed her coat and placed it over her shoulders, rubbing her back a bit before pulling his hand away. "Maybe we should go inside."

She didn't move. "Maybe."

He reached up with one hand and put his fingers in the silky curls behind her ears, cradling her head in his hand. It fit so perfectly there; always had. She smiled up at him, full lips parting just a touch to reveal those crooked teeth, and the last of his resolve melted away. He lowered his head toward hers, his lips brushing hers lightly.

"Diz," he said. He could feel her breath mingling with his, and he moved closer, pushing her back against the wall, bending his knees to her level as he pressed against her. She moaned into his mouth, and he closed his lips down on hers, breathing in the heady mix of sweetness and spice that was Dana. Only Dana.

He felt her arms wrap around him, one hand curling around the back of his neck and up into his hair, the other snaking under his jacket, running up his chest. He cradled her face in his hands and gently pulled her lower lip between his teeth. She moaned again.

More.

Her hand moved from his neck, moving slowly downward.

Oh. God.

He pushed his tongue into her mouth, tasting her with force this time. She pushed back.

Not yet.

Nick pulled back to catch his breath. He opened his eyes, and there she was, eyes half-closed, warm breath floating over her plump, red lips . . .

So beautiful.

She pulled him in for another kiss. She was so good, felt so good . . .

Not until she knows everything.

He unclenched his fingers, pulling them away from the silkiness of her hair, feeling like his heart was being pulled out of his chest as he did it.

Dana opened her eyes and looked up at him. Now was definitely not the time to tell her the whole story about the move to California, but if he let things go too far before that, she might never forgive him. If he could just hold off until tomorrow, until Babs was home safe, until he'd called Melanie and told her their deal was off . . .

"Are you okay?" she said, her eyes starting to show

concern. He smiled down at her and touched her face, so soft under his fingers.

There was no way in hell he was going to screw this up now.

"I'm great," he said, his heart pounding so loudly in his ears that he almost didn't hear the sound behind them. He looked to his right. "What was that?"

He turned around, his body blocking hers as he looked out from behind the potted tree. A guy with spiked red hair and a blue jacket carried a canvas bag past them, his head swaying back and forth as he scanned the terrace.

"Nick?" Dana whispered.

"Shhhh." Nick reached behind him, found Dana's hand, and squeezed it. The guy glanced their way. Nick held his breath. The guy moved on. Nick released Dana's hand and felt her grab at his back as he moved forward. He turned around and looked at her. She read his face and let go. Nick silently moved out from behind the tree.

"All right, bird," the guy said in a soothing voice, opening the canvas bag in his hand as he approached the birdcage. "Let's take this nice and slow, okay? Everything's gonna be just fine."

It was dark, but based on voice and movement, Nick figured the guy to be a little younger, midtwenties or so. He moved quietly, cautiously, like someone with some experience in the area of breaking and entering. He was a bit shorter than Nick, but Nick had had his ass kicked by enough shorter guys to know that didn't mean much. Nick glanced around for a weapon, but froze where he was when the guy suddenly stopped and sniffed in the air.

"Oh. Crap." The guy raised one arm, sniffed underneath, shrugged, then looked to the bird. "That you, bird? Hell. No wonder you're almost extinct."

Nick was about three feet behind him. If he caught the guy by surprise, he might be able to take him out with one punch. Just then Horshack let loose with a screech to wake the dead. The guy jumped up and cursed.

"What the—?" he said.

Nick closed the distance between them. Now or never.

"Kinda takes you by surprise, doesn't it?"

The guy spun around. Nick pulled his arm back and put everything he had into the punch, catching the guy on the jaw. He went down to the ground with a thud, narrowly missing the bird, which gave a short screech and flapped its wings as it skittered around its cage.

"Oh, my God." Dana ran out from behind the tree and stood by Nick. "Are you okay?"

"I'm fine," he said. The guy, however, wasn't looking so good. Nick knelt down, using his left hand to feel for a pulse in the intruder's neck. He breathed a sigh of relief as he felt the heartbeat, full and strong.

He looked up at Dana, who was watching him, her eyes wide and frightened.

"It's okay," he said. "He's okay. We're gonna need to secure him before he wakes up, though."

"Does he have a gun?"

Nick went through the guy's pockets. Set of keys. Pack of cigarettes. Lighter. Some money.

"No gun."

Dana moved closer, staring down at the guy. "Who is he?"

Nick straightened up and brushed off his jeans. "Bird thief, I'm guessing."

"Do you think he knows anything about Mom?"

Nick shrugged. "Maybe. I don't know."

"What do we do?"

"You ever play good-cop, bad-cop?"

Dana met his eye, and they both let out a little chuckle.

"I didn't mean that way," Nick said. The guy grunted at Nick's feet, bringing his attention back to the problem at hand.

"We're gonna have to move fast," he said, then jerked his chin toward the penthouse. "Babs should have something we can secure him with in the laundry room."

Dana blinked, as though torn from a train of thought, and nodded. "Okay. Yeah. I'll go check."

Nick smiled. "Great. Thanks."

Dana took a step backward, her eyes still on Nick, then turned and went into the penthouse. Nick watched her go. There was a small squeak down at his feet. He looked down and saw Horshack nipping lightly at the bars of its cage.

"Excellent timing, Horshack," he said. "Maybe you can rub some of that off on me, huh?"

Horshack gave a tiny squawk that sounded like the bird version of, "Fat chance."

Fifteen

When Finn's consciousness began to ebb back in, the first thing he noticed was a stiffness in his jaw. Then, the weight of his head, which felt heavier than usual. He pulled his chin up slowly from where it had been digging into his chest and groaned. He was sore as hell. He tried to reach up to rub it with his hand, but couldn't move his arm. He opened his eyes and saw that his arm was duct-taped to something. He tried to move his other arm. No dice.

Whoa. This can't be good.

He felt something tugging on his ankles and raised his eyes. There was a woman with her head near his knees, who seemed to be the source of the ankle tugging. Hmmm. Maybe things weren't so bad after all.

"He's waking up." A man's voice cut through the fog in Finn's head. He blinked and raised his head higher. There was a tall guy, dark hair, wearing a leather jacket, standing about three feet away. Finn squinted. He remembered that leather jacket. It had come at him on the terrace, along with the fist that knocked him out.

"Hmmm?" The woman at Finn's knees looked up, screamed, and jumped back. Finn groaned and squinched his eyes shut.

"Can I suggest a 'no screaming' rule?" he grunted. "Because getting knocked in the head gives you a hell of a hangover."

The woman moved over next to Leather Man. Finn shifted around to try and see what he'd been taped to, fighting the shooting pains in his head as he moved. Looked to be an office chair. He raised his eyes back to the couple, who were staring at him. Leather Man had his arms crossed over his chest, giving a decent tough-guy impression, although the punch he'd landed on Finn had already accomplished that quite well, thankyouverymuch.

Finn gave a short chuckle. "There's got to be a better way to earn a living, know what I mean?"

"Hi," the woman said, smiling at him. "We're really sorry about the head injury. You okay?"

Finn looked at her, and it occurred to him he'd seen her before. He took another long look at Leather Man.

"You were in the elevator," he said.

"What?"

"Nothing." This was definitely the couple he'd seen coming out of the elevator earlier that day when he'd cased the place. But his source said Mrs. McGregor lived alone.

Which meant these people didn't belong here any more than he did.

"Fucking birds," Finn grunted.

"I'm sorry?" the woman said.

"How the hell did you get to the bird before I did?" Finn wriggled against the bonds at his wrists and legs. They were tight. "Okay. Fine." He pulled on a smile and looked up at his captors. "Look, the security system was hot when I got here, and the method I used bought me maybe fifteen minutes." A lie. He'd disabled the system when he'd come in earlier that day. But a good the-cops-are-coming bluff was typically effective with the thieving crowd. "So let's get the bird, get out, and talk about it somewhere else, what do you say?"

They stared at him blankly. After a moment, Leather Man took a step forward, looking humorless and pissed off. "What do you know about Babs?"

"Mrs. McGregor?" Finn asked. "Nothing, she bought the supplies for the bird, I figured out she had a Kakapo, I came up to get it, and somehow, you two beat me here. Fair and square. Fine. Now I'm thinking it's time we all get the hell out of Dodge, what do you say?"

He struggled against the tape again. Good God, you really could do anything with duct tape. The woman knelt before him and smiled.

"Look, just tell us where she is, and we'll let you go," she said. Finn glanced down at her, then up at Leather Man.

"Is this your first job? Because I have to tell you, you guys are getting low marks on the part where you *leave before the cops come.*"

"Forget it." Leather Man shook his head. "He doesn't know anything."

Finn raised his eyebrows. "Well, I think that's a snap judgment."

The woman stood up and walked over to Leather Man. "Sure he does. He has to."

Finn blinked as it occurred to him that maybe these guys weren't bird thieves, which meant they were something else, and Finn really didn't care to find out what. He wriggled his wrists under the duct tape.

"Jesus!" he yelled, as the tape ripped at his arm hair, leaving behind tiny, tingling prickles of fire. "Fucking hell, that hurts!"

They paused to look at him. Finn tried to replace his grimace with a smile.

"Right. Lady present. Sorry." They continued to stare at him. Finn nodded encouragement. "Don't mind me, really. Continue with the discussion. Please."

She turned back to Leather Man and let out an exasperated sigh. "So, what are you saying? That this is a coincidence? Wrong place, wrong time?"

"Let me put in a vote for that theory," Finn said, staring down at the tape on his arms. It was definitely time to start bartending again. Maybe Aldo would hire him back at the Liar's Den. Finn bit the inside of his cheek and slowly turned his wrist under the tape, causing more prickles of fire.

Leather Man put his hand on her arm. "If he was with whoever took Babs, he'd know who we were. Also, it was a man and a woman on the phone, and already I can tell that this guy is smarter than the guy I talked to on the phone."

Probably not by a wide margin, Finn thought as he struggled against the duct tape. Christ. He should have listened to his guidance counselor and become an accountant. Finn yanked the last hairs off his wrist and gained a little mobility, but the tape was still too tight for him to slide his hand under.

Shit.

The woman sighed. "So, maybe this guy is a lackey."

"Lackey?" Finn muttered under his breath. "What is this, a Bogart film?"

"Maybe." Leather Man glanced at Finn, then back to the woman. "But why send the lackey in to steal the bird they're getting tomorrow anyway? Why would they go to that trouble?"

She threw her hands up in the air. "I don't know. Despite my association with you, I'm not an expert in the deranged workings of the criminal mind."

"What is that supposed to mean?" His eyes narrowed. "You think I'm a criminal?"

Finn pulled his arm up as far as he could. The tape stretched a little, which was good, but not enough, which was bad. And there was still the problem of his ankles . . .

The quiet got his attention. He looked up to see them staring each other down, *High Noon*–style. This could be good. If they took it to the bedroom, Finn just might have a shot of getting out of here without major bodily injury. He decided to keep still. His chances were greatest if they forgot he was there.

Leather Man was the first to speak. "I'm not a criminal. What I do—which I do for *your mother,* by the way—is almost always perfectly legal."

Great. So Mrs. McGregor was a crime boss now?

"Fucking birds," Finn muttered.

"I know." She sighed, still talking to Leather Man. "I'm sorry. I didn't mean . . ."

"All I'm saying," Leather Man said slowly, "is that we can question this guy all night, but I don't think it's going to get us anywhere."

"So then . . . what?" she said, sounding helpless.

"We trade the bird in the morning, just like we planned," he said, running his hand down her arm. They watched each other in silence as Finn watched them, starting to put the pieces together.

Babs Wiley McGregor was being held with the bird as ransom.

Babs Wiley McGregor, by all appearances an extremely wealthy woman, was in need of some assistance.

Finn relaxed a bit. Whatever he'd stumbled into tonight was not going to be easy to get out of. But there was a quarter million dollars of bird out on that porch and a very rich woman in jeopardy. One way or another, Finn felt it was a good bet he'd be getting something out of this deal.

And he was definitely a gambling man.

Dana threw a glance over her shoulder at the bird thief, who was casually inspecting his bound wrists. She got the feeling he was paying close attention to her and Nick, though. Something in his eyes made her feel like he wasn't someone you turned your back on. Nevertheless, she turned her back, looked up at Nick, and mouthed *What now?*

"Excuse us," Nick said to the thief, then placed his hand lightly on the small of Dana's back and guided her down the hallway into the guest room. Once inside, he flicked on the light and shut the door.

"How are you doing?" he asked.

Dana sat down at the edge of the bed and nodded in the direction of the living room. "You think it's safe to leave him out there by himself?"

"Unless he's got lasers that shoot out of his eyes and eat through duct tape, I think we can steal a quick moment, yeah." Nick leaned back against the door. "You okay?"

"Me?" Dana shrugged. "Let's see. My mother's been kidnapped, I'm the proud caretaker of a big, fat, smelly green chicken, and I've just duct-taped a bird thief to an office chair." She pulled on a grin. "I'm super. You?"

Nick gave a small laugh, and Dana couldn't believe she'd gone six years without making him laugh. It felt so good just to amuse him. How could she have forgotten how good that felt?

"Believe it or not, this is not out of the ordinary for Babs." He paused. "Well, minus the kidnapping."

"And she wonders why I don't come down more often." As soon as the words were out, Dana regretted saying them. Whatever was between her and her mother didn't matter now; she just wanted her home safe. "So, what's next?"

"You go out there and good-cop him."

Dana feigned a shocked expression. "Isn't that illegal in some states?"

Nick shot her an unamused look. "Take him out on the terrace. Give him a smoke. Talk to him. Be his buddy. See if he knows anything about Babs."

"And if he does?"

Nick shrugged. "If he can tell us where she is, we go get her. Otherwise, we make the trade in the morning, as planned."

"In which case I have to find a socially graceful way to de-duct-tape a strange man. And me without my Emily Post."

He grinned. "If anyone can do it, you can."

"Damn straight." Dana pushed up off the bed, then paused, deciding to address the thing that had been bugging her. "You know, what I said about you being a criminal . . . I didn't mean . . ."

Nick made a dismissive face. "Oh. Yeah. I know."

"It's just that we have to be divided in order for good-cop, bad-cop to work, right?"

"Yeah. Right. Absolutely. So when you go out there—"

She touched him on the arm. "I mean it. I didn't mean it."

He smiled. "I know."

She smiled back. "Okay. So while I'm out there charming the figurative pants off our little friend you will be . . . ?"

Nick's eyes got serious. "I'll be right inside ready to beat the hell out of him if he gives you any trouble."

"Good plan." She put her hand on the doorknob, but Nick didn't move. "You can double-check me on this, but I think I need to be able to get out of this room in order for your master plan to work."

Nick watched her, still not moving.

"About before," he said finally, the sides of his mouth quirking up as he kept his eyes on a point decidedly to Dana's left.

Dana pulled her hand off the doorknob. "I thought you said you weren't mad about that."

"I'm not talking about *that* before." His eyes raised to hers, the little sparkle lighting them at the edges. "The *other* before."

"Oh." Dana blinked, couldn't help but smile a little. "Which before are you talking about? By-the-elevator before? Hotel-room before? Or out-on-the-terrace before?"

He let out a small chuckle. "Good point."

Dana sighed, thought for a moment. "I don't know what to say about before. Any of the befores. I think I need to sleep and eat and get my mother out of quasi-mortal danger before I'll even begin to know what to say about the befores."

"Yeah," he said. "That's what I meant. I just wanted to say, don't worry about it."

Dana raised her eyebrows. *"Don't worry about it?"* What's that supposed to mean?"

"Just what you said. We've got other things—"

"Let me tell you something, Nick. There are a lot of perfectly acceptable things to say about a kiss. *We'll talk about it later* works. *I just couldn't help myself because you were so irresistible* is a start. *Don't worry about it* is basically the postkiss equivalent of *Assume crash positions.*"

Nick thunked his head against the door and looked at the ceiling. "I had to open my mouth . . ."

"I mean, if you tell me not to worry about it, then there's obviously something to worry about, and granted, our whole situation here makes Courtney Love look stable, but—"

He reached behind her neck with one hand and kissed her, long and deep, then pulled back, resting his forehead on hers as he caressed her jawline with his thumb.

"So," she said when she got her breath back, "was that because I'm so irresistible you just can't resist me, or because you wanted to shut me up?"

"Little of both. Now go do your thing so we can get rid of that guy and"—he paused, his fingers still on her face, making Dana's knees go weak—"start worrying."

She laughed and looked up into his eyes and thought, *I love this man.* It felt less like an earthshaking revelation and more like someone finally took the blinders off. It was at that moment she knew she absolutely had something to worry about.

"Oh, God," she said under her breath.

Nick's eyebrows quirked together. "You okay, Diz?"

No. I'm assuming crash position.

"Sure," she said, nudging him out of the way and pulling the door open. "Never better."

Babs knelt in front of her door and leaned one ear against the wood as she fiddled with the bobby pins. It had been a while since she'd picked a lock, but her understanding was that it was a lot like sex.

Or riding a bike.

She still couldn't believe Vivian had actually brought her bobby pins. Idiot. For someone so manipulative, Viv sure did have her blind spots.

Click. One tumbler down, three to go. Babs angled the second pin while holding the first where it was, smiling as she worked the lock. Despite the fact that she was thoroughly pissed off at Gary and Vivian, and she was worried about Dana being worried about her, she had to admit that part of her was enjoying the adventure. She'd always said, a little danger and intrigue was good for the soul.

Click. Babs chuckled to herself. She'd forgotten how much fun picking a lock could be. She'd found someone to teach her how a few years back, and it had become something of a hobby since. She'd successfully gotten past all the locks in her home and had even taught Nick.

Recently, she'd given it up for knitting, but she had to admit, it was coming in a lot more handy right now than a pair of baby booties would.

Especially considering the fact that there wasn't a whole lot of hope for grandchildren at this point. But that was a worry for another day.

Click. Three tumblers down.

One to go.

She smiled, pushed the door open, and padded out into the hallway.

Oooh, she thought to herself as she headed down toward Vivian and Gary's bedroom, *I'm gonna enjoy this.*

Sixteen

⌒

Dana pulled the last of the tape off the bird thief's right arm, then glanced through the window at Nick, who sat on the couch with his arm over his eyes. He wasn't sleeping, she knew. He was listening. Not that he could hear what they were saying out there, but all Dana had to do was yell his name and he'd be out there bad-copping that thief right over the terrace wall.

It was nice to know.

The thief raised his newly freed arm and shook it out. "Ah. The joy of circulation."

He grinned at her, and Dana couldn't help but smile back. He was younger than her and Nick, although probably not by too much. Mid to late twenties, maybe. Light red hair spiking out from his head in product-induced gravity defiance. The subtle beginnings of laugh lines at the edges of his eyes. The whole bird-thief thing aside, he seemed nice, not scary like the big, bald guy. As far as break-ins went, they definitely could have done worse. Dana shook a cigarette out of the pack and handed it to him.

"Thanks," he said. "I owe you one."

Dana flicked the lighter and held the flame to the tip of the cigarette. "Then tell me what you know about my mother."

The thief watched her as he inhaled deeply, then released a stream of blue smoke before smiling at her. "I'm Finn, by the way."

He tucked the cigarette into his left hand, then held out his right hand to her. Dana stared at it for a moment, shrugged and shook it.

"I'm Dana. That's Nick. Where's my mom?"

He gave her a sympathetic smile, and Dana felt like a bit of a sucker for totally buying it.

"I really don't know. She came in, ordered supplies, and left. I didn't see anyone take her. That's all I've got. Sorry." He grabbed the burning cigarette with his free hand and lifted it to his lips, motioning toward the bird with his head. "I do, however, know something about that bird there."

Dana looked over her shoulder at the bird. "Really? Does it taste like chicken?"

"Doubt it."

"Looks like chicken."

He chuckled. "Can't argue with you there."

"Smells like fruitcake on fire."

"You're really big on the tangents, aren't you?"

She turned back to face him and raised an eyebrow. "I'd have myself diagnosed with ADD, but I don't have the patience for the testing."

Finn chuckled and took another drag off his cigarette, eyeing the bird as he did.

"If you don't mind my asking, how did you get a hold of a Kakapo in the first place if you don't even know what it is?"

The very thought of explaining it all exhausted Dana. "It's a long story."

Finn smiled, glanced down at his taped arm. "Doesn't look like I'm going anywhere."

Dana let out a small laugh. "Guess not. My mom, she does these favors for people and . . . I don't know. I don't really understand what she does or why she does it. I never have."

Finn nodded. "No one ever understands their parents." He grinned at her, shrugged. "For what it's worth, she seemed like a nice lady."

"Yeah," Dana said. "She is. Nuttier than a can of cashews, but real nice."

Finn exhaled a stream of blue smoke. "You smoke?"

"Used to."

"Want one?"

"No thanks," Dana said. "I quit after college. Nick didn't like it. And tracheotomies are so unflattering."

"Good point," Finn said. He glanced through the window at Nick, then looked back at Dana. "So, you guys married, or . . . ?"

Dana sighed. "Definitely *or.*"

He nodded, took one last drag, and dropped the cigarette to the ground. Dana smushed it out with her toe.

"Thanks," he said. "Now how about letting me go? I think we've established that I don't know anything about your mother, and the fingers on my left hand are getting kinda numb."

"Fair enough." Dana pushed herself up off her chair. "I'll go get Nick."

"Before you do, could you just do my other arm?" He smiled up at her. "Seriously, I'm in some pain here. Then you can go get him and he'll be out here before I can even think about giving you any trouble."

Dana eyed Finn for a minute. He seemed genuine enough. And he was right; she so much as sneezed, and Nick would be out there in a nanosecond. She sighed, knelt in front of him, and went to work untaping his left arm.

"I probably should have asked this before untaping you," she said, "but you're not going to report us or anything, right? The man said he'd kill Mom if the police got involved. And prison uniforms?" She gave a dramatic shudder. "Let's just say I'd have to start smoking again."

Finn smiled. "How's this? I'll trade my breaking and entering for your assault and duct-taping. We'll call it even."

Dana pulled the last of the tape off his left wrist. "Works for me."

Finn leaned down and started working on his ankles. Dana stood up, brushed off her knees, and froze when she heard Nick's voice behind her.

"Dana?"

Well, crap. Dana looked up to see Nick standing next to the terrace door, arms crossed, his face taut with anger.

"What the hell are you doing?" he asked, his eyes flickering from Finn to her. Dana pushed herself up from where she was kneeling on the floor.

"Just coming to get you," she said, trying to decide if

he was really angry, or just playing the bad-cop thing. "He doesn't know anything."

"Hey," Finn said indignantly.

"About Mom," she amended.

"So you decided to just untape him, out here, all by yourself?"

"Yeah. Pretty much."

"Look, man, I wasn't gonna hurt her," Finn said from behind them. Nick pointed a menacing finger at him.

"Stay out of it, Sparky," Nick said. His jaw muscles were working overtime; this was no bad-cop routine. He was really mad. Dana put her hand on his arm and lowered it.

"His name is Finn, and it's okay, Nick."

Nick turned his attention back to Dana. "You should have gotten me first."

"We talked. He told me all about the chicken—"

"Actually, it's a parrot," Finn said.

"Fine. Parrot. It's a Cockapoo—"

"Kakapo," Finn corrected.

Gah. "Whatever. What I'm saying is, I think he's okay. You know, for a thief. He has honest eyes."

Nick let out an exasperated sigh. "Honest eyes? The guy breaks into the place to steal from your mother, and you're springing him on account of *honest eyes*?"

Dana made a face. "Well, of course, if you say it like *that*, it sounds really stupid, but . . ."

"Hey," Finn called out, his tone less playful than it had been just moments before. "Guys."

Dana turned to see Finn settling on the table, legs dangling on either side of the birdcage before him, cigarette in his mouth. He flashed the lighter, inhaled, and blew out a puff of smoke.

"I appreciate that you've got this whole sexual tension thing going on, and it's sweet, really." He took another drag off the cigarette. "But my understanding is that you've got a woman out there in the grips of a bad guy, and I think maybe we should focus on that."

"We?" Nick glanced at Dana, then took a step toward Finn. "What's it to you?"

"Bird's worth a quarter mil." Finn glanced down at the Kakapo sleeping under his feet, then back up at Nick. "What do you think it is to me?"

Nick stared at Finn for a moment, then slowly turned his gaze Dana. *"Honest eyes."*

"Oh, shut up," Dana muttered.

"Look, Sparky," Nick said, his eyes locking down hard on Finn, "if you're under the impression you're going to get any money out of this, you can think again."

Finn let his eyes roam around the terrace pointedly, then landed them back on Nick.

"Let's see. Beekman penthouse. Lady in trouble. Rare, powerfully valuable bird that you have no idea what to do with." He took a long drag off his smoke. "Hell, yeah, I'm getting some money out of this." He tossed the cigarette to the ground, hopped off the table, and stomped it out. "And the name is Finn."

Nick started to advance on Finn, but Dana put her hand out to stop him.

"You're really not making me look good here, Finn," she said.

"Look," Finn said, "all I'm asking is that you hear me out, and then if you don't think I can help you, I leave. No hard feelings."

"Little late," Nick muttered. Dana stepped in front of him.

"Help us?" Dana asked. "We're gonna trade the bird for my mother in five hours. You're gonna help us with that?"

Finn shrugged. "Sure. Why not? But that's not what I'm talking about. What I'm talking about is after your mother is back safe. I'm talking about following the people who took her—"

"Oh," Dana said, excited, "and knocking them down and pulling their hair?" She glanced from Finn to Nick and shrugged. "Or, you know, the manly version of that?"

Finn paused, thinking, then shrugged again. "Sure. Why not? But first, I steal the bird back."

Nick let out a hostile chuckle and muttered, "Honest eyes, my—"

Dana took another step closer to Finn, intrigued. "Then what?"

Finn hopped off the table. In the cage, the chicken let out a little squawk. "I have a buyer all set up—$250,000. I'll split it with you, half for me, half for you. All you have to do is let me in on your trade so I can follow them when it's done."

"So, $125,000 each then?" Dana asked.

That's enough to re-open the winery.

"If my math serves," Finn said.

With no cosigning.

"No," Nick said to Finn. "I'm assuming you know where the door is."

"Wait," Dana said. "We should at least talk about this."

No guilt over running to Mom to save me.

"There's nothing to talk about," Nick said. "See you later, Finn."

Of course, if I do this, I'll have to admit that my apple didn't fall far from Babs's tree . . .

"Looks to me like Dana's still thinking about it," Finn said.

. . . which I'd have to admit eventually anyway, so no loss there.

"Yeah," Dana said, raising guilty eyes up at Nick, "I kinda am."

Nick's eyes narrowed as they locked on her. "What do you need $125,000 for?"

She shrugged. "Who doesn't need $125,000, right? And tell me that screwing over Boris and Natasha doesn't make you all tingly inside?"

"One minute," Nick said to Finn, then pulled Dana a few feet away. He leaned his face down toward hers and spoke in low tones. "What's going on?"

Dana took a deep breath and stared up at Nick. She didn't want to tell him she'd nearly flushed the family business all the way down the crapper, but it was time to show her hand.

"My grapes got sick."

Nick's eyebrows knit. "They what? When? With what?"

"Got sick, last year, with some disease, I don't know. I paid a guy with thick glasses a lot of money to tell me, and he told me but I still didn't understand because I'm not a guy with thick glasses."

Nick blinked. "You've lost me already."

"Yeah. I do that. Anyway, I had to close the winery this season, and I need a hundred thousand dollars, which the stupid banks up in stupid Syracuse don't want to give me, so I came down here to ask Mom to cosign a loan for me, but she got all weird about the microscope going up her nether regions and if I don't find a way to save the winery then Melanie Biggs is going to buy it and that makes me crazy inside because she's evil and I hate her. You know why she wears her hair down all the time, don't you?"

Nick sighed. "Mark of the beast?"

"Back of her neck. So now here's this guy, and this bird, and once Mom's back, what's the harm in letting him get me a little money? I mean, aside from the fact that it's illegal."

Nick's eyes narrowed. "Has Melanie made an offer?"

Dana blinked, jarred by the backtracking in topic. "Yeah."

Nick's grip on her arm tightened. "Recently?"

"Circling in like a shark. And I realize that by even considering this I'm moving into Babs-level crazy, but I'm desperate, Nick." She glanced down at his hand. "And losing the feeling in my lower arm. What's up with the death grip?"

"Sorry." He released her arm. His face was tense, which didn't surprise her. Roles reversed, she'd want to kill him. All things considered, she thought he was showing admirable restraint.

"Let's just talk about it with him a little more," she said. "Just talk."

Nick opened his mouth to say something, but then his eyes rose to something over Dana's shoulder. Dana turned just as Babs slid the door open and stepped out onto the terrace.

"So, the party's out here, is it?" she said, smiling brightly.

Seventeen

"Mom?" Dana stared at her mother, too stunned to speak. Babs was wearing a fine navy blue suit, and despite having been held captive at gunpoint for most of the day, looked pretty damn good.

Talk about unflappable, she thought. *Wish I'd inherited those genes.*

"Yes, dear, it's me. So sorry for all the hassle today. It's been an adventure, to say the least." She looked at Finn and smiled. "CHEZ ANIMAUX?"

"Just making a delivery."

"At midnight? My, you people are dedicated."

Finn grinned. "We do our best."

"He's a bird thief," Nick said flatly.

Babs looked from Nick back to Finn, and her smile widened. "No. Really?"

Finn shrugged.

"Interesting," she said, eyeing him for a moment, then

an object next to him caught her attention. "What's my office chair doing out here?"

"Long story," Dana said. "Bigger question—and don't take this to mean that I'm not happy to see you, because I really am—what are you doing here?"

Babs beamed with pride. "I broke out."

Dana took a moment to digest this. "You broke out."

"Also a long story," Babs said. "I really need a drink to tell it."

"Let's go inside," Nick said, stepping out from behind Dana and walking toward Babs. He put his hand on her arm and squeezed.

"Scotch and soda?" he said.

"Sounds perfect," Babs said, smiling up at him. "Only skip the soda."

Nick smiled, kissed her lightly on the forehead. "Good to have you back safe."

He makes it look so easy, Dana thought. *Why can't I be that way with her?*

Babs patted Nick's hand, and he released her arm. He shot a pointed look at Finn, then at the bird, then back at Finn. Finn took the hint, hopped off the table, and headed inside. Dana stood where she was for a moment, then walked over to Babs, putting her hand on her mother's arm the way Nick had. The gesture felt awkward when she did it, but it was all she had at the moment.

"I'm so glad you're okay," she said, feeling sincere but sounding stiff. Damnit. What the hell was wrong with her? "Are you okay? Were you scared?"

Babs shrugged. "Not really."

Dana let her hand drop from her mother's arm. "I would have been scared."

"Oh, there was a moment, when he shot the sculpture, where my heart skipped a beat. But for the most part, I was fine." She smiled at Dana. "I knew you'd save me."

Dana felt a knot of emotion form in her throat. "I didn't."

Babs squeezed Dana's hand. "But you would have."

Dana smiled. Babs smiled back.

"Well," Babs said after a moment. "Drink?"

"Please."

She followed her mother inside and sat next to her on the couch. Nick set Babs's scotch on the coffee table and looked at Dana.

"Gin and tonic?" he asked.

"Twist of lime."

He nodded and headed back to the bar, and Dana felt her heart give a little leap as she watched him walk.

Oh, man, she thought, gaining control of herself. *Somebody needs to douse me with a hose.*

"I'll just have a water," Finn said. Nick froze and gave him a black look.

"And me without my to-go cups," he said flatly.

"Actually," Babs said, "I'd like the thief to stay."

Everyone, including Finn, raised eyebrows at that one.

"I think you might be able to help us . . . um . . . I'm sorry, what is your name?"

Finn walked over to her and held out his hand. "Dermot Finnegan, Mrs. McGregor. You can call me Finn."

Babs smiled and shook his hand. "It's nice to meet you officially, Finn. And please, call me Babs."

"Absolutely, Babs." Finn looked at Nick. "Water. With ice, if you have it."

Nick remained silent as he served the drinks, then

settled in the chair next to the couch. Finn settled on a barstool, and Babs started in on her story, beginning with getting the phone call from Vivian outside CHEZ ANIMAUX. By the time she got to the end of her story—the climax of which included stealing her purse back from Vivian and Gary's bedroom while they slept—Dana wasn't sure which was hitting her harder, the alcohol or the fact that her mother could pick her way out of a locked room with a couple of bobby pins.

"Unfortunately," Babs said, settling her empty glass on the coffee table, "it's not over yet."

"It's not?" Dana asked. "What else do you need to do? Defuse a ticking bomb with a paper clip and a wad of Juicy Fruit?"

Babs's eyebrows knit together. "No. Why would I do that?"

"Forget it." Dana sipped her drink. "So, you were saying? Not over?"

Babs sighed. "I'm afraid not. Vivian and Gary are not the kidnapping types, trust me; but they're stupid and desperate, and that's a very, very dangerous combination. When they wake up in the morning, they're going to come looking for the bird."

"Unless I go looking for them first," Nick said.

"Oh, they're hardly worth the assault charges," Babs said. "No, I'd actually like to handle this myself. But in order to do that"—she looked at Dana—"I'm going to need your help."

"Okay," Dana said. "Sure. What?"

"I'd like you to take the bird up to the winery."

Dana paused to digest this before responding. "You want me to take the stinky chicken to my winery?"

Babs looked to Nick. "Would you go with her, Nick? Keep her safe?"

"You mean keep you both safe," Nick said, his eyes firm on Babs, "because you'd be coming with us."

"No, actually," Babs said with finality, "I'll be going to pay Gary and Vivian a visit."

Nick gave a staccato laugh, then looked at Babs with all seriousness. "No, you won't."

"Don't worry. It's perfectly safe. I disabled Gary's gun on my way out."

"What?" Dana said. "How in the hell did you do that?"

"Stole it from his drawer, filled the kitchen sink with water, dropped it in. He'll find it in the morning." She sighed. "I'm kinda sad I won't be there when he does."

"I don't like you going there by yourself," Nick said.

Babs reached over and patted him on the hand. "I know you don't, dear. If it's any comfort, I think you'll like what I have to say next even less." She looked at Finn. "Do you have any plans for the weekend, Finn?"

Finn cocked his head to the side. "I think I can clear my dance card. Why?"

"I'd like you to go with Dana and Nick. I'm going to offer Vivian and Gary the bird at a high markup, payable in cash tomorrow afternoon. If for any reason they can't or won't do it, I'll need you to sell the bird. My understanding is it's worth about a quarter of a million dollars, which should be enough. Do you think you can find a buyer in that bracket, Finn?"

"Wait. Enough?" Dana said. "Enough for what?"

"Funny you should ask—" Finn began in response to Babs, but Nick held up his hand.

"Cool your jets, Sparky," Nick said, then looked at

Babs. "She has to convince me to do this first, and that'll take a lot of convincing."

"Am I invisible here?" Dana said, putting her hand on Babs's arm. "Enough for what?"

Babs met her eye. "Enough to save the winery."

Dana went silent. Babs looked at Finn and smiled. "And to cover Finn's broker's fee, which I'm sure will be reasonable . . ."

"It hovers around 50 percent," Finn said.

"Fifty thousand if we need you to sell the bird," Babs said, "twenty-five thousand for your time if I get the money from Gary and Vivian."

Finn eyed her for a moment, then gave a brief nod. "Deal."

"But . . . wait." Dana put her hand to her forehead, hoping that would delay its impending explosion. "Mom, all I need is a cosigner—"

"I know," Babs said, "and I can't cosign for you, darling, I'm sorry."

"What do you mean you can't cosign?" Dana said. "I mean, you absolutely have the right to say no if you don't want to, but you're not saying you don't want to; you're saying you can't. I don't understand."

Babs eyed Dana for a moment, then sighed. "I don't have any money."

Dana stared at her mother as though she'd just started reciting the Gettysburg Address. In Klingon. "But . . ."

"Bryson was broke when he died." Babs took a sip of her drink. "His real-estate partners owned the penthouse and everything in it. They've been very kind to let me stay here and keep my pretty things, and I have enough of a stipend from Bryson's life insurance that I'm perfectly happy, but I don't have the kind of resources to withstand a microscope up my nether regions for that sort of money, darling. I'm sorry."

Dana blinked, feeling numb. She looked at Nick. "And you knew this?"

"Yeah," Nick said, then shot a look at Babs. "You never told her?"

"It's none of her business," Babs said, then reached over and patted Dana's knee. "Sorry, darling."

"No," Dana said slowly, still stunned. "You're right. It's not my business."

Babs leaned forward, her elbows resting on her knees. "So, you see, if Vivian and Gary won't pay handsomely for the bird—*and* my selective amnesia about being kidnapped and held at gunpoint—then I will simply call you all up at the winery and you sell the bird and everything works out perfectly then, right?"

"Not right," Dana said. She put her glass down and stood up. "If you think I'm going to let you put yourself at risk—"

"Let's understand each other, Dana," Babs said, her face as serious as Dana had ever seen it. "You're not *letting* me do anything. That winery has been in the hands of a Wiley for three generations, and as long as I draw breath, it'll be in the hands of a Wiley. If you refuse to help, that's your choice. But if it's my safety you're concerned about, I'll certainly be in more danger with the bird here than if it's upstate with you."

Dana looked at Nick, who shrugged reluctant agreement.

Babs turned to Nick. "There's a twenty-four-hour car rental place on—"

"I have a van," Finn said.

Babs smiled. "Perfect. Can you do the deal upstate, Finn?"

Finn shrugged. "For that bird? I can do a deal from anywhere."

"Wonderful."

"I don't trust him, Babs," Nick said, then shot a look at Finn and bit out, "No offense."

"None taken. First impressions are a bitch," Finn said, his eyes landing coolly on Nick.

"I completely understand, Nick," Babs said, "but I believe that everything happens for a reason. What are the chances of us having a bird thief at our disposal at the exact moment we need one? Very slim." She cocked her head to the side and evaluated Finn with a smile. "And I have a good feeling about him."

"Gee," Nick said flatly, looking at Dana, "do you think he has honest eyes?"

Dana gave him her least-amused look. Babs stood up. Nick and Finn followed suit.

"The three of you should get going, then," she said. "It's a long drive. I'll call you tomorrow and let you know the verdict, then I'll come straight up and we can celebrate. If you'll excuse me, I'm off to bed. It's been a positively exhausting day."

She kissed Nick on the cheek, hugged Dana, and waved at Finn, then disappeared into her room. Dana stared after Babs, trying to process what her mother had said.

"Dana?" Nick said. "We really should get going."

"One minute," Dana said, then followed after her mother, ignoring Nick as he called after her.

Back in her room, Babs settled on the chair before her vanity and stared at herself in the mirror.

She suspected she was getting too old for this lifestyle. It was one thing to manage the favors and listen to Nick's stories over a bit of scotch after the fact. Being kidnapped at gunpoint, however, was a bit much for the system. When Nick first announced he'd be leaving, she'd thought she could probably handle the favors on her own. Accept jobs that didn't require the physical ability Nick brought to the table. She was clever; she figured she could do it, with a few adjustments for age and temperament.

Looking at herself in the mirror, she wondered if she'd been realistic. Sure, she'd gotten the best of Gary and Vivian, but together they couldn't intellectually challenge a lobotomized Great Dane. If she'd found herself facing a gun held in the hands of someone who had half a brain, what would she have done then? Could she have handled it?

She sighed. She'd been tired before, but she'd never felt old. She didn't much care for it.

The door opened, and Dana walked into the room. Babs put on a smile and twisted in her chair to face her daughter. Based on the look on Dana's face, the day's challenges weren't over just yet.

"Did you need something, darling?" Babs asked, pulling one earring off and laying it on the vanity.

"So that's it, then?" Dana said.

"Yes, that's it. Are you hungry? I'm starved. I'm thinking Chinese."

Dana crossed her arms over her stomach. "You're just

going to decree that this is the way things are, no discussion?"

"We had a discussion. This is the decision."

"Not *my* decision."

"You're right. It's *not* your decision, Dana. I told you, I do this with or without you. If your concern is for my safety, then you'll help me."

"My concern is for your sanity," Dana said. "I don't like these people, they're dangerous. You said so yourself."

"And gunless," Babs said. "I'll be fine."

"I don't want you going back there."

Babs stood up from the vanity and turned to face her daughter. "I know. I heard you. And I'm sorry if you don't like it—"

"You're not sorry," Dana said. "You do what you want, and you pretend to be sorry later."

Babs closed her eyes. It had been too long a day, and it just kept getting longer. "You are planning on getting over that someday, aren't you, Dana? What's it been since I left your father? Thirteen years?"

Dana's eyes flashed. "This isn't about Dad—"

"Isn't it? Isn't it always about your father? You and I used to be close. We used to be friends. Now every time we're in a room together, it's like he's there with us, whispering in your ear about how awful I am."

"That's not true. This is about today, about you putting yourself in danger and not giving a good goddamn how I feel about it."

"Because it's *my* life," Babs said. "Mine. Just because I'm your mother does not mean I belong to you. I am a full-grown, adult person, and I make my own choices."

"And to hell with anyone else," Dana said, storming toward the door.

"He was a drunk when I met him," Babs said. Dana froze, her hand on the doorknob.

Babs was silent for a moment as she debated whether or not to continue down this path, then realized there was no way back, so she kept going. "He was charming then, because he was a fun drunk. It became decidedly less charming as the years went by."

Dana turned to face her, but said nothing. Babs went on.

"I know you know this. I know I only protected you from so much of it." She pulled her shoulders back and straightened her stance. "You were in college, and I left, and I don't regret it."

"For better or worse," Dana said. "Did that mean anything to you?"

"Your father had chosen his path a long time before that, and he wouldn't stray from it."

"In sickness or in health, Mom. Just words, I guess."

Babs felt her throat tighten, and fought it by raising her head up high. "If you think I didn't love him, you're wrong. I did. But he was killing himself, and I wasn't going to sit there and watch him do it."

Dana turned to face Babs. "No. You left that for me."

"You were an adult," Babs said. "That was your choice."

"You took away my choice."

"And I suppose he was completely innocent?"

Dana dropped her eyes to the floor. "I'm not stupid. I know what he was. But you just left. He loved you, and you destroyed him."

"He destroyed himself," Babs said. "All I did was

refuse to let him take me with him, and, dammit, I'm done apologizing for that."

They stared each other down for a moment. Babs was the first to look away, pulling off her other earring and dropping it on the vanity.

"So, what's your decision, Dana?" she asked, after the silence became overbearing.

"What?" Dana said. "About the bird?"

Babs nodded. Dana shook her head and sighed, then raised her eyes to Babs's. She looked tired, defeated, and sad.

"I'm going to take it back home and wait for your call, because it's either that or lose my winery, and it's not like you've given me any choices."

Babs watched Dana, trying to imagine how the three-year-old who couldn't stop laughing had grown into such an angry young woman. What had actually done it didn't matter much, though. Babs would always feel like it was her fault, even if it wasn't, and she would always be trying to make it up to Dana, even if she couldn't.

And she did have to consider the possibility that Dana was only angry around her. Cold comfort, that.

"Well," Dana said, "I guess I'd better go get my things."

"Yes," Babs said. "It's getting late."

Dana let herself out of the room, closing the door behind her with a gentle click. Babs sat down at her vanity and stared at her face in the mirror, then raised her eyes heavenward.

"Don't worry about the winery, Frank," she said. "I'm on it."

A realization hit her, and she let her eyes float toward the floor.

"Hope all those 'priest walks into a bar' jokes are going over well down there," she said, smiling sadly. "Because if they're not, you owe me twenty bucks."

Eighteen

The black outlines of trees sped past on either side of the highway as the *Chez Animaux* van made its way upstate. Nick tightened his grip on the wheel and glanced in the rearview mirror. He could see Dana's outline in the back of the cargo van, where she and the bird had both been sacked out since they'd gotten on the road three hours earlier. He was glad she was getting some rest, but at the same time he wanted desperately to talk to her. He didn't know what he wanted to say, exactly, but she'd hardly said two words since she'd come out of Babs's room, and it bugged Nick not knowing if she was okay.

"She's fine," Finn said, from the passenger seat.

Nick trained his eyes back on the highway in front of him, saying nothing.

"She seems like a nice girl," Finn said. "What's the story with you two, anyway?"

Nick shot him a look. "None of your business."

"Hey, man, I'm just making conversation. We've got at least another hour on the road before we get where we're going." He paused, stared out the window. "Don't make me resort to Twenty Questions. I hate that shit."

"Go to sleep," Nick said. "That should pass the time for you."

"Turns out, I'm nocturnal," Finn said, pulling his feet up and resting the soles of his boots against the dash in front of him. He reached into his pocket and pulled out a cigarette.

"You smoke?" he asked, holding the pack out to Nick.

"No," Nick said. "And Dana quit, so don't smoke around her anymore."

"She quit like fifteen years ago."

"Twelve." Nick shot Finn a sideways glance. "And how did you know, anyway?"

"We had a little girl-talk out on the terrace," Finn said, shooting a look back at her. "And she's sleeping now, anyway."

"What part of 'no' do you not understand?"

"I'm just saying, I think she'll withstand the temptation."

Nick shot him a cold look. Finn huffed and tucked the cigarette back in the pack.

"Whatever your problem with me is, man, you might want to think about getting over it," Finn said. "Whether you like it or not, we're working together on this."

Nick glanced back at Dana again. They hit a bump in the pavement, and the bird gave a little squawk. Dana didn't move. Nick smiled lightly. The woman could sleep through anything.

"You really should just marry her and get it over with," Finn said.

"What, do I need an English-to-Sparky translator? None. Of. Your. Business."

Finn sighed. "Just making an observation, killing some time."

Nick flicked at the dashboard. "What kind of van doesn't have a radio?"

"All I'm saying is, she's obviously into you, and you're obviously into her . . ."

"Who the hell makes cars without radios? Ten-speeds come with radios now."

". . . and this little dance you two are doing is going to end up in the sack eventually . . ."

Nick shot Finn an irritated look. "Don't you need a girl to have girl-talk?"

". . . and from all the googly eyes shooting around when you two are in a room together, I'm just saying give her a ring already and put the rest of us out of our misery."

"Pushing you out of a moving van would do a helluva lot for putting *me* out of my misery."

"Would you settle for me shutting up?"

"It'd help."

"Good, cause as it turns out"—Finn reached into his pocket and withdrew his pack of smokes—"smoking keeps me quiet."

Nick grunted an insult under his breath, then gave a brief nod. "Fine. Roll the window down."

"You're the boss, Hoss." Finn pulled a cigarette from the pack. "So, what's your deal, anyway?"

Nick tightened his grip on the wheel. "I thought you were going to keep quiet."

"Oh. Fine print." Finn flashed his lighter and took a drag off the cigarette. "I'll keep quiet about the girl. But when I'm working with someone, I like to get to know him."

"Great," Nick said. "Here's my deal. I don't like you. I don't trust you. You do anything to screw with us on this bird thing, and I'll kill you with my bare hands. That settle your curiosity?"

Finn exhaled out the window. "Long as we understand each other."

Nick shot a look at Finn. "So, what's your deal?"

Finn exhaled out the window. "Me? I'm a bird thief."

"I see." Nick glanced at the green sign on the side of the road. It would be another sixty miles until they got to the winery. The closer they got, the tighter the tension in his neck became. It had been six years since he'd set foot on the property, but heading back felt strangely like going home.

"You really should marry that girl," Finn said, cutting into Nick's thoughts.

Nick rolled his shoulders to release the tension. "Already tried."

"No shit?" Finn sounded genuinely surprised.

"No shit."

"What happened?"

"Didn't happen." Nick motioned toward the dash. "Even the cheapest cars come with AM."

Finn looked over his shoulder at Dana. "You should ask her again."

Nick shot him a sideways glance. "What's it matter to you?"

Finn blew out another puff of smoke and shrugged. "Beats Twenty Questions."

Ask her again. Nick would have to be crazy and stupid even to consider it. It was no comfort to him that he knew he was a little of both.

Finn let out a long exhale. "So. I'm thinking of something."

Nick sighed. "Animal, vegetable, or mineral?"

The rumbling of gravel under the wheels of the van shook Dana awake. She opened her eyes and pushed herself up, looking out the window. They were already on the long gravel road that curled around the edge of the vineyard, leading to her log home. She'd hoped she'd have a little more time to get used to the idea of Nick being there again after all this time, but there they were.

Already.

"What time is it?" she asked.

Finn turned around in the passenger seat and shot her a smile. "Hey, sleeping beauty. How ya feeling?"

Dana gave him a weak smile. "I smell like bird. Time?"

Finn shrugged. "I'm guessing around four in the morning."

"Three forty-six," Nick said, glancing at his watch. Dana tried to catch his eye in the rearview mirror, but he wasn't looking at her. She leaned forward between the two front seats and watched as Nick pulled the van up to the house. Finn looked at her and smiled.

"I'll get the bird," he said.

Nick pulled the keys out of the van and tossed them at Finn, who caught them clumsily.

"*I'll* get the bird. Dana, you get Finn set up for the

night." He finally met her eyes in the rearview. They were smiling. "That okay by you?"

Dana smiled back and nodded. She scooted out of the back of the van and walked Finn up the steps to her porch as she felt around in her bag for her keys.

"Sleep well?" Finn asked.

"I'll tell you when I wake up." She unlocked the door, and Finn pushed it open and held it for her. They walked in, and Dana flicked on the lights and tossed her purse on the coffee table.

"Nice," Finn said, touching one hand to the bare log walls. "Very rustic."

"Rustic," she said. "Isn't that city-speak for creepy?"

"No," Finn said, smiling. "I grew up in Vermont. I like the country. Just not enough to actually live in it."

"Well, that's a glowing endorsement if ever I heard one." Dana pointed toward the sofa. "That's a pull-out. I'll go get the sheets."

Finn nodded and started removing cushions. Dana walked down the hallway to the linen closet, only noticing the shaking in her hands as she reached for the sheets.

Good God. She'd hoped the nap would get all the ickiness out of her system from her fight with Babs, but there it was. Not to mention that she was here with Nick, back to the home they'd shared for three years. She hadn't been here with him since the night of the would-be wedding, when she'd walked in on him and Melanie. Seeing him in the city had been intense, but this . . .

This was real.

She shook out her arms and stretched from side to side, hoping to slough off some of the bad mojo that clung to her. Babs had been right about one thing—what had happened with her parents was history, and she needed to let it go. Their marriage had been their marriage, and just because she didn't personally know anyone who'd gotten married and hadn't ended up a shriveled mockery of the person they once were didn't mean that she and Nick . . .

Oh. Wait. Nick? How did Nick hop onto the marriage thought train? They'd kissed a few times. That didn't mean he was thinking marriage again.

Oh, God, she thought. *What if he's thinking marriage again?*

She took in a deep breath and exhaled through her nose. Nick wasn't crazy. Nick wouldn't be thinking marriage yet. If ever, considering how well everything had worked out the first time.

Relax. Just let it happen as it happens. Get a rubber band, put it on your wrist, and snap it whenever you think a what if? *thought.*

She was trying to remember where she kept her rubber bands when she heard the front door open, followed by a squawk from the bird and a terse exchange between Nick and Finn. She pulled some clean bedding out of the closet and headed back into the living room, where Finn had the sofa bed pulled out. Nick was standing by the front door, the cage with the sleeping bird on the floor at his feet. She started to unfold the fitted sheet when Finn reached to take it from her.

"Let me get that." He gave her a kind smile, and she smiled back. She didn't care that he was a bird thief or that he probably couldn't be trusted or that Nick seemed to really, really hate him. She liked him. He was nice.

And he did have honest eyes, dammit.

She looked up at Nick while Finn worked on the sofa

bed. Nick gave her an unsure smile and glanced in the direction of the master bedroom. The bedroom they used to share. Dana's stomach took a roller-coaster tumble, and she tried to smile back, but feared she looked plastic, like one of those models who show off the cars at the mall.

"I'll just put the bird in there, then?" Nick asked.

"Sure," Dana said. "Sounds great."

Nick hesitated for a moment, then picked up the cage and went into the bedroom. Dana watched as the door shut behind him.

"Do you have any cigarettes left?"

Finn cocked one eyebrow at her. "Thought you quit."

She grabbed a pillow and stuffed it in a case. "Yes. I did. I did. I quit."

Finn flicked the blanket out and laid it on the sofa bed. "Hey, I'm not being righteous. I'll happily give you all the smokes you want, if you're sure you really want them."

Dana fluffed the pillow in sharp movements. "No, no. You're right. I don't want to smoke. Thank you. I'm just a little . . . tense." God. Why was she so tense?

Finn sat down on the edge of the bed. "Look, Dana, I don't know what's going on with you guys, and to be honest, I think my head would implode if I tried to figure it out. But if whatever it is is too much, either one of you is welcome to come out here and bunk with me."

She raised an eyebrow at him. "Oh, really? And which one of us did you have in mind?"

He grinned. "Well, if I had to choose . . ."

She laughed and held the pillow out to him. "Good night, Sparky."

Finn pushed up off the arm of the sofa, took the pillow

from her, and tossed it on the bed. When he turned back to face her, his expression was serious.

"Look," he said. "I mean it. If things get too intense for you in there, I sleep like the dead, I have it on authority that I don't snore, and I won't make a move. You've got my word."

Dana looked into his eyes for a moment.

"You really mean that, don't you?"

Finn looked at her, his face totally sincere. "Yeah."

"You're really not hitting on me?"

"Nope."

"Why not?" she said, feeling slightly stupid for being offended, but there it was. "I'm not that much older than you. Am I not attractive or something?"

Finn gave her a confused look. "Did you want me to hit on you?"

"No." Dana glanced toward the bedroom door, then looked back at Finn, speaking in low tones. "It's my hair, isn't it? I have cargo van hair."

Finn rolled his eyes. "You're fine. You're gorgeous. And trust me, if it wasn't for the fact that you've got a huge neon sign over your head blinking OCCUPIED, I'd be thinking about it." He sighed, jerked his chin in the direction of the master bedroom. "Go on in. Come back out if you need to."

She smiled at him. "Thanks. You've been really sweet."

"Yeah," he said, turning away from her and pulling the covers back on the sofa bed. "I'm the damn poster boy for sweet."

Nineteen

Nick settled the cage in the corner of the room, then looked around and sighed. Jesus. He never thought he'd see this place again, yet now that he was there, it was just like nothing had changed.

In fact, nothing had. The same yellow curtains hung from the same wooden rod over the window. The same blue-and-white quilt lay smoothed out over the bed, and the same stupid picture of a bunch of babies in buckets hung on the wall. Even the slightly crooked angle was the same.

Dana must really like those babies.

He shrugged off his jacket and tossed it on the bed, retreating to the bathroom, which was at least a little different. The yellow ducky shower curtain she'd bought all those years ago—in direct defiance of Nick's requests for something less juvenile—had been replaced, by a curtain with yellow and orange duckies. Nick chuckled to himself as he turned on the cold water and splashed it on his face. Stubborn, beautiful, crazy. That was his girl.

He rubbed the towel over his face and leaned his back against the wall. *His girl.* He hadn't thought of her like that in so long. Yet it was all so easy, falling back into the old habits with her. Kissing her, arguing with her, laughing with her. Wanting her. He wasn't sure anymore which way was up, how he was supposed to act. He could only fall back on instinct, which insisted he grab on and not let go. Time would only tell how well that would work out for him.

He tucked the towel back up on the rack and glanced at himself in the mirror when he saw *it* hanging on the back of the bathroom door. He spun around and looked at it directly, to be sure he wasn't imagining it.

He wasn't.

The dress. She had the wedding dress—*the* wedding dress, from their wedding—hanging in the bathroom. He reached out and touched it lightly, remembering how Dana had taken his breath away when he'd first seen her in it, walking toward him down the aisle.

God, she'd been so beautiful.

"Jesus," he muttered to himself as he ran his hand over his face. "I need to get some sleep."

At that moment the door opened, and the dress and door came flying at him, smashing him on the nose.

"Ow, hell!"

Dana poked her head around the door, her eyes wide. "Nick? Oh, God, are you okay?"

"Ah! Damn!" He stumbled back and sat on the toilet as Dana rushed in after him.

"I'm so sorry," she said, putting her hands on his face. "Are you okay?"

Nick kept one hand over his nose, blinking as his vision returned. "I'm find."

"Find?" She rolled her eyes, tugging lightly at his hand. "Let me see."

"I'm. Find," he insisted, resisting her tugs.

"Oh, stop being a big baby and let me." She won the struggle and pulled his hand away, kneeling before him and inspecting his face carefully from all angles.

"You're find," she said.

Nick grinned at her. "Told you."

She stayed where she was for a moment, staring up at him, both hands resting on his legs. Nick's heart started beating so loudly he was sure she could hear the excitement she aroused in him. Hell, if her hand moved over an inch, she'd feel it.

She smiled up at him. "This is weird, isn't it?"

He reached up and smoothed one hand over her hair. "Yeah. Kinda."

"But a good weird," she said as she leaned her face into his palm.

He moved forward and kissed her lightly on the lips. "The best."

They kept their eyes locked for a moment longer, then she got to her feet. Nick stood up, his eyes still on hers. One hand reached out, of its own accord, and grabbed for hers, their fingers twined together, the connection sending warmth shooting through his body. She smiled, reached blindly behind her for the doorknob. Nick saw the dress tilt on the hanger as Dana grabbed a handful of the fabric. Her eyes widened.

"Oh, God." She pulled her hand out of his and glanced at the dress. "This looks bad, doesn't it?"

Nick laughed. "Well, it's a little Miss Havisham for my taste, but . . ."

Her face darkened, and Nick knew instantly that he'd said exactly the wrong thing.

"No." He held up his hand in a feeble stop gesture. "Wait."

She turned and walked out of the bathroom. Nick closed his eyes and exhaled a long breath before following her.

He was so going to get his ass kicked.

When he walked out, she was pulling the blue quilt off the bed and tossing it onto the hideous papasan chair she kept in the corner.

"Dana," Nick said, catching the pillow that came flying at his head. "I didn't mean—"

"You should be comfortable on the chair," she said tightly. "And you know, the only reason I even said we'd both sleep in here is because I still don't have a bed in the extra room upstairs."

"Dana—"

"Although actually, now that I think about it, you can go up there and sleep on the treadmill. Bye."

"Cut it out," he said, tossing the pillow on the chair and taking a step toward her. "I'm not going anywhere until we iron this out."

"Iron what out? There's nothing to iron. Nothing even remotely crinkly here." She gave him a flat smile. "Good night."

"Dana, it's been a long day and I'm too tired for all the random chatter. Just tell me why you're upset."

She put a thin veil of indifference over her obvious anger. "I'm not upset. Why would I be upset? Just because you seem to think I'm some crazy old maid who can't get over the past? I mean, geez, why would I be upset over that?"

She sat down on the bed, spun her legs under the covers, threw herself down flat on her back, and shut off the light. Nick sighed, walked over to the bedside, and flicked on the light.

She shot up in bed and poked her index finger at him. "One stupid little moment of clarity—which, by the way, wasn't nearly as clear as I made it sound—and you just think you're God's gift, don't you?"

"Shut up, Diz."

Her finger dropped a level. "What?"

He let out a tired laugh and sat down on the bed next to her, taking her hand in his. "I said shut up."

She yanked her hand out of his. "Wait a minute. I'm the insulted party here. You don't get to—"

"Shut up," he said again. She opened her mouth to speak, but he put his fingers to her lips, and she quieted. "I made a joke. I didn't mean it. I'm very tired and I didn't mean anything by it and you know that."

He lowered his fingers and took her hand again.

"I wear the dress for work," she muttered.

"I don't care," Nick said.

"See, I had to get a job at this old folks home and—"

"I don't care. Just shut up."

They stared each other down for a moment, then Dana looked away. Nick released a breath.

"Diz, we're here."

She watched him expectantly for a moment, then let out a frustrated huff. "That's it? Your big statement. *We're here?*"

"Yeah," he said, keeping his eyes on hers. "We're here. Again. Right where we once were, with the curtains and the bed and the stupid bucket babies."

Dana shot a glance up over her shoulder. "I hate those babies."

"Then why do you still have them?"

She turned back to face him. "You don't remember?"

He shook his head and shot a dubious look at the babies. "Must have blocked it out."

"Crazy Lulu from the Chamber?"

Nick laughed as he caught the edge of the memory. "The one with all the hats?"

"Yeah. She gave it to me, then called to say she was dropping by and couldn't wait to see where I'd put it—"

"Oh, God, that day you were in the basement for an hour? That's what you were doing?"

"Yeah. So I tossed it up on the wall with mere minutes to spare." She glanced back up at the picture. "I've just been too lazy to take it back down, I guess."

"That was like, eight years ago," Nick said.

Dana turned to him and held out her hand. "Hi. I'm Dana. Obese cats marvel at the extent of my laziness. Have we met?"

Nick took her hand and pulled her palm to his lips. "Yeah. We have."

"Really?" she said on a light sigh. "Handsome guy like you, you'd think I'd remember."

"You'd think," he said, leaning forward and kissing her lightly on the lips.

"Oh, yeah," she said, when he pulled away. "It's coming back to me."

He glanced toward the chair. "I should probably—"

"No, you shouldn't," she said, grabbing a fistful of his T-shirt and pulling him to her. "That chair is stupid."

She kissed him, and she was so soft, and so inviting, and it would be so easy, and feel so good . . .

But he pulled back anyway.

"Agh," she said. "Now that's just rude."

He ran his finger along her jawline and smiled. "I really need to sleep on the chair."

"Blah blah blah, whatever." She ran her hand self-consciously over her hair. "It's the cargo van hair, isn't it?"

"Your hair is fine," he said.

"Then what's up with the chair?"

Nick sighed. "Dana, if I sleep in that bed with you, there will be no sleep, trust me. Even if you tell me no and I manage to hold myself back . . ." He watched her for a moment, looking up at him with those eyes, her hair all mussed and her lips so full . . . He exhaled and got up off the bed. "I really need to sleep on the chair."

"Something's wrong," she said.

"Nothing's wrong," Nick said, then thought again. "Unless . . . is something wrong?"

"Yeah," she said. "Men *always* want sex, *always,* so if a man makes an excuse—especially one like timing, I mean, get serious—then it's because he just doesn't want to, and that means something's wrong, because men *always*—"

"I want to," he said, the exhaustion from the internal battle showing in his voice. "You have no idea how much I want to. Napoleon wanted Russia less than I want you right now. But what I don't want is to screw this up again. I don't want . . ."

He trailed off. He didn't want to tell her all the things

he was afraid of, the millions of ways he was sure he'd make a mess of it all and lose her again. That wasn't an option. Somehow, some way, he was going to make this work. He was going to marry this woman and wake up next to her every day for the rest of his life or die trying.

Which, he thought looking at her as she stared up at him, *just might end up being the case.*

He leaned over and kissed her lightly on the lips.

"Good night, Dana," he said, reaching one thumb up to gently smooth out the furrowing between her brows. "And don't worry."

"I won't," she said, offering a conciliatory smile. "I know. You're right. The timing is bad and things have been intense and we'll both still be here in the morning, right?"

"Right."

"But you don't need to sleep in the chair, do you?" she said, tugging her lower lip between her teeth. He wondered if she had any idea what that gesture did to him. "I mean, couldn't you just crawl into bed here with me and hold me? We could make a rule. Clothes on. I'll even get more clothes . . ."

He was kissing her before she could finish the sentence and she clutched at him, pulling him down on top of her, and the bedding between their bodies did nothing to keep it from feeling so good that all he wanted to do was sink into her and never have another stupid thought about what was right ever again.

But the thoughts came anyway, and he managed to pull himself back from her and stand up, dragging her into a sitting position on the bed as she still clung to his arm. A moment later, after they'd both caught their breath, she let him go.

"Um, there's extra pillows in the armoire," she said, "if you need them."

"Thanks," he said. "I'm just gonna . . ."

He gestured toward the chair with his head. She nodded. "Yeah. You should."

"Yeah." He smiled at her, and she smiled back. He started back toward the chair in the corner.

"You're walking kind of funny," she said, a light laugh in her voice.

"Shut off the light, will ya?"

"Sure you don't want to untuck that shirt?" she asked.

"Don't think I won't get even with you, Diz," he said, throwing himself down in the papasan and pulling the blanket up over him.

"Promises, promises," she said, then flicked off the light.

Twenty

At eight the next morning, Babs found herself standing in front of the large, heavy door of Vivian and Gary Belle-fleur's East Side town house.

Well. It was now or never. It wasn't Vivian and Gary's habit to be up much before noon, and she suspected they'd probably gone right back to sleep when they'd woken up in the morning to find her gone. The idea of waking them up was pleasing.

She hit the doorbell. Moments later, Vivian pulled the door open. Her hair and makeup were done, but her eyes looked tired.

"Oh, hell," Vivian said.

"Good morning, Viv," Babs said. "Mind if I come in?"

Without waiting for a response, she stepped past Vivian and went inside.

"Let's make this short and sweet, Viv, because quite frankly, I lack the patience. I've got it, you want it. You give me $250,000, cash, this afternoon, and I'll give it back."

Vivian glanced toward the living room. "Babs—"

Babs clutched her purse to her stomach and held her ground. "Do we have a deal or not? And don't even think about trying that kidnapping nonsense again. The people who have the bird are under strict orders to immediately call the National Conservation Society in New Zealand if you so much as look at me cross-eyed."

"Did I hear something about a bird?"

Babs blinked. The voice coming from behind her belonged to a man, but it definitely wasn't Gary; for one, the voice was deep, and two, it was accented. She turned and found herself staring straight into a broad chest, covered in a black T-shirt and a denim jacket. She angled her head upward.

Big, bald guy. With an accent. This was the original thief, the one Nick had mentioned in the letter.

"Oh," Babs said, "this can't be good."

"This is Simon Burke," Vivian said flatly. "He's with the New Zealand Kakapo Wildlife Conservation."

"Where's the bird?" he asked, his voice oddly menacing for a conservationist.

"I'm sorry," Babs said. "Bird?"

He gave her a smile that was completely devoid of mirth. "Perhaps you didn't hear me." His hand moved from his pocket and Babs looked down to see a gun pointing at her. "I asked where the bird was."

Babs let out a huge huff. "Good God. What is it with you people and the guns? Couldn't someone just come up from behind and knock me out with some chloroform? Sake of variety?"

Simon stepped back and motioned toward the living room with the gun. Vivian led the way.

"Watch you don't trip over Gary," Vivian said, motioning down to where Gary was lying on the floor, bleeding from the head. Babs gasped and froze.

"Oh, my God," she said. "Is he . . . ?"

Vivian plopped down on the couch. "No. Gary got an attitude, and Simon knocked him in the head with the gun. Gary's like a small dog that way. No concept of size ratios."

Babs looked at Simon, who had the gun trained on her at the moment. "So, you Kiwis take your conservation very seriously, then?"

Simon motioned toward the couch with the gun, and Babs sat down next to Vivian.

"I like you less and less with every moment that passes, Vivian," Babs muttered.

"Gee," Vivian said flatly. "I'd be upset about that if I wasn't about to die a horrible death."

"Where's the bird?" Simon asked.

Babs remained silent. Vivian crossed her arms over her stomach and slumped back on the couch like a petulant teenager.

"Stupid bird," she muttered.

"Look," Simon said. "I will shoot you."

"I don't understand," Babs said, trying to stall until she thought of something clever. She had a feeling she'd have to do a lot of stalling. "This sort of behavior surely isn't sanctioned by the Conservation Society."

Simon leveled the gun at her. "Where is the bird?"

"He's not easily distracted, is he?" Babs said under her breath.

"Nope," Vivian said. "I offered to sleep with him, and he didn't even blink."

Babs gave Vivian a look of disgust and decided that once this was over, she was going to have to become much more selective about the people she spent time with. She turned to Simon and stood up.

"Okay. Simon. Look, the same rules apply to you as Vivian. If the people who have the bird hear that I've so much as caught a cold, they will call the Conservation Society immediately." That wasn't exactly true and had only occurred to her in the cab ride over, but Babs had always been exceptional at poker, and what did she really have to lose? "So unless you want those people to know you're over here acting like a big bully, you'll put that gun away and let us come to a reasonable solution."

Simon eyed her for a moment, then slowly lowered his gun. It wasn't put away, but it was at least pointed at the floor, a decided improvement.

"I've got a reasonable solution for you," he said. "You call whoever has the bird and tell them to bring it here."

"I can't," Babs said, trying not to look as though she was making it up as she went along, although that was exactly what she was doing. "The bird's in a secure location, out of the city."

"Pfft, what'd you do?" Vivian asked. "Send it upstate with Dana?"

Babs stiffened. "Perhaps you should knock Vivian out, too. You and I can settle this just between us."

"Hell, no," Vivian said, shooting forward. "I'm cooperating. Totally." She looked at Simon. "Wiley Wines. In the Finger Lakes. I'd start there."

"Do you really think I would be so stupid as to give the bird to my daughter?" Babs said.

Vivian sighed. "Look, you said she was here, and the bird's out of the city. Doesn't take a genius to put it together."

"And you're certainly no genius."

"Damn straight, sister." Vivian blinked. "Wait—"

"Vivian," Simon said, his eyes on Babs, "do you have a car, luv?"

"You bet. I'll get the keys," Vivian said, getting up and grabbing her purse from off the coffee table.

"Wait," Babs said, shooting up off the couch. "I told you, the bird isn't there."

"Maybe," Simon said, "maybe not. But your daughter is."

Babs felt her heart go cold. "What are you saying?"

"I think you know what I'm saying, pet," Simon said, a cold smile at the edges of his eyes. "Either the bird is there, and I get it, or your daughter is there, and I get her; and then you'll make sure I get the bird. Won't you?"

Babs gripped her purse tightly. "I'll kill you before I let you touch her."

Simon looked her up and down, and gave a condescending laugh. Babs felt her fury erupt, but she knew it was impotent. The man was twice her weight, half her age, and had a gun.

Vivian huffed. "Are we going or not?"

Simon motioned toward the front door with the gun. "Ladies first."

It was daylight when Nick opened his eyes, the sun bouncing through the yellow curtains to give a glow to the log ceiling overhead. For a moment, he was disoriented, trying to sort out which of the events swimming in his head were dream and which were reality.

Dana mumbled something about apples in her sleep, and Nick lifted his head to see her adjust her head on the pillow before falling silent again. He pushed himself up off the creaky papasan as quietly as he could, walked over to the bed, and watched her sleep.

She was so damn beautiful. So beautiful, so funny, so crazy, such a pain in the ass. He wondered what she was dreaming about, what was going on in that insane head of hers, and whether he was there with her. He hoped so.

I love this woman. He sighed and ran his hand over his hair. *Assume crash positions.*

He turned and headed into the bathroom. He pulled out the extra toothbrush Dana kept in the medicine cabinet and was rinsing before it struck him that something wasn't right. He dropped the toothbrush in the sink and ran out into the bedroom.

The cage, and the bird with it, was gone. He grunted a curse and pushed through the door into the living room.

The sofa bed was put back together, linens folded neatly in one corner. No sign of Finn.

"Dammit," Nick muttered. "Shit."

There was a noise to his left, and he wheeled toward the dining area. The cage was sitting on the table. Inside, the bird pecked away at his food. The hotel towel was gone, replaced by fresh newspaper. Nick sighed as his heart rate slowed down. He turned, wandered through the living room, and pushed his way out to the front porch, where Finn sat with a cigarette, watching the scenery.

"Nice out here," he said.

"Yeah," Nick replied.

"You okay, Hoss? You look a little pale."

"I'm fine."

Finn cocked his head to one side as he watched Nick. "You thought I stole it, didn't you?"

"Now why would I think that?" Nick asked flatly.

Finn smirked up at him. "Look, man, I just figured the bird could use some food and water."

"Of course."

"Not my fault you two sleep like the dead."

"'Course not." Nick looked out in the direction Finn was staring and saw the industrial building of the winery, fronted by the rustic gift shop and tasting bar.

"That's her place?" Finn asked.

"Yeah," Nick said.

Finn shrugged. "It's nice."

Nick pulled the screen door open.

"I'm gonna make some breakfast, so if you're hungry—" Out of the corner of his eye, he saw Finn's head turn toward him.

"What?"

"Nothing," Finn said, putting his cigarette out on the sole of his boot. "I just realized we had an entire conversation in which you didn't call me Sparky or tell me to mind my own fucking business."

"Oh. Yeah," Nick said, stepping into the doorway of the house. "I need coffee."

Dana gave her hair one last scrub with the towel and wiped out a circle on the steamy bathroom mirror so she could make eye contact with herself. She was smiling.

"Stop that," she said to herself. "You look like a teenage girl who just got a note in study hall."

Still, the reflected self grinned back at her.

Good God, she thought. *I'm just pathetic.*

She stepped out into her bedroom. Still empty. She could hear Nick and Finn talking in the living room, accented by the occasional screech of the chicken. Everyone seemed to be getting along, and if her nose wasn't deceiving her, there was some bacon frying going on.

A perfect morning. Something about the sunshine and the sleep and the fact that she'd be getting something to eat in a minute made her feel . . . she wasn't sure. Happy? Fresh?

Hopeful. That was it. *Hopeful.* Things had seemed so dire the night before when in reality, they weren't so bad. She'd sort things out with Babs after they got the bird and the winery out of the way. And things with Nick were good, friendly and easy, just like old times.

Except he'd never planned a move to California in old times. Dana craned her neck from side to side. Well, they'd jump off that bridge when they came to it. Maybe they could do long-distance, or if the winery crashed and burned she could start fresh with him . . .

She put her hand to her chest. Her heart was beating wildly, the typical response to the wave of excitement and mind-numbing fear running through her at the thought of really starting over with Nick.

Be Scarlett, she thought. *Think about it tomorrow.*

She took a few deep breaths to slow her heart rate,

dropped the towel, and stepped into a yellow T-shirt and jeans. She reached for the doorknob to go out, then stopped as a dumb smile spread over her. She rolled her eyes at herself as the smile hardened into her face, like one of those perma-smiles worn by clowns and the criminally insane. Oh, man. There was no way she could face him like this. She closed her eyes, breathed deep, tried to think of something seriously bad, but all she could see was that sparkle at the edge of Nick's eyes when he looked at her . . .

Oh. This was bad.

A strange tune played behind her, and she opened her eyes. She turned toward the chair, a rumpled mess of her quilt and Nick's leather jacket. She went to it, reached in the pocket, and grabbed the phone. She glanced at the caller ID and froze in the middle of the room.

No.

It couldn't be.

The phone continued ringing. Dana looked at the door, then back to the phone, her heart pounding and sinking at the same time.

She swallowed, hesitated, hit the ANSWER button.

"Hello?"

Twenty-one

⌒

Nick shoved two eggs from the frying pan onto Finn's plate with the spatula. Maybe it was the coffee, maybe it was the sunshine, maybe it was just knowing that he had a shot at getting his life back, but Sparky was beginning to grow on him.

"So, I'm in the room," Finn was saying, "birdcage in my hand, tiptoeing out, when she walks in and asks me what I'm doing."

"Who?" Nick asked. "The mother or the daughter?"

"Daughter. The mother would have totally kicked my ass. That was one scary broad. Pass the salt?"

Nick slid the salt across the counter to him. "So what happened?"

Finn chuckled as he salted his eggs. "I started talking crazy. Just random whatnot. *The clock strikes at midnight* and *Sally sells seashells by the seashore,* that stuff. I convinced her she was dreaming, she went back to bed, and I sold the bird the next day for five grand."

Nick laughed. "When I was getting this thing"—he motioned toward the bird with the spatula—"Vivian comes into the room, negligee flowing—"

"Wait, *negligee*?"

"Hand to God," Nick said.

Finn laughed. "Are you kidding me? What kind of woman wears a negligee anymore?"

"Vivian types. Not sure it's worth it. Anyway—"

Nick stopped as he heard the door to the bedroom close. He smiled, pushing the rest of the eggs onto a plate for Dana.

"Ah, the lady rises," he said, glancing at his watch. "And before noon, though not by much. I hope you're in the mood for over-easy—"

Nick stopped talking and dropped his smile when she came into view.

"Dana?" Finn said. "You okay?"

Nick knew the answer by the look on her face.

She was a country mile from okay.

Finn hopped up off the stool by the kitchen counter and took a few steps toward her. She passed by him and headed straight for Nick, holding out his cell phone. Nick's stomach took a swan dive, whistling in the wind as it lunged for his toes.

Melanie.

"Shit," he muttered under his breath.

"You have a call," she said.

Nick took the phone from her, keeping his eyes on her as he held it to his ear. She crossed her arms over her stomach, staring at him, her eyes cold.

"Yeah," he said into the phone.

"Nick?" Melanie's voice grated at him through the phone, her tones so over-the-top innocent that he instantly knew she'd said something horrible to Dana. "I was just calling to see how things are going."

"Melanie." He rubbed his thumb and forefinger over his eyes, pinched the bridge of his nose. "How'd I know?"

"I can't believe you're at Dana's. It's such a coincidence. I'm just—"

"Melanie, I don't have time right now."

"Oh. Well, Nick, I was just saying that I'm just about—"

"I quit, Melanie."

There was a pause on the phone. "I'm sorry, Nick? This cell phone is giving me fits. You'd think if they could put a man on the moon, they could—"

Nick looked up, caught Dana's glance, and held it, looking at her as he spoke. He knew it wouldn't make a difference, but he was still stupid enough to hope.

"The deal's off, Melanie," he said. "I'm not coming to California."

"I can't understand a word you're— Look, I was trying to tell you before, I'm like five miles down the—"

He flipped the phone shut and laid it gently on the counter, his eyes never leaving Dana's. There was a moment of gut-wrenching silence, then she spoke.

"You know, I don't even know what to say," she said. "And I think we all know what a big deal that is for me."

"Dana, it's not what it looks like."

"Oh, good, because it looks like you were about to move to California to be with Melanie Biggs."

"Hey, look at that." Finn checked his watch and hopped

off the stool. "Smoking time. I'll be out on the porch, if anyone—"

Nick shot him a glance. Finn gave an I-get-it wave.

"You won't need me," he said, then slipped out the front door. When Nick returned his gaze to Dana, her eyes were on the floor.

"Melanie Biggs," she said with a small laugh. "Of all the people in the world, you had to pick Melanie Biggs. What? Was the chick who slept with my prom date unavailable?"

There was an excruciating moment of silence in which Nick tried to think of a good place to start, but he knew there was no good place to start.

"I was going to tell you," he said finally.

She raised her eyes to his. They were cold blue steel. "When? When the wedding invitations went out?"

"It's not like that."

Dana gave him an over-the-top smile laced with sarcasm. "Gee, Nick, you might wanna tell her that, because she had the sound of a woman looking to borrow something blue."

"What did she say to you?" he asked. Dana opened her mouth to respond, but he held up his hand to stop her. "It doesn't matter. Whatever it was, she lied. She offered me a job, and I took it. That's all."

"You took a job." Dana shook her head and stared at him, perfect dismay on her face. "From Melanie Biggs. What could possibly be worth working for—oooh, d'ja get good dental?"

Nick felt anger cut a swath through him. "I knew you'd react like this. This is exactly why I didn't tell you."

"I asked you," Dana said. "Yesterday at Murphy's, I asked you why you were going to California."

Nick dropped his eyes to the floor. "I didn't lie."

"A lie by omission is still—"

"I know!" he said, then took a breath and lowered his voice. "I know."

"Do you?" she said. "Do you know what it felt like to walk in here and see you with her?"

"Dana, that was six years ago. And I told you, I didn't—"

"And I can believe you, I guess. Just trust you at your word. Because God knows you'd never lie to me."

Nick took a step closer to Dana. She didn't step back. That was good. That was something.

"Look at me," he said. She kept her eyes on a spot just above his left shoulder, so he shifted into her line of view. Her eyes met his. "You can believe me. There has never been anything between me and Melanie Biggs."

She shifted on her feet and looked away. Nick sighed. She believed him. Now, of course, came the really hard part.

The forgiveness.

"I'm sorry," he said, putting both hands on her arms. "But you have to talk to me about this. Give us a chance to work through it. You can't just run away."

Her head shot up. "Why not? Since I'm so good at it and all."

Nick shook his head. "Dana—"

She pulled her arms out of his grip. "That was your point, though, right? You were throwing that at me, trying to deflect attention from the fact that you are involved with the most evil woman to walk the planet since . . ."

Dana paused, threw her hands up in the air. "I can't even think of an example. That's how bad she is."

"I know," he said. "And let me repeat, for the record, I'm not involved with her. I haven't been. It was a job, that was all. We made a deal to . . ."

He trailed off. The last thing he wanted was for Dana to know that she'd played any part in the deal with Melanie.

"A deal to what?" she asked. "Save my winery?"

He blinked and looked up. "What did she tell you?"

"Did you really think she'd let you save me, Nick?" she said. "Did you think she'd let you be my hero?"

Nick let out a long breath. "I just wanted to get out of New York, and when I was on the fence, she used you as leverage."

"And you believed her?"

"I needed to get out of New York, Dana. It was just a business deal."

"She went ahead and made moves on this place anyway. You had to know she would."

"I didn't," he said. "Until you told me last night, I thought she'd honored the agreement."

"Nick, it's Melanie. Melanie doesn't honor agreements. Geez. What do you need? A copy of *Satan for Dummies*?"

Nick didn't say anything. Dana shook her head.

"She manipulated this entire situation to make sure you and I would never speak again."

Nick threw his hands up in the air. "What? That's crazy. You think she's behind the bird, and your mother?"

"No," Dana said. "But if you went out to work for Melanie and she bought my winery anyway, exactly what would you be able to do about it? You'd already be out there, working for her. And by then, you and I would absolutely have no chance of ever . . ." She trailed off.

"But why?"

"I don't know. She probably still wants you, Nick. You were likely the only man ever to send her packing half-naked. Melanie takes stuff like that very seriously. I beat her out for sophomore class president, and you see how obsessed she's been with me all these years. She's nuts."

Nick felt the realization wash over him. Dana was right. Jesus. "What the hell is wrong with women? Can't you just knock each other's teeth out in a bar like men and get it over with?"

"I wish," Dana said. "If I thought one well-placed right hook would end it with Melanie, she'd be carrying her teeth in a jar right now."

Nick shook his head. "I'm so stupid."

"Yeah," Dana said, her voice softening.

He leaned his head down toward her. "So, are we okay?"

Dana eyed him for a moment. "Well. I'm still a little skeeved out from talking to Melanie. And I'm mad about you not telling me, but I'll get over it, I'm pretty sure. I just . . . I'm gonna go to the winery and be alone for a little while, okay?"

Nick nodded, reached over to the kitchen counter for a plate, and handed it to Dana.

"Take this with you. It might be cold, but at least it's something. You haven't eaten in a while." He snapped a paper towel off the roll and handed it to her. "Do you want coffee? I can pour you some."

"Nick," she said, taking the towel, "I'm trying to hold on to a little righteous indignation here. You floating all over me like a mother hen doesn't help, know what I mean?"

"Oh. Sure. Yeah." He paused for a moment, unsure. "So, no coffee then?"

She let out a half laugh, half sigh. "No. I'm just gonna take my plate of cold eggs and cold bacon and go sulk in the winery for a little while."

She turned and started toward the door, then stopped and shot a look at him.

"For the record," she said. "I'm not running."

Nick nodded. "I know."

"I'm just taking a moment for myself."

"I know," Nick said, smiling.

She smiled back. "Just wanted to make that clear."

She turned and headed toward the door. As she passed, the bird gave a squawk and fluttered in its cage.

"Shut up, chicken," she said, pointing her fork at it. "Nick makes a mean marsala."

Simon dialed on a cell phone from the back of the SUV. Babs glanced to Vivian as Simon put the phone to his ear.

"You don't have to do this," she whispered. "You're driving. You can turn the car around."

Vivian shot her a sideways glance. "No way. I want my bird."

"Are you crazy?" Babs said, only realizing after she said it that the answer was pretty obvious. "How do you think you're going to get the bird away from him?"

Vivian sighed as though Babs was the stupidest person in the world. "The same way I get things from Gary. I put ice cubes in my mouth, then I unzip—"

"Oh, dear God," Babs said, holding up her hand. "My fault for asking."

Vivian glanced at Simon in the rearview and smiled to herself. "See how tense he is? My guess, he hasn't had a good roll in ages. That bird is good as mine."

"You would really sleep with him? He almost killed your husband."

"Oh, please, it's a little knock to the head. Gary will be fine." Vivian bit her lip. "I'm a little worried about getting the blood out of that rug, though."

"Gee, Gary's a lucky guy."

Simon flipped the phone shut and leaned forward, placing the barrel of his gun between the front seats as he did.

"Enough talking. You"—he indicated Vivian with the gun—"drive. And you"—he looked at Babs—"shut up."

"Who was that on the phone?"

Simon gave her a black look and tilted the gun barrel toward Babs. "*Shut up* is an American phrase, isn't it?"

"Oh, stop," Babs said, trying to keep her breathing even so she'd look calm. "You're not going to shoot me in the car. It'd spook Vivian, and she's not a great driver to begin with . . ."

"Hey," Vivian protested.

". . . and I'm sure you don't want the police to notice us," Babs said over her, "so put the gun away. You're just being a big bully with that thing."

Simon didn't put the gun away, but he did point it away from Babs. It was a small victory, but a victory nonetheless.

"So, let me see if I understand this correctly," Babs said. "We get to Dana's, you see there's no bird, and you take my daughter hostage in order to coerce the information out of me, is that right?"

Simon shrugged. "Something like that, yeah."

"Okay," Babs said. "Consider me coerced. Turn the car around, Vivian. The bird is back in the city at my apartment."

Vivian gasped. "Oh! You bitch! I've been driving this stupid thing for two hours! I hate driving."

"Sorry, Viv. Promise to make it up to you when we get to my place. I'll give you some ice."

Vivian shot her a look, and she shot it back. Vivian glanced up in the rearview at Simon.

"So, am I turning the car around?"

Babs deliberately met and held Simon's eyes. She had no idea what she'd do if they actually turned the car around and went back to her place, but she'd have two hours to figure it out. At any rate, she wanted him as far away from Dana as she could get him.

"No," Simon said. "Keep driving."

Babs tried to look nonplussed as she turned to face forward, but her heart was racing. "Fine by me. It'll only be that much longer before you get your bird."

"I have a little time," he said, "and I want to hear what your answer is when I've got a gun to your daughter's head. Just to be sure."

"Ugh, God!" Vivian said. "Does that mean I'm going to have to drive all the way there and back? That's like ten hours total!"

"Oh, for heaven's sake, Vivian," Babs snapped, "reassess your priorities, will you?"

"There's no need to be snotty about it, Babs," Vivian said. "We're stuck here, we might as well be civil."

"Sorry, I've had a few too many guns in my face during the past two days to feel particularly civil right now, Viv."

Vivian gave an indignant grunt. "You are just never going to let that go, are you?"

"Hey!" Simon yelled from the back, pointing his gun at Vivian's head. "You, drive. And you, shut it."

Babs clenched her teeth and fell silent. Simon huffed and leaned back in the backseat.

"I swear, this is the last time I kidnap women," he grumbled.

Twenty-two

Nick didn't realize he'd finished the dishes until his hand reached for a plate that wasn't there. His mind had been on Dana, wondering how long he'd have to wait before it'd be okay to go to the winery and find her. Now that the truth about Melanie was out, it was driving him crazy not to be with Dana, figuring out where to go next.

He tossed the dish towel onto the counter and looked out the window. It was a scene he'd been living without for a long time. He would have thought he'd be over it by now, but the familiarity of it, his own longing for it, struck him square in the chest. Rolling green hills, trees singing out in yellows, reds, and browns, harmonizing one last melody to the sky before the snows came in November and silenced them. The crisp fall air, full of grapes and earth.

He had a shot. He could have it all again. All he had to

do was go after her, tell her they belonged together, and they could sort it out together.

He turned around, leaned against the sink, and looked at the front door. He could see the top of Finn's head through the window. So be it. If he had to beg in full view of Finn, then he had to beg in full view of Finn. He clutched the towel in his hand and moved toward the door, his heart pounding as he pushed through.

Finn was on the porch, sitting in one of the Adirondack chairs, reading the local weekly paper.

"Wow," he said, glancing at his watch. "You held out for fifteen minutes. Good for you, man."

"I'm going to the winery," Nick said, tossing his cell phone at Finn. "Come get me if Babs calls."

"Fine," Finn said, tucking the phone in his pocket. "But if you ask me, she seemed like she needed a little time."

"None of your business, Sparky," Nick said, moving down the front steps.

"Ah," Finn said, turning the page. "Just like old times."

Behind the bar, Dana put the empty plate in the sink and stared out through the window, remembering how her father used to stand in this very spot and watch her walk to the school bus every morning. When she and Nick were engaged, she used to imagine watching her own child through that window someday. Of course, those thoughts were eventually overshadowed by the image of the child having to pick up the pieces after she and Nick destroyed each other, which tended to put a damper on the fantasy.

She walked through the empty room, her hand running along the smooth counter, her feet making that familiar scuff sound against the worn, wooden floor. She closed her eyes and breathed in deep. Wood. Dust. Wine. Smells that had been as much a part of her as of the winery. Where did she end and it begin?

And, finally, the question she'd been avoiding for months now: Did she even really want it?

"I hate this part," she muttered to herself as she absently ran her fingers over the bar. She'd always used her father, her grandfather, the Wiley history, as an excuse not to look any deeper into why she wanted that place. Was it just obligation that kept her there?

Did she really have a choice, like Mom had said?

No. There it was, deep inside her, that *No* stomping its feet and holding its breath, insisting that Dana do everything in her power—including letting her mother risk her life—to keep this place. Why? Did she really want it?

It was time to figure out what she wanted, before Nick got there—she knew he'd be coming—and touched her and sent her head spinning so far out into orbit that she couldn't think straight. She had to know, now, what it was she really wanted, and what she was willing to do to have it.

And she had to admit that part of her was so angry with Nick and her mom because they tried to save something she wasn't sure she wanted saved. If they'd just butted out, she'd be able to let the place go knowing she'd done everything in her power to save it. No guilt, no obligation. She'd be free of all of it.

But now . . . now she was torn. She didn't want Melanie

to have the place, she knew that. But if Melanie took it, if it was beyond Dana's power . . .

"Oh. God. I need a drink."

Dana went behind the bar and knelt, running her fingers along the bottles.

"Let's see, what goes with confusion, heartache, and internal conflict?"

She gasped as she realized exactly which wine this moment called for. She popped up from behind the bar, punched the register open, and grabbed the keys to the cellar from under the money tray.

Talk about perfect timing.

Nick knocked on the door to the gift shop. There was a yellowed note, CLOSED FOR THE SEASON, written in Dana's hand and stuck in the window.

But no sign of Dana.

He cupped his fingers against the windowpane, shielding the sun from his eyes. Still couldn't see much. He tried the knob again.

Damn. He stepped back, looked around, tried to remember where Dana used to hide the spare set of keys.

He paused.

Oh, yeah. Keys.

He pulled his set out of his pocket, rifled through for the gold-colored one he'd kept but hadn't used in six years, and stuck it in the lock. It turned easily, and a moment later he was inside. He shut the door quietly behind him, giving his eyes a moment to adjust before moving on. The lights were off, but there was enough sun coming in from the windows for him to see that he was alone.

He walked down the length of the bar, peeked through the open door into the office. "Dana?"

No answer. He came back out to the bar, crossed the room to the window, pushed the curtain aside to see if she was heading back toward the house.

Nope.

It was then that he noticed the door to the cellar was ajar. He pushed it open, made his way down the stairs into the center of the musty room. Random office supplies and gift shop merchandise took up the open area to his right as he descended the stairs; immediately in front of him was a series of wine racks, set up like bookshelves at a library, sporting all the different varieties of Wiley Wine.

"Dana?"

There was no answer, but the sound of clinking glass came from somewhere in the wine racks. At the back wall, light from a flickering candle fought a small battle against the cellar's darkness. He made his way slowly past the racks, to the very last aisle. Dana sat on a stool next to the back wall, next to a large wooden wine barrel, which was serving as a table.

"Dana?"

She stared into the tiny flickering flame that came from a tapered candle sitting on the center of the upturned barrel. She had one hand on the neck of a bottle of wine, the other holding a full wineglass. She took a drink and slowly lowered the glass, her eyes on her hands.

"Perfect timing," she said, holding the bottle out with a small smile. "I just started it."

He glanced at the label and a wash of memory hit him. "The Merlot."

"We're a year and a few days past what would have been our fifth anniversary, but what the hell, right?"

She nodded toward the wall, where another stool hung from a series of thick wooden pegs. He pulled it down and sat across from her, watching her as she poured a glass for him. He laughed.

"You knew I'd be coming," he said.

She handed him his glass. "Of course. I asked for some time alone. I'm actually very impressed with your restraint."

"Sorry," he said. "I just didn't want you to—"

"Ah, ah, ah," she said, holding up her glass. "Before we get into it, a toast."

He held up his glass. "To what?"

She chuckled lightly. "Don't know. I hadn't thought that far ahead."

"Okay," he said. "Here's to not knowing."

They clinked glasses and each took a sip. It was good, the Merlot. Dark. Rich. Ages old. The night before the wedding, they'd found two bottles of Grampa Wiley's inaugural harvest Merlot in the cellar. They'd decided to drink one that night, and have the other on their twentieth anniversary. It was so good, though, that by the end of the first bottle, they'd negotiated the second one down to their fifth anniversary.

"I love you," she said. Nick had been so wrapped up in the memories of that night with the first bottle that he almost didn't hear her. He started to speak, but she held up her hand and hushed him.

"I do. I always have. I think now I've made it pretty

clear to myself that I always will. It's the only thing I know right now, and I'm kinda clinging to it. Hope you don't mind."

"Dana—"

"Shh. Please. Let me get through this first, then I promise I will shut up and let you speak. But I have to say these things out loud because if I don't, then I won't unravel all this crap I've got in my head, and I have to do that before we can move forward. Does that make sense?"

Nick nodded.

"Oh. Well, I obviously haven't had enough wine yet then." She took another sip, set the glass down on the barrel. "I'm thinking of selling this place to Melanie."

"What?" Nick said. "That's just crazy."

"Oh, shit," Dana said, slapping one hand down on her knee. "I said her name. Now I have to go put five bucks in the kitty."

"Hey, if it helps, I think you've had enough wine," Nick said. "I'm not understanding anything you're saying."

"Me, either," she said. "It's just . . . I love this place. I do. But there's so much *here,* you know? There's Grampa Wiley who built the place, and Mom who conceived me here, and Dad who died here. Mom and Dad fell apart here. You and I imploded here." She met his eye and was silent for a moment, then went on. "I let my mother put herself at risk for this place. Why? So I could thumb my nose at Melanie? I mean, who cares? She's just evil incarnate. What's the big?" She paused, blinked. "Oh. Crap. I said her name again. Ten bucks."

Nick leaned forward and took her wine from her. She moved forward and took it back.

"I'm trying to think, Nick. Thinking without wine gives me a headache."

Nick leaned back and smiled. "Fine. Can I talk yet?"

"No," she said. "I have to figure this out. I have to know what I want."

"Right now? Why?"

"Because Mom is risking her life to get money for my winery, and when she comes to me with that money, I have to know what I'm going to do."

He sighed, took a drink of wine. "Fine. Let's start with what you know, then. What do you know you want?"

She stared down into her glass and laughed into it. "You."

Nick smiled. "You got me. What else?"

She looked up at him. "I have you?"

"Yeah," he said, his smile fading. "You do."

"But . . . your life . . . your job . . . and don't think I've forgotten that you almost moved to California to work for Melanie." She cringed. "Fifteen bucks. Dammit."

Nick couldn't help himself; he laughed. There she was, at the absolute lowest point he'd ever seen her, slouching over a glass of wine in a dark cellar, getting drunk at noon, and he loved her so much he thought he might die from it right there on the spot.

He got up, took the wineglass out of her hand, and set it on the barrel.

"I think you've figured out enough," he said.

Dana gave him a confused look. "Wait. I haven't gotten to the part about panty hose versus no panty hose."

He took both her hands in his and pulled her up to standing.

"And I have to figure out how I feel about trade with China. What are you doing?"

He smiled, cupped her face in his hands.

"What do you think?" he said softly, his eyes searching hers in the candlelight. "I'm shutting you up."

Then he lowered his face down to hers and kissed her with everything he had.

Twenty-three

Wine on his tongue. His hands in her hair. Spicy, warm, heavenly. Dana felt her entire body relax against his, followed by a buildup of energy and heat radiating from her abdomen that made her knees buckle a bit. She pulled back and looked up at him, at his beautiful eyes, half-closed and simmering, at his mouth, soft and slightly open, his breath rushing forward over his lips, mingling with hers. Her heart did a gymnastic flip, and she smiled at him.

"If you think that's gonna shut me up, you've got another thing—"

She stopped as his lips found hers again, more insistent this time. His tongue slid over hers as he pushed her back against the wall. Good thing. She was about five seconds away from falling over.

He tugged at her T-shirt, pulling it slowly out of her jeans. His hand slid flat and warm against her stomach, his fingers reaching down into her jeans, undoing the top button.

"So," she exhaled, "I guess the timing is good now?"

"To hell with the timing," he said, and suckled on the curve where her neck met her shoulder.

Oh. God. Yeah. That.

She slid her hands up his chest and over his shoulders, under his jacket, pushing it down his arms to the floor, savoring the feeling of him under her fingers. When his hands returned to her, they circled her waist and lifted her, pressing her against the wall, their hips aligned as she wrapped her legs around him. She dove into his kisses, his mouth hot on hers, spicy with wine.

She slowly lowered her legs and slid down his body. She undid the top button of his jeans and was going for the zipper when one of his hands grabbed hers, the other lifting her chin to look in his eyes.

"Unless you think the timing is bad," he said.

"Oh, God, shut up." She reached up and pulled him down to her in a kiss, her other hand working his zipper as his hands made quick work of removing her jeans and panties. He bent down to guide her feet out of them, then slowly moved back up, pressing her against the wall as he kissed his way up her thighs, stopping for a short exploration before moving up to her stomach. She clutched at the wall, grateful for the support. Her knees were all but useless. He straightened up, lifting her again, pressing her against the wall, settling her on top of him as she curved her legs around him.

Oh. God. Yes.

Dana closed her eyes, waiting for him to go inside, to push it all away, to make her feel what only he could make her feel, but he suddenly went still, the only sound, only movement, coming from the staccato puffs of their breathing.

Dana opened her eyes. Her face was level with Nick's, mere inches away. Her hands were clutched at the back of his neck, her body arching, aching for him. She could tell by the strength of him underneath her that he wasn't pausing for lack of interest. She looked at him, her eyes darting over his.

"What . . . ?" She barely got the word out. He shook his head, put one finger to her lips. She groaned. He shifted under her, lightly, and her body flamed up, beyond her control. But then, he stopped again. She clutched her hands behind his neck and looked in his eyes, trying to figure out what he was thinking.

"Oh," she said. "Still on the pill. Recent checkup. Ready for takeoff."

He chuckled. "Good to know. But that's not . . ."

She touched his face. "Then what?"

"Do you want the winery?"

"What?" He shifted again and she rode a quick wave, then opened her eyes and looked at him again. "This really isn't the time. I can't think . . ."

"I know," he said. "That's why I'm asking you now."

He moved his hips and slid under her, just about to enter her, when he paused.

"Oh, God," she breathed, "please remind me to kill you later."

"What do you want?" he asked.

"I think you know what I want, you rat," she said.

"Just tell me—"

"I want the winery," she said. "I love this place, and losing it will break my heart."

He smiled down at her. "Well, there you go."

He took her mouth, suddenly, pushing all her thoughts away. She felt herself flowing into him, no difference between where she ended and he began. He pushed into her, filling her, driving her. She clutched at him with one hand, the other clinging to the wall as he moved with her, wave after wave, building up the heat and intensity until they both were screaming in it, shuddering together, as one, his face on her shoulder, her hair flying from her neck in time with the rhythm of his breathing. He nipped at her shoulder playfully, then pulled back, smiling at her.

"You're a rat," she said.

"I'm a rat that loves you," he said.

She smiled. "Really? You really do?"

He looked at her like she was crazy. "Of course. Idiot."

"Well, I couldn't be sure until you said it, but now you've said it, and I have to admit I like the way it—"

"Marry me."

She froze. Did he just . . . ?

"Yes," he said, answering her thought. "I just asked you to marry me."

"Nick . . ." She sighed. "It's kind of a hard question to answer when you're still . . ."

She glanced downward. His fingertips dug tighter into her hips, and he lifted her up off him and settled her down on her feet.

"Guess I should have asked you when I asked about the winery," Nick said as he pulled up his jeans.

She pulled on her underwear and turned to face him. "That's not fair."

"No, it's not," he said, setting himself down on one of the barstools. "I know that. But . . . I don't understand you. We love each other."

"Yes. We do." She stepped into her jeans. "Why does that have to equal marriage?"

"Because it does," he said. "Because I don't want to go through it all over again. Because I need to know you're gonna see this through."

"Jesus, Nick. We've been back together for ten minutes."

"We've known each other for seventeen years, Dana."

"I know," she said, her voice hitting a high pitch as she tried to figure out her argument. "It's just that this, being back together, is sudden and we should take some time—"

"I don't need time," he said.

"Well, I do."

He watched her for a moment, then shook his head. "I know I'm rushing things and I know this isn't fair and dammit, Dana, I just don't care. I can't do it again."

"What? What we just did? Give it twenty minutes."

"No," he said, his face serious. "Lose you."

Dana closed her eyes. Oh, God. She did not want to go there now. Why now? Things were good there for a nanosecond.

She opened her eyes to see him still watching her.

Guess it has to be now.

"Marriage is no guarantee against things falling apart, Nick," she said. "Hell, look at my parents."

"We're not your parents," he said.

"This is like the worst déjà vu of my life."

"Just answer me. Are you gonna marry me or not?"

"Are you going to listen to me? Marriage—"

"Freaks you out," he said. He put his hands on her arms and lowered his face toward hers. "I know. But I'm not asking you about marriage in general. I'm asking you about marriage to me. It comes down to basic trust, whether or not you believe that I'll be there for you. If you don't, I think I should know now."

Dana slumped in his grip. "Nick . . ."

"I'm not going through it again, Dana," he said, releasing his hold on her and straightening up. "I can't."

Dana's heart sank to her feet. "So this is what? An ultimatum?"

He met her eye. "Guess so."

She felt her entire life crash into her chest until she couldn't breathe. Her eyes filled with tears, and she knew what she was going to need to get out of there fast before she fell apart into a huge puddle of sobbing stupidity.

"Then no," she said. "If you have to have an answer right this moment, the answer is no."

She started to walk away, but he caught her arm. She swallowed hard against the knot in her throat and stared straight ahead.

"I don't want to see you leave," she said as the tears fell down her cheeks. "Just give me enough time to get to the house before you go. I think it's the least you can do."

She wrenched her arm from his grip and moved out of the cellar as fast as her wooden legs would carry her.

Twenty-four

Finn drummed his fingers on the surface of the table. His eyes went to the clock on the wall, to the bird, then to the keys to the van lying on the table next to the cage.

He drummed his fingers harder, then stood up.

"See, here's the thing, Horshack," he said, then stopped and eyed the bird. "Mind if I call you Horshack? No offense. It's the beak. The resemblance is uncanny."

The bird cocked its head to the side. Finn shrugged, started pacing.

"Horshack it is, then. My question for you is this: What kind of idiots leave a valuable parrot and keys to a van in the care of a known bird thief? Huh?"

He raised questioning eyebrows at the bird. Horshack looked away from him and nipped at the bars on its cage.

"Don't avoid the question," Finn said. "You know I'm right. I mean, I think I made it perfectly clear to both of them that I'm completely untrustworthy. Haven't I?"

He leaned against the table, his back to the bird, his eyes on the kitchen counter where Nick's cell phone sat.

"He chased her out, leaving me to mind the store, knowing I've got a buyer downstate just waiting. What the hell did he think was gonna happen?"

Silence. Finn glanced over his shoulder at the bird, which watched him for a moment in silence. He turned around, eyes landing back on the cell phone.

"Take it from me, Horshack. In this life, there's only one person who's gonna get your back, and that's you. I know that. Everybody knows that. And if I don't do this now, I'll be working birds into my sixties. For what? For people I've known less than a day? People who knocked me out and duct-taped me to a chair?" He shook his head, exhaled. "That'd just be stupid."

He walked over to the window, pushed the curtain aside, let his eyes wander down the long gravel trail leading from the winery to the cabin. There was no sign of either Dana or Nick.

"Loyalties are for idiots and martyrs," he said. "You stop to help anyone but yourself, all you get for your trouble is a solid asskicking."

He glanced at the bird, then looked back out the window one more time before letting the curtain fall back again. "Really. It's a proven fact. I believe Nietzsche said it first."

Finn exhaled. This was it. Time to make a choice.

But there was no choice. There was only one thing to do, and he was going to do it. He walked over to the counter and picked up the phone, then dialed a pager number and punched in a code indicating the time and place the deal would go down. He flipped the phone shut, tucked it in his pocket, and swiped the keys off the table.

"Time to move, Horshack," he said, grabbing the handle to the cage. "And let this be a lesson to you not to trust people you hardly know."

Dana reached for the knob in the gift shop, then hesitated and looked over her shoulder.

Good God, she'd done it again.

She'd run. Again. From Nick, the one thing in her life she'd ever been sure of. What the hell was she thinking?

She thunked her head against the doorframe, then headed toward the cellar door, stopping in the middle of the room.

Wait. Think about this. If you tell him you're going to marry him, you have to do it.

She closed her eyes, visualized the dress, visualized saying "I do," visualized the honeymoon, visualized more really hot wall sex. All good.

Then she visualized the divorce lawyers, the crying children, the angry messages she'd have to leave on Nick's lonely bachelor answering machine demanding alimony payments and child support.

Her chest constricted, and she felt her heart crack.

It just wasn't fair. Why was he demanding this of her now? Couldn't he at least wait a few weeks, a few months, a year? He knew how she felt about marriage. She'd told him.

But she'd never really explained. Never made him listen. She'd always gotten angry and run out of the room. And there she was, doing it again. She knew she wanted to be with him forever, to wake up next to him every day. He'd asked her to separate marriage to him from marriage in general. She stood still for a moment and thought about it.

Did she trust him to hang on even when things weren't great? If she became a drunk like her father, did she believe that Nick would abandon her? She knew the chances of that happening were slim; she paid careful attention to what she drank, but still. She could slide into something equally awful. No one knew what was going to happen, how life would change them.

So. Fine. If she became cruel, or distant, or thoughtless, would Nick leave her out there on her own, or would he reach down into the pit and drag her out?

Her vision blurred and her throat clamped up as she realized the answer.

He would drag her out. Even if he had to do it with her kicking and screaming and fighting him all the way, he would drag her out. And she would do the same for him. Maybe the secret to being married was choosing someone who loved you enough to kick your ass if necessary.

Well, it wasn't exactly the platform for a self-help book, but it was good enough for her. She drew in a deep breath and took another step toward the cellar door, stopping when she heard the door to the shop open behind her.

"Sorry, we're closed," she said, turning on her heel, expecting to see some wandering wine tasters. Instead, she saw Babs, some blond woman Dana'd never seen before, and Scary Bald Guy behind them.

Holding a gun.

"Oh, for Christ's sake," Dana began.

"Dana," Babs said, her eyes dark. "I was hoping you wouldn't be here."

Scary Bald Guy's eyes narrowed as he looked at her. "I know you."

Dana backed up a step. "No, you don't. Lots of people think that because I have one of those faces—"

"You were in the bar. With a man. It was you," he said, obviously putting it together. "Where's your bloke?"

Dana crossed her arms over her chest. "I don't know. Day hire. I imagine he's in the city."

Scary Bald Guy smiled and turned the gun on Dana. "I want my bird back."

Dana looked to the blonde standing next to Babs. "Vivian, I presume?"

Vivian nodded. "And this is Simon. He'd really like the bird back. I think you should give it to him."

Dana looked at Babs. "I really don't like her."

Babs raised one hand. "Preaching to the choir, darling."

In the cellar, Nick poured himself another glass of the Merlot.

He was such an idiot. He gave stupid a new meaning. From this day forward, stupid people would give him a wide berth on the sidewalk, their eyes full of pity and disdain.

"Christ," he said, downing a long swallow.

He had no idea what had come over him. He'd known marriage freaked Dana out, and what the hell was wrong with living in a little sin? The greater good—that he and Dana would be together—would be served, and if she ever got over the fear of marriage, at least he'd be there when it happened.

Something had clicked in him, though, when they were

up against the wall. Some deep fear of finding himself back in New York, working that wine bar, living without her. He'd just wanted a promise that it wouldn't happen again, that she wouldn't run from him.

So he drove her away.

"Great move, Einstein," he muttered, finishing off the glass. He glanced up at the stairs. Maybe it wasn't too late to find her, take it all back. Sure he wanted to marry her, but he wanted to be with her more, and if it meant waiting, he'd wait. Maybe if he told her that he could make up for being an idiot.

Maybe.

He reached for the wine and took a swig directly from the bottle.

"Okay, Simon," Dana said, turning her attention from Vivian to Scary Bald Guy. "Let's go get your stupid bird."

Simon raised his eyebrows at Babs. "Well, isn't this a surprise? She had it the whole time."

Babs glared at him. "Shut up, Simon."

He moved the gun closer to Babs's head and looked at Dana. "I want that bird, and I want it—"

"Agh!" Dana grunted in frustration. Simon looked at her, surprise on his face. "Didn't you hear me? I don't give a rat's ass about that stupid bird. I hate the shit of it. I hate the way it smells. I hate the way it sounds like a ten-car pileup when it's pissed off. I hate the way its beady little eyes follow you around the room as it plots your untimely demise. I *want* you to have it. Far as I'm concerned, you can't take it fast enough. So if you're done taunting my mother, can we just go and get the stupid thing?"

"Fine by me, pet," he said. He jerked his head to indicate Vivian and Babs. "But I'm not gathering a harem here, and I'm not stupid enough to turn my back on any one of you."

Dana eyed the cellar door. If this went on much longer, Nick would come out and significantly raise the stakes. The less threatened this guy felt, the safer they all were. She had to get them out of there fast.

"It's okay," Dana said. "They'll stay here. I'll go with you. If they try to interfere, you'll shoot me. They stay here and behave, I come back, and everybody's happy." She turned and looked at Babs. "That works, right?"

"No, it doesn't work," Vivian snapped. "That's my bird, and I want it back."

Dana shot a look at Vivian. "Newsflash, Vivian. Simon gets the bird. It's over."

"And what about me?"

"Nobody cares," Dana said, then turned to Simon. "Let's go."

"No!" Vivian said. "You're not giving him my bird!"

Babs grabbed Vivian by the arm. "Get over it, Viv. It's done!"

Vivian yanked her arm from Babs's grasp. "The hell it is! I want my bird!"

A gunshot sounded and all three women screamed and turned to see Simon holding the smoking pistol, pointed upward.

"The next time anyone talks," he said, "it won't be a ceiling that takes a bullet."

Dana stared up at the chunk taken out of the log ceiling.

"What the hell, Simon!" she yelled. "Switch to decaf, will ya?"

At that moment the cellar door whipped open, and Nick flew into the room.

"Oh, crap," Dana muttered.

"Dana!" Nick froze as his eyes landed on Simon. "What's going on?"

"Nick, so good to see you," Babs said. "We're just having a bit of a domestic dispute."

Simon tilted his head and eyed Nick. "Guess the day hire's still on the payroll, eh, pet?"

Nick moved to Dana's side, put his hand on her arm. "Are you okay?"

"No, I'm really pissed off, and I haven't had nearly enough wine to deal with this," Dana grumbled. She pointed up. Nick's eyes tracked up to the small hole in the ceiling, then back down to Dana.

He let out a rough sigh. "But you're okay."

"I'm fine. I think he just took a good two grand off my asking price for this place, though." She turned to Simon. "Can we go now?"

Nick's voice came low and tight from behind her. "Dana. What are you doing?"

She turned and met his eyes. "I'm giving him the bird."

"Which isn't yours to give," Vivian grunted.

"Shut up, Viv," Babs said.

Nick grabbed Dana's arm. "Fine. We give him the bird. You stay here. I'll go with him."

"Don't think so, mate," Simon said, pulling Dana toward him. "I get the feeling she's the key to keeping you all quiet over here."

"She's not going anywhere with you," Nick said, taking a step forward.

"Nick. Stop."

Nick looked down at Dana, his eyes tight and angry. Dana sighed.

"It'll be okay. I'll give him the bird. I'll sell the winery. I'll figure it all out. But right now, I just want it all to be over."

Simon stepped up next to Dana, grabbing her by the arm and pointing the gun at her head. "We're gonna go get my bird now. And just to be clear, I see the police, any of you lot, or so much as a bloody raccoon coming after us, and the little pet gets it. Understand?"

Nick's jaw muscles tightened, and Dana knew that he was going to come after Simon if she didn't get them out of there right then. She put her hand on his arm.

"Just let me go, Nick. I'll be back in a few minutes and it'll all be over, okay?"

Nick kept his eyes on Simon. "Anything happens to her, I'll kill you."

"You lot stay here like good little girls and boys, and you won't need to."

Without taking his eyes off Nick, Simon motioned toward the door with gun. "Ladies first, pet."

Dana tried to make eye contact with Nick, do something to soften the moment, but his attention was glued to Simon. Dana turned and headed out the door. If everything went as it should, she'd have the chance to make it up to him.

And if not . . . well, she chose not to think about that.

Twenty-five

Dana's hands shook as she turned the front doorknob.

Just because the van is gone, she thought, *doesn't mean Finn ran off with the bird. I mean, it was a dirty van. Maybe he's off getting it cleaned. Polished. Waxed.*

She pushed the door open and glanced at the empty kitchen table.

Or maybe the bastard ran off with the bird.

She motioned for Simon to sit at the table. Simon shook his head.

"Where's my bird, pet?"

Dana laughed, feeling beads of sweat trickling down her lower back. "It's not here. What do you think I am? Stupid?"

Simon raised one eyebrow. "Smells like it was here."

Dana rolled her eyes. "Well, of course it *was*. Until I had it removed to a safe place. Now I just have to make one phone call—"

She moved toward the kitchen, but was stopped by Simon, who pulled her close to him and looked in her eyes as he spoke.

"One thing I didn't mention when we made our little deal, pet, and that was that if you screw me over—"

Dana sighed. "I get shot. Don't worry. I picked up on the subtext."

Simon held her eyes for a moment longer, then released her arm. She exhaled and walked to the kitchen phone. She glanced behind her. Simon was watching her from the living room, but he hadn't moved any closer. Great. Easier to bluff from a distance. She turned and dialed Nick's cell number on the phone.

"Hello?"

Finn. Bastard stole Nick's phone, too. "Good. You have the phone."

"Dana?"

"It's time to bring the bird back," she said.

"Yeah. Uh. About that. You know, I'm a bird thief, and you guys just left me alone with the—"

"How long until you get here?"

"What? I'm not . . . I'm . . . I've screwed you guys over. Ultimate betrayal. Get it? I've got the bird now."

"Simon and I will be expecting you in . . . what . . . a half hour then?" Dana turned her back to Simon so he wouldn't see her chewing her lower lip. Shit. Shit shit shit.

Finn's tone tightened a bit. "Who's Simon? Dana, are you okay?"

"No," she said. "I said a half hour."

"What—?"

She hung up the phone and turned back to face Simon. "Nothing to do but wait."

She forced a smile and tried not to panic. Either there was some decency in Finn, and he would return with the bird and save her life . . .

. . . or she was totally, completely, unequivocally, absolutely screwed.

"Hey," she said, clapping her hands together. "Who needs a drink?"

In the bar, Nick glanced up at the clock. It had been ten minutes. Through the window, all he could see was the red SUV parked out front. How long did it take to get the bird and get gone? They'd been in there for way too long.

"Would you ask him to stop that pacing?" Vivian said from her barstool. "He's making me motion sick."

Babs walked over to Nick and put her hand on his arm. "What do you think?"

"I think they've been there too long," he said.

"I need a drink." Vivian stepped off the stool and went behind the bar.

Babs glanced through the window at the house, then back up at Nick. "Can you get over there without him seeing you?"

Nick thought for a moment. There was a back path through the vineyard, but the plants were thin this time of year. He was pretty sure he could get through without being seen, though.

He nodded. "Yeah. I think so."

"Okay," Babs said. "Then go."

"God," Vivian said, popping back up from behind the bar. "Don't you people have anything but wine?"

"Open a chardonnay and shut up," Babs said, then

turned back to Nick. "I'm counting on you, Nick. You keep her safe."

Nick nodded, pulled the door open, then turned back to Babs for a brief second. "Lock the door behind me, and don't let anyone in, okay?"

"Go get her," Babs said. Nick walked out, shutting the door quietly behind him and cutting around the back to the vineyard.

She lives through this, he thought to himself as he ducked and ran down the back path, *I'm gonna kill her myself.*

Vivian watched Babs lock the door behind Nick, then poured two glasses of chardonnay and set one on the bar for Babs. Babs returned and took the glass, playing with the stem between her fingers as she stared at the bar.

"I'm sorry about your daughter, Babs," Vivian said sweetly. "I'm sure she'll be just fine."

Babs eyed her suspiciously. "Thanks."

"Darla seems like a very nice girl."

"Dana."

"Whatever. And you know what I think would be a great idea? Why don't we go over there and help Neil save her?"

Babs gave her a disgusted look. "Give it up, Vivian. The bird is gone."

Vivian stomped her foot. "That bird is worth $25 million to me, Babs."

Babs gave Vivian a dark look, took a drink, set her wine down on the bar, and pushed herself off the barstool.

"I'll be right back," she said. "Between that car ride and

the past fifteen minutes, my bladder is launching a formal protest. You so much as move from that spot, Vivian, and I'll stab you to death with a corkscrew, I swear it."

Vivian watched as Babs walked slowly toward a door in the corner of the room. Once it was shut, Vivian tiptoed across the room to the cellar door. She flicked the lock on the outside and turned the inside knob. It held. She knelt and checked it out.

Yep. The only keyhole was on the outside. Even Babs wouldn't be able to get out of this one. Probably.

The water shut off in the bathroom. Vivian left the door slightly ajar and hurried back to her place behind the bar, settling her elbows on the bar just as Babs stepped back into the room.

"Did I hear something moving around out here?"

Vivian grinned. "Oh, I was just checking out the merchandise. There's some lovely stuff. I think I'd like to pick up a couple of T-shirts while I'm here."

Babs eyed her warily. It didn't matter. Let her be suspicious. All she had to do was figure out a way to get Babs in that cellar, shut the door, and make it over to the main house before her bird went bye-bye. This nonsense about waiting around for Cheekbones to save the day was just stupid. Even if he did, he had no motivation to get the bird for Vivian, and dammit, she needed that bird.

And come hell or high water, she was going to get it.

Vivian grinned at Babs and lifted the bottle of wine.

"You know," Vivian said, "I've made a decision. You're right. Dana's safety is more important than my stupid inheritance."

Babs gave her a tired look.

"Really?" she said flatly.

"Absolutely," Vivian said. "Things will work out, I believe that. Gary can work for a living doing . . . something. And sure, we'll lose the house and all our pretty things." She fought the lump in her throat to make her voice sound contrite. "And I'm sorry that I let Gary kidnap you. That was just crazy. And very rude. I apologize."

"What do you want, Viv?"

Vivian smiled. "This chardonnay is cr—" She stopped herself and redirected. "Not very good. Everyone knows they keep the best stuff in the cellar at places like this. What do you say you and I go raid the cellar and drink to Dana's safe return?"

Babs sighed. "Will it shut you up?"

Vivian grinned. "Absolutely."

Babs shuffled off the barstool. "Let's go."

Bent at the waist, Nick scrambled the last bit between the cover of the vineyard and the back of the house, then froze, listening. He could hear the soft tones of Dana's voice, and he exhaled. She was safe.

For the moment, anyway.

Silently, he crept close to the back door. Simon was speaking. Nick couldn't hear what he was saying, but Simon seemed calm. Nick poked his head around the back window, where he could see a bit through the curtain. Dana and Simon were sitting at the table.

Drinking wine.

Nick blinked, looked again.

Yes, they were drinking wine. And the bird wasn't there, at least not where Nick could see it. He ducked behind the house again.

Where was it?

He glanced to either side and snuck around the side of the house, coming up behind the carport . . .

. . . where the driveway was empty. Where was the van?

Nick groaned as it hit him. *Sparky.*

"Honest eyes, my ass," he muttered to himself. Dana was in there with a murderous Kiwi, and Finn had run off with the bird. Great.

Nick pressed himself against the wall. Think. Think. He hadn't seen the gun out, so probably Simon had it tucked in the back of his jeans. If he busted in the back door, he could probably get to Simon before . . .

The sound of a car pulling up the gravel drive stopped him. He crept along the side of the house and peeked over, expecting the van. Instead, a silver Lincoln Continental pulled to a stop in front of the house. Nick squinted as he watched the driver.

No. It couldn't be.

The door opened, and two long legs sporting stiletto heels swung out. Dark gray skirt with a dark gray blouse, buttons open to reveal the top of a silk camisole and some generous cleavage. Platinum blond hair fell to her shoulders, framing a heavily made-up face.

Melanie.

Dana downed the last of her wine and glanced at her watch. She had maybe fifteen minutes before Simon started asking questions, found out she didn't have the bird, shot her, and left her for dead.

She poured another glass.

"So, then we knocked him out and duct-taped him to an office chair," Dana said, trying to pull off a convincing, relaxed laugh. It came out more like a choking cackle. "As it turns out, we should have left him there."

Simon raised an eyebrow. "Really? Why's that?"

Dana froze for a moment, then smiled and shrugged. "Long story. But we've been talking about me enough, Simon. Why don't you tell me a little about yourself?"

"Me? I'm the quiet type," Simon said.

"That's nice."

Dana took another drink and tried to smile. She was going to die. She was going to die because of a big, fat, smelly, ugly, stupid green chicken.

And she was going to die without ever getting the chance to tell Nick how stupid she was about the whole marriage thing, how much she wanted to grow old with him and have fat children who would give them fat grandchildren and what the hell good was a stupid moment of clarity if it took a Kiwi with a gun to her head to make her see clearly?

Heat struck behind her eyes and she sniffled, pushing it back. Now was not the time to get all weepy because she'd been too stupid to marry the man she loved. Now was the time to get killed by a bald Kiwi with anger-management issues.

"So," she said, trying to keep her voice level, "you ever been married, Simon?"

Before he could answer, there was a knock at the door. Dana jumped and gave a little squeal of surprise.

"Little skittish, there, pet?" Simon asked. He reached behind his jacket, Dana guessed so he could have quick access to the gun that would be killing her momentarily. "Answer it."

"Sure," Dana said, standing up on wobbly legs. "Sure, that's what I'll do."

She crossed the room to the front door. The image through the glass wasn't Finn. With those breasts and that hair, there was only one person it could be, and it couldn't be her.

Except it was. Dana took a deep breath, put her hand on the doorknob, and opened it.

"Melanie," she said flatly.

Melanie put on a tremendous, and thoroughly fake, smile. "Dana! So good to see you! You look gorgeous, sweetie, but then you always did." Melanie peeked around Dana's shoulder and her smile widened. "Hello. That's not Nick."

Melanie pushed in past Dana and made her way across the room to Simon, her arm outstretched. Dana kicked the door shut and followed.

"Hi," she said. "I'm Melanie. So nice to meet you."

"Where's the bird?" Simon asked.

Dana glanced at the wine bottle on the table. All she had to do was distract Simon, then she could hit him with the bottle, grab Melanie, and toss them both out the back door. But how to distract him?

"Bird?" Melanie said, her perfectly plucked eyebrows crinkling daintily. She and her tremendous breasts turned to face Dana. "What's this about a bird?"

Tremendous breasts. Dana smiled.

No. I can't. It's too evil.

"Oh, wait. Am I interrupting something . . . kinky?" Melanie tilted her head at Dana, blinking innocence. "And where is Nick? Does he know about you two?"

Dana smiled wider. Evil be damned. If anyone had

earned this, it was Melanie. And Dana was pretty sure she could pull it off without getting Melanie shot. She nudged Melanie and her breasts toward Simon.

"This is Simon, Mel," Dana said. "He's here for the bird. Go get it, will you?"

Melanie gave a confused laugh and rested the fingers of her right hand gently over her throat. "I'm afraid . . . I don't know—"

Simon blinked at Dana, then looked at Melanie, his eyes pulled by testosterone toward Melanie's breasts. Dana smiled. Finally, those things were coming in handy.

"I knew it," Dana said. "You took the bird and sold it yourself, didn't you, Mel?"

Melanie gave her a confused look. "I have no idea what you're talking about."

"Sure you do." Dana stole another glance at the wine bottle, catching something move at the back door. She stared for a moment, and her heart exploded in her chest.

Nick.

Oh thank God.

Nick met her eye through the window. He nodded toward Simon, and Dana nodded back, knowing what he needed her to do. She stepped closer to Melanie, keeping Simon's attention away from the door behind him.

"I think I've had enough of this," Melanie said, backing away from Simon. Dana grabbed Melanie's arm, turning her so that her breasts were facing Simon.

"She did it," Dana said. "She double-crossed us. She's a big, fat double-crosser."

"Hey!" Melanie shrieked. "I am *not* fat!"

Simon's cyes narrowed and locked on Dana. "What are you playing at here, pet?"

"Nothing," Dana said. In her peripheral vision, she could see Nick rising at the back door, waiting on her signal to jump in. "She took the bird and sold it and kept the money for herself. I think you should shoot her."

"What?" Melanie screamed, turning to Dana. Dana tossed Melanie at Simon, who instinctively reached out and caught her. At that moment, Nick burst in, tackled Simon and brought him to the ground, landing two quick punches before Simon pushed him off. Melanie scrambled across the room to Dana's side. Dana reached down and pulled her up as the men fought.

"What the . . . hell was . . . that?" she said breathlessly, swiping at her skirt.

"A little fun," Dana said. "Mostly distraction."

Nick swung at Simon, clocking him across the chin. Melanie clutched at Dana's arm, shrinking behind Dana like a frightened kitten.

"What's going on here?" Melanie shrieked. "Why is that man hitting Nick?"

"I'll tell you later," Dana said, trying to move closer to the wine bottle, but Melanie only tightened her grip. "Let me go. I need to help him."

"No!" Melanie said, yanking Dana back. "That man has a gun. You have to protect me!"

"I don't care about you," Dana said, yanking Melanie with her as she tried to wrench her arm away. "What the hell are you doing here, anyway?"

"I thought I'd pay an old friend a visit," Melanie said, peeking up over Dana's shoulder to get a glimpse of the fight.

"Well, go visit her then!"

Simon gut-punched Nick, sending him back a few feet. Dana and Melanie both shrieked, "Nick!" in unison.

"Hey!" Dana said. "Don't you call his name!"

"What, you don't own him!" Melanie shot back.

"Good God, Melanie, it was tenth grade!" Dana yelled. "Get over it already!"

"I should have won that election!" Melanie yelled back.

Dana narrowed her eyes at Melanie and opened her mouth to say something when the sound of a gunshot rang through the house, followed closely by shattering glass and both Dana and Melanie yelling, "Nick!"

Babs jabbed her metal nail file in the doorjamb, pushing it against the bolt. She couldn't believe she'd been stupid enough to go into the cellar with Vivian. It wasn't until Vivian excused herself to go to the bathroom that Babs caught on, and by then it was too late.

"I swear, if I have to pick one more stupid lock this week, I'm calling it quits and moving to Florida," she muttered to herself.

Something clicked. She pulled on the door.

Nothing.

Hell.

"I can retire. I can live in a retirement community, like all the other retired people, and get old and die cranky."

The nail file slipped out of the lock and wedged itself into the wall. She closed her eyes and gritted her teeth.

"You have to calm down, Babs," she coached herself. "You know you can't pick a lock angry. It just never works."

She reached up and dislodged the nail file from the

wall. The trick to flipping a lock, her teacher had said, was attitude. Believe you could do it, and you could do it.

All she had to do was get her zen back. She took in a deep breath and released it, visualizing all the tension in her shoulders flowing out with her breath.

"Happy thought," she said. "I need a happy thought."

She closed her eyes and visualized Vivian in her favorite leather Gucci duster, tied to a chair, and being dunked repeatedly into a vat of ice water. She smiled, slowed her breathing, and opened her eyes. She slid the nail file into the doorjamb, angled it up under the bolt, and scraped at it.

Nothing.

"Dammit," she said, and tossed the nail file, listening as it clattered down the steps. She crossed her arms over her chest and sulked, staring at the wine bottles shelved by the hundreds before her.

"Oh, the hell with it," she said as she got up and trudged down the steps. "There's gotta be a corkscrew here somewhere."

Twenty-six

Finn pulled the van up to the house, parking behind a silver Lincoln, which was parked behind a red SUV. He shook his head and shot a look at Horshack, who sat on the passenger seat in his cage.

"Looks like we're a little late for the party," Finn said. He put the car in park and stared at the house. It wasn't too late to turn back. He could probably leave another message for his buyer and push the meet time back. Or find another buyer. It wasn't too late to—

A gunshot sounded, and Finn ducked in the van as one of the house's side windows exploded.

"Shit." Finn let out an exasperated sigh and released his seat belt. "All that stuff I told you about loyalty being for idiots and martyrs still stands, Horshack."

Finn shot out of the van and up the front steps. He flattened himself against the wall and peeked through the window. Nick and some huge bald guy were scrabbling over a gun on the floor. Off to the side, some Marilyn Monroe wannabe was clutching Dana's arm and ducking behind her. Finn closed his eyes, swore, and pushed the front door open, knocking into Dana and Marilyn.

"Hey, who the hell are you?" Marilyn asked as he pushed past her.

"The village idiot," Finn said, and stepped into the fight. Nick had his shoulder digging into the bald guy's windpipe as he bore down on the guy with his weight and struggled with both hands to pry the gun out of the guy's hands. Finn walked around, gave the guy a swift kick in the 'nads, and heard the gun drop as the guy cried out in pain. Nick kicked the gun away with one foot, hauled up on his knees, and gave the guy a swift shot to the head, knocking him out.

Finn stepped back, giving Nick a little space as he got to his feet. Breathing heavily, he wiped some blood off his lip with his fist and turned his eyes on Finn. Finn grinned.

"Hey, I have an idea," Finn said. "But I'll need some duct tape and an office chair."

Nick narrowed his eyes at Finn, and fury erupted through him. He grabbed Finn by the shirt and bashed him up against the wall.

"I should kill you now," he said.

Finn stared at him in disbelief. "What the hell, man? You have short-term memory loss or something? I just saved your ass!"

Nick pulled Finn back and bashed him against the wall again. "You stole the bird!"

Finn threw his arms up. "Yeah. Bird thief. Remember?"

"You put her in danger," he said, indicating Dana with his chin. "You could have gotten her killed."

"Yeah, and I came back," Finn croaked, straining against Nick's arm, "a decision I'm beginning to regret."

"Let him go, Nick," Dana said from behind him.

Nick exhaled. "Fine." He released Finn and walked over to get the gun off the floor. He put the safety on and tucked it in the back of his jeans, then looked to Dana. She met his glance, a trace of guilt in her expression.

Good.

"You okay?" he asked.

"Yeah," Dana said. "Really super. You?"

"Really pissed off." He took a step toward her, not sure which he wanted to do more—take her by the shoulders and shake her or pull her into her arms and never let go. Instead, he chose to clench his fists at his sides. "What were you thinking, going off with him like that?"

"I'll just go find some rope and get this guy secure before all the yelling wakes him up," Finn said, heading down the hallway.

"I was thinking the bird would be here," she said. "I was thinking it would all be over and I could hole up in front of the television with some Ben & Jerry's and work on getting really fat."

"He could have killed you," Nick said, the words shooting through his gut as he said them. "Did you even think about that?"

"Once I got here and the bird was missing, yeah, I thought about that a lot, actually."

Nick moved closer to her and looked into her eyes. "Yeah, well, sitting out there, watching you in here with him, I guarantee you I thought about it more."

Dana looked away, and Nick knew she got it. He unclenched his fists, and she raised her eyes to his.

"Nick—" Dana started, but was interrupted by Melanie, who situated herself on Nick's other side.

"What exactly is going on here, anyway?" she said, putting her hand on Nick's arm. "Nick, why did Dana try to have me shot?"

"I didn't try to have you shot, you stupid cow," Dana said. "I was distracting Simon so Nick could come in and save us."

"She told him to shoot me!" Melanie screeched.

Finn returned with the rope and raised an eyebrow at Nick. "Wanna help me out here?"

"Oh, God, yes," Nick said, stepping out from between the two women. Finn had just handed him the rope when Melanie spoke again.

"Who's that?"

Nick glanced up to see Melanie looking out the front window.

"Who's what?"

Melanie pointed. "The woman driving off in that van."

Finn ran to the front window as the sound of screeching tires echoed from out front. He cursed and banged his fist against the wall.

"Oh," Melanie said, pointing one heavily manicured nail at Finn, "was that his van?"

Twenty minutes later, Dana handed Finn the keys to the SUV. She glanced through the back window; Simon was lying on his side, still unconscious, bound at the ankles and knees, with his hands tied to a rope that went around his waist. They'd also bound him around his upper arms and chest, just in case. It had been Finn's idea to take care of Simon himself, and Dana wasn't going to argue. No real damage had been done, and explaining the events of the last forty-eight hours to the police was something she'd gladly avoid if possible.

"Did you get Vivian's address?" she asked.

Finn squinted in the sun as he looked at her. "Yeah."

"Okay, then," she said.

"Okay."

She followed him as he walked to the front door of the SUV and opened it.

"Finn."

He turned his head to look at her. "Yeah?"

She hauled off and punched him hard in the biceps.

"Jesus!" he said, rubbing his arm. "Give a guy a warning, will ya?"

"That's for taking the bird," she said, then smiled. "Thanks for coming back."

"No good deed goes unpunished." He laughed and shook his head, getting in the SUV. He nodded toward the house. "Now get in there before Blondezilla makes mincemeat of your boy."

Dana gasped. "You could tell she was evil? You only spent a few minutes with her."

Finn shrugged. "What can I say? I'm a student of human nature."

Dana smiled. "I knew I liked you."

Finn chuckled and gave a wave before shutting the door and starting up the SUV. Dana took a deep breath and headed back into the house. As she opened the door, she caught Melanie's whining tones.

". . . don't understand how you can turn this opportunity down. What can I say to change your mind?"

"Nothing," Nick said. He was kneeling on the floor, sweeping up a glass that had broken in the tussle. He looked up as Dana came in.

"He gone?"

Dana nodded. "Yeah."

"Good riddance." Nick stood up, emptying the dustpan into the kitchen garbage he'd pulled out into the room. "I think I got everything, but you might want to give the floor a going-over with the vacuum before you walk around barefoot."

Dana crossed her arms over her stomach. "Okay."

He held her eyes for a moment, then turned to put the garbage, broom, and dustpan away.

"What if I gave Dana the money to reopen the winery?" Melanie said suddenly.

Dana turned to face her. "Why are you still here?"

Melanie walked toward Nick, who stood in the kitchen, staring at her.

"I mean it, Nick. I'll give Dana the money, if you agree to come to California."

Dana gasped in horror. "Wait. What?"

Melanie tossed a smug glance at Dana. "I know you're in trouble. I know you went to the bank, and they turned you down for a loan to get this place back up and running."

"What?" Dana screeched. "How did you—"

Melanie raised one eyebrow and smirked. "Bernard Higgins. At the bank. Old friend."

"You don't have friends," Dana said. "And Bernard Higgins? So very fired."

Melanie rolled her eyes. "Whatever." She turned to Nick. "So, Nick, what do you say? I give her the money, you come out and manage Brigstone for me."

"No," Dana said, her stomach roiling with rage. "He says—"

"No strings attached?" Nick asked.

"What?" Dana said, her world going quiet as she looked at Nick.

He can't be serious.

Nick stared Melanie down. "You'll give her the money she needs, free and clear?"

He's serious.

Melanie's face lit up. "Absolutely. She won't owe me a dime."

"No. I won't," Dana said, shooting a stern look at Nick. "Because he's not going."

Nick kept his eyes on Melanie. "A hundred thousand dollars, Melanie. No taking it back. Once it's hers, it's hers."

Melanie stepped forward, holding her hand out to Nick. "I'll have my lawyers draw up the paperwork. It'll be a gift. I won't be able to get it back even if I want to."

Dana felt her stomach turn. "But . . . Nick . . ."

Nick eyed Melanie. "I know a guy in the city. He'll draw up the paperwork."

Melanie let out a tinkling laugh. "Why? Don't you trust me?"

Nick shot her a black look.

"Fine," Melanie huffed. "Have him send it to my lawyer, and if he moves fast, we can have Dana on her feet by the end of next week."

"Wait a minute," Dana said, stepping in between them.

"I'm on my feet, and I'm saying no." She turned to look at Nick. "What the hell are you doing?"

Nick's jaw muscles worked and he held up his index finger to Melanie.

"One minute, Mel," he said. He walked out of the kitchen, grabbed Dana's arm, and led her outside, closing the door behind them. He put both hands on Dana's arms and leaned toward her.

"Dana—"

"No," Dana said. She put her hand to her chest, trying to relieve the sensation that it was being crushed. "How can you do this?"

"Dana, listen to me—"

"No," she said. "I know we had a fight, but . . ."

Nick glanced inside at Melanie, who quickly pretended she was inspecting her manicure. Dana threw her arms up to release herself from Nick's grip, and took a step back. "Are you really going to take that deal?"

Nick looked back at Dana. "Yes, but—"

"Well," Dana said, trying to keep her voice even. "Then I guess we don't have anything to talk about."

"We would, if you would just listen—"

"Am I crazy? Or were you asking me to marry you not two hours ago?"

Nick's face tightened. "Yeah. And as I recall, you turned me down and threw me out."

"No, I . . . well, yeah, okay, I did, but you didn't give me a chance to . . ." She stomped her foot and took a breath, trying to get her thoughts together. "You gave me an ultimatum."

He closed his eyes and sighed. "I know. I did. And it was totally unfair, and I'm sorry. But this—"

"I don't want to hear about this. I'm horrified that you would even consider this."

He huffed in frustration. "Would you let me finish a sentence?"

"Not if it's going to end with, 'I'm going to California with Melanie,' no."

His eyes narrowed as he looked at her. "You just don't trust me at all, do you?"

"Should I?" Dana said, trying to keep the hysteria out of her voice. "You're about to make a deal with Melanie Biggs, Nick. What's there to trust?"

He looked away. "Apparently, nothing."

"Well, fine, go on in there and negotiate my life for me, Nick. But don't expect me to be here when you're done."

He stuffed his hands in his pockets and glared at her. "Fine. I won't."

"Fine, go!"

"I'm going!"

"Fine!"

He stomped to the door and slammed it behind him. Through the window, Dana watched as Nick walked over to Melanie and shook her hand. She was very proud of herself that she managed to walk all the way to the winery and get Babs out of the cellar before she burst into uncontrollable sobs.

Twenty-seven

Ten days later, Dana knelt on her mother's terrace and stared into the cage at the two birds nestled together on one bar swing.

"They're cute," she said. "What are they?"

"Lovebirds," Babs said, sitting down on her lounge chair. "I'm going to bring them out here every afternoon. They like the fresh air."

"Oh, they tell you this, do they?"

"We speak the language of love," Babs said with a grin, then sipped her gin and tonic. "Speaking of which . . ."

Dana held up her hand in warning. "Don't."

"What?"

"You were going to bring up Nick."

"I was not."

"Yes, you were. I can tell when you're about to talk about Nick because your right eyebrow raises just a notch above the left."

Babs's right eyebrow raised a notch. "I was just going to say that I saw a moving truck outside the wine bar today."

Dana snapped her fingers. "I knew it!" She lowered her hand. "Really? A moving van?"

"I didn't go inside. I am completely loyal to you, darling. But I thought maybe you might want to go over there and talk to him."

Dana looked down. "Mom, I told you. It's over."

"Then why are you still here?"

"You know why I'm here. I'm just taking a break until the money goes through."

"Which it did yesterday."

"Yeah. So? What's your point?"

Babs sighed. "It's not that I don't absolutely love having you here, dear. I do. We've hardly fought over anything during this whole extended visit."

"Except *Butch Cassidy and the Sundance Kid.*"

"I'm telling you, they didn't die, they got away," Babs said with a smile. "But that's not the point. The point is . . ."

". . . you want your adult daughter out of your guest room. I get it. I'll pack." Dana pushed herself up from her kneeling position, then sat down next to Babs on the lounge chair. "Right after tonight's episode of *Queer Eye,* I swear I'm outta here."

"You're not a very good listener, you know that, Dana?"

"I blame my mother."

Babs smiled softly. "Go see him, Dana."

Dana leaned her head on Babs's shoulder. "Mom. I can't."

"Why not?"

"Because he made his choice."

"Did you make yours?"

Dana raised her head. "What's that supposed to mean?"

"It means exactly that. Did you ever tell him you wanted to marry him?"

"Well. No. But . . . Melanie. And the ultimatum—"

Babs patted her daughter's hand. "Dana, if I've taught you anything, it should be that you shouldn't live a life with regrets. If you let Nick go to California without telling him how you feel, it'll always be there, hanging over your shoulder, nagging you."

"Kinda like a parrot?"

"I'm not joking, Dana." Babs pushed up off the lounge chair. "I have some errands to run. I want you to think about what I've said. Will you promise me to think about it?"

She stared down at Dana, an expectant look on her face.

"Okay," Dana said. "I'll think about it. I promise."

Babs smiled. "That's all I ask."

She picked up the cage. The birds tweeted sweetly as Babs hustled them inside. Dana stood up and walked over to the terrace railing, staring out into the city as the late-afternoon sun painted it orange.

Nick was really leaving. She'd kinda hoped that he'd track her down at the penthouse, come by in a surprise move and tell her he'd changed his mind, he wasn't going to California. When she'd checked her account the day before to find the hundred thousand there, it felt like all the air had rushed out of her world.

He was really going.

She stared down into the street and thought about what her mother had said about regrets. She was already full of them. She regretted running out on Nick at their wedding. She regretted letting six years go by before telling him she still loved him. She regretted telling him no when he asked her to marry him at the winery, and she regretted letting him make the deal with Melanie.

And now came the choice. She could allow one more regret to land on the pile, or she could go tell him she loved him and beg him not to go to California and take the chance of getting moving van tread marks all over her heart.

It was pretty much a no-brainer.

Finn skimmed through the *Times* want ads at his kitchen table. He'd found a couple of decent prospects, but nothing that would pay as well as the birds. Still, if getting knocked out, duct-taped, and almost shot didn't get him to quit birds, nothing would.

And that thought was just too damned depressing.

There was a knock at the door, and he dropped his red pen and pushed up from the table. He peeked through the security viewer and chuckled to himself before flipping the bolt and opening the door.

"I'll be damned," he said.

"Very likely." Babs McGregor said, stepping inside and pushing the paper against Finn's chest as she walked past him. "I read in the paper where a conservation guy named Simon Burke was found on a cargo ship to New Zealand. Thought you might find that interesting."

"Come on in, Babs. Good to see you."

"Apparently, he e-mailed a confession to the New Zealand Kakapo Wildlife Conservation, stating how he stole a Kakapo with intent to sell it, but then changed his mind. That's how they knew to look for him on the ship."

"No kidding." Finn held up a Dunkin' Donuts box. "Donut?"

Babs sat down at the table. "Jelly, if you have it. Darnedest thing, though. They can't figure out how he got himself into the belly of the ship, considering he was all trussed up like a Sunday pig. And apparently, he's not talking."

Finn put a plate with a jelly donut down in front of Babs. "What a world."

"Also interesting—it seems a Kakapo, missing since 1973 and presumed dead, was on the boat with him."

"Sounds like quite the tale." Finn sat down opposite Babs and watched as she bit into her jelly donut. "Good?"

"Mmmmm," Babs said, then daintily dabbed at her mouth before speaking again. "And I saw Vivian."

"Really? Where?"

"On the street by her house, arguing simultaneously with her lawyers and the people who were moving her stuff out onto the street."

"You must have enjoyed that."

"You have no idea how much. Unfortunately, I think she's going to be able to have the old coot declared insane and get the money anyway, but she'll be living on government cheese between now and then, and that makes me happy inside."

"Not to change the subject, but what brings you here, Babs?"

"I have this burning curiosity . . ."

"I hear they have an ointment for that."

"Why'd you send the bird back?"

Finn didn't say anything. Babs leaned her elbows forward on the table and eyed Finn.

"I mean, there you were. Bird thief. Valuable bird. A buyer at the ready. All that money. And yet, you chose to put the bird on the boat. Why?"

Finn met her eye. "I have no idea what you're talking about. I sold that bird. Went to Fiji. This conversation is actually just a figment of a vibrant but somewhat deranged imagination."

She smiled. "You grew a conscience, didn't you, Pinocchio?"

Finn leaned back in his chair. "Impossible."

"You knew there were only eighty-six of them left on the planet, and you felt bad."

"That's it. No more *Murder, She Wrote* reruns for you."

Babs grabbed a napkin and dabbed at her lips. "You know what I think?"

"I have a feeling I'm gonna find out."

She grinned. "I think someday you're gonna be a real boy."

Finn pushed himself up from the table.

"Well, not to be rude, but this real boy has to go to real work if he wants to make real rent." He walked over to the door and grabbed his *Chez Animaux* jacket from the hook on the back of the door.

"Yes," Babs said, reaching into her purse and pulling out a slip of paper. "You do."

Finn nodded toward the paper. "What's that?"

"Nothing really. Just a little favor I need done.

Finn paused for a moment. She didn't look like she was kidding. "You're asking me for a favor?"

"It's for charity," she said with a bright smile, then leaned in slightly and winked at him. "Good for your karma."

Finn chuckled. "Lady, my karma ceased to be an issue a long time ago."

"Blah blah tough guy blah," Babs said. "Don't worry. I'll see you receive a generous fee for your services. But I need your help and you need a job and I believe what we have here is a case of fortuitous timing."

She pushed the piece of paper toward him. Finn eyed her for a moment, then took it from her. He unfolded it and read, then raised his eyes to hers.

"You want me to steal a baseball glove?"

"Not steal, pick *up*," Babs said. "So, what do you say? Are you interested?"

"Can you guarantee I'll never have to look at another bird again?"

Babs shrugged. "I'll do my best."

"Good enough," Finn said, and hung the jacket back on the hook.

Twenty-eight

Dana got out of the cab at the end of Nick's street. She figured the walk would be good for her. And if she chickened out and wanted to run the other way, there'd be time for that, too.

Just in case.

She walked slowly down the street, her eyes on the moving van parked in front of Murphy's, right next to Oscar the hot dog guy. The back of the van was open, and when she got close enough, she could see boxes inside labeled in Nick's hand with black magic marker. KITCHEN. BEDROOM. MUSIC AND DVDS.

"Oh, God," Dana said, as her stomach did a flip.

"Yeah, guy's been living there six years, and that's all he's got," Oscar said. "Sad."

"Dana?"

She turned to see Nick standing behind her, a box marked BATHROOM in his arms. He just watched her, not smiling, not calling her Diz, not giving her anything to indicate if she was about to completely humiliate herself in front of God, Manhattan, and Oscar the hot dog guy.

"Did you need something?" he asked.

"No," she said, her voice registering at an embarrassingly high pitch. She cleared her throat and continued. "No. I just wanted . . . to wish you luck."

"Oh," he said. "Really?"

"No."

They stared at each other for another moment, then Nick said, "Is that it? 'Cause I have to be out of the place by midnight."

"Don't go to California."

There was a painfully long moment of silence in which Nick said nothing. He seemed genuinely surprised, but still. He could say *something*. Dana waited, her heart beating louder and louder until she finally worked up the nerve to go on.

"The money went through," she said. "I checked my account yesterday and the money's there and I can walk away and go back to the winery and live my life."

Nick's face was tight. "Good. That's great."

"I don't want it."

His eyebrows knit. "What?"

"Not if it means losing you," she said. She felt her throat start to close on her and her eyes heat up and people were starting to gather, but she didn't care. "I would rather give her every dime back and live out here in that box with you than be in the winery without you."

Nick walked over to the van and pushed the box inside, then leaned against it and crossed his arms over his chest. "You mean that?"

She nodded. She reached out, grabbed his hand, then knelt on one knee as the crowd started to "Awwwww."

"Dana?" he said, his fingers tightening on her hand.

"It's a cheesy gesture, I know," she said. "But I'm going with it."

Nick glanced at the crowd, then back at Dana. "You don't have to do this."

"Yes. I do. Remember how I ran out on you at our first wedding?"

"Yeah, but . . ."

"And when you proposed again, I yelled at you and threw you out of the winery?"

"Yeah."

"Trust me, Nick. I've earned this."

He smiled. "Okay. Go ahead."

She looked up at him and smiled, trying to remember everything she'd planned to say in the cab ride over.

"I've had a lot of time to think about us, and here's the thing. Marriage scares the hell out of me. When I think about it as an institution, I break out in a cold sweat. But when I think about you . . . I don't."

He raised an eyebrow and smiled down at her. "This is your big romantic speech? Cold sweat?"

"It gets better. Where was I? Oh, yeah." She shifted on her knee and tightened her grip on his hand. "Every time we've been about to make it work, I think about marriage and divorce and I run because I don't trust marriage. But you, I trust. I know you don't think I do, but I do. And I'm not running this time, Nick. You can pack up that van and go to California, and I don't care. I'll follow you until you believe me. For better or worse, Nick. It's you. Only you." She felt the tears fall over her cheeks, and it sounded like someone in the crowd was crying as well, but she kept her eyes on Nick. "Will you marry me?"

The crowd went "Awwwww" again.

Nick squeezed her hand. "Get up."

He pulled her up to standing and wrapped his arms around her, kissing her until her leg muscles went weak as the crowd around them cheered.

"All right," he said to everyone. "Show's over, people."

"So . . . ," Dana said, moving his chin with her finger until he was looking at her again. "That's a yes?"

He reached up and nudged a curl away from her forehead. "What do you think?"

"Oh, thank God," she said, and swiped some tears off her face. "I was going to have to kill myself if I got turned down in front of Oscar the hot dog guy."

"Diz, you're crazy, and you're a massive pain in the ass, but I love you." He pulled her close and kissed her lightly on the lips. "I'd never turn you down in front of Oscar the hot dog guy."

"That's good. I guess." She looked up at him through her eyelashes. "Do you need to call Melanie and tell her you're not going?"

"I'm proud of you. You waited a whole fifteen seconds before bringing that up."

"I'm sorry. I'm trying to get past my pettiness, but I'd really love to hear you tell her she lost."

He shook his head. "She already knows I'm not coming."

"Wait," Dana said. "She already knows?"

"Yeah," he said with a smirk. "She called me to tell me the money went through, and I told her I wasn't going."

Dana blinked, trying to put it all together in her head.

"But . . . but . . . but . . . if you weren't going, what's with the van?"

Nick pulled her hand up to his lips and kissed the palm. "I was on my way up to your place. I was basically going to give you the same speech. Only, I had this." He reached into his pocket and pulled out a battered, but familiar, ring box.

"Oh, my God. Nick . . ." Dana reached for the box and opened it, pulling out her diamond engagement ring. "You still have it?"

"What can I say?" he said, taking it from her. "I've got hidden depths."

"You were really going to ask me to marry you?"

"Yeah."

"Again?"

"Yep."

"You just don't learn, do you?"

"Apparently not." He held the ring up and raised his eyebrows at her in question. "May I?"

She squealed and held out her hand.

"We'll take our time," he said as he slid it on her finger. "It can be a long engagement. Ten, fifteen years, if that's what you need."

She sniffled. "I was thinking next flight to Vegas."

He laughed. "That's fine, too."

"But what about Melanie? The winery?"

He shrugged. "It's paid off, right?"

"Right."

"No strings, right? Legally yours?"

"Yeah, but . . ."

"I reviewed the paperwork myself, Dana. There's not a word in there about me. Melanie gave you a gift, and frankly, I think it was damn nice of her."

Dana gasped as it hit her what Nick had done. "Wait a minute. You lied."

"Yep."

"You never had any intention of working for Melanie."

He shook his head. "Nope."

"You screwed over Melanie Biggs!" She threw her arms around his neck and hugged him. "I didn't think it was possible to love you more than I did, but you've proven me wrong."

"I tried to tell you on your deck that day, but you wouldn't let me get a word in edgewise," he said, putting his hand on her hips as she slowly slid down the length of his body. "But this way is good, too." He motioned in the direction of his apartment with his chin. "You know, I haven't taken down the bed yet."

Dana smiled up at him, put her arms around his neck, and placed her lips next to his ear.

"Race ya," she said.

A Note About the Kakapo

The Kakapo is a real parrot, in real peril. Native to New Zealand, this unique and fascinating bird now has a worldwide population of only eighty-six. While I tease the Kakapo mercilessly in this book, I've grown quite fond of it, and would encourage anyone interested in learning more about it, or donating to assist in its recovery, to visit the Kakapo Recovery Programme's website at http://www.kakaporecovery.org.nz. Thank you.

More
Lani Diane Rich!

Please turn this page
for an exciting preview of

Ex and the Single Girl

Available in trade paperback

November 2005.

CHAPTER ONE

Fat white flakes clustered around the edges of my living-room window as another Syracuse winter flipped late March the bird. I sat with my feet curled under me on the cheap futon in my tiny one-bedroom, lit by the flickering colors of the BBC version of *Pride and Prejudice*, which I was watching for what was probably around the eighteenth time. My hand was draped casually over a bag of Cheetos, which I planned on trading in for the chilled chardonnay in my fridge as soon as I could locate the motivation to get up.

". . . allow me to tell you how ardently I admire and love you."

I sighed. I couldn't help myself. Nobody knows how to do lovers in a snit like Austen. Darcy paced, lecturing to Elizabeth all the reasons she was unworthy of him. Her eyes widened, then narrowed.

Things were just about to get good.

Ring.

Dammit. I exhaled heavily, shooting my bangs up off my forehead, and glared at the phone, which hung at a defiant angle on my kitchen wall. Almost three years, and I'd never drummed up the wherewithal to straighten it.

"In such cases as these, I believe the established mode

is to express a sense of obligation." Elizabeth's eyes lifted and met Darcy's. They were cold. "But I cannot."

Ring.

"Shit, piss, and corruption," I grumbled, searching around for the remote control, even though I hadn't seen the thing in weeks. "I sat through three hours of parties and pianofortes for this scene."

Beep. My voice crackled through my garage-sale answering machine, creaking with the cold I'd had when I recorded the outgoing message in February. "Not here. Do your thing."

I'm a big fan of brevity. My mother, however, is not.

"Portia, darlin'." Mags's voice was like honey, sweet and slow to move. I never noticed her accent until I moved to upstate New York, where words that start out as one syllable tend to stay that way. I shed my own drawl on the train ride out of town, although I'm told it comes out when I've been drinking.

"Are you there, baby? You should answer the phone. It's not right to sit and listen to people talking and not answer the phone. Vera says that sort of thing absolutely ruins your karma."

"Vera thinks hairspray ruins your karma," I muttered, hopping off the futon and sweeping my arm underneath the mammoth cushion for the twentieth time that week, as though repetition of the ritual would make the damn remote magically reappear.

Mags released a stage sigh, the kind regular people only hear during plays by Tennessee Williams. "I guess I can assume you're not there. Well, please, baby, call me the second you get this message. It's *urgent.*"

Urgent. The word didn't have the same meaning for

Mags that it did for most people. *Urgent* could have meant that she had misplaced her unholy red pumps and needed me to talk her through the search. It could have meant that one of her favorite movie stars from the forties had died, and the entire family needed to lift a glass in unison to the Great One's memory. One *urgent* call resulted in my losing two hours of my life to gossip about Felicia Callahan getting fired from the Catoosa County Chamber of Commerce for stealing four staplers and thirty-eight dollars petty cash.

"I need you to call me tonight, baby, the very moment you get home."

I tossed the futon cushion back down and got up to hit the PAUSE button on my tiny TV/VCR. On an average day, I spent more time looking for the stupid remote than it'd take for me to get up and walk over to the TV, but it was the principle of the thing. It had disappeared around the same time Peter left, and having it at large meant Peter might find it in his things and return it. The very thought of him showing up on the doorstep with nothing to say but "Here's your remote" was the stuff of which nightmares are made.

The machine beeped again, and I released a breath I hadn't realized I was holding. I wandered into the kitchen, curling the top of the bag of Cheetos and tossing it onto the counter, where it began its determined work of uncurling. I didn't care. I'd done my part. I grabbed the corkscrew with one hand as I opened the fridge with the other.

Tick-tock. Darcy's waiting.

Freeze-frame.

This is the pre-epiphany moment, the mental snapshot of myself that I revisit on occasion, mystified at how much I failed to notice. There I was, wearing the oldest flannel robe in existence, my unwashed hair sticking up in all directions out of a lazy ponytail, my glasses smudged and crooked, a bottle of wine in hand with little splotches of Cheeto residue on the neck, and I had no earthly idea that anything was wrong.

It hadn't been that bad when Peter'd been around. I'd been clean, lively, happy. I smelled good. I flossed. But then one day—Valentine's Day, if you can stand the irony—I came home to a half-emptied apartment and a half-ass good-bye note scribbled in the title page of a book. And not just *any* book. *Peter's* book. The one he'd written during two years of late nights and early mornings while I encouraged him, making coffee and providing sexual diversions. The one that had hit the shelves and stayed there, neglected, while Steeles and Koontzes flew from either side. The one that I read over and over, gushing over his talent every time.

I'd found it lying on the bed, the front cover held open with my Itty Bitty booklight, the title page etched with his deliberate handwriting.

I'm sorry. I wish you all the best. Love, Peter.

A simple note, vague as hell, fodder for hours and hours of painful dissection. What did it *mean*? Why would he sign a later-babe note with *Love, Peter*? Isn't love pretty much a moot point when one is being dumped? And where had he gone? Had he run off with another woman? Another man? Had he simply decided that he would rather be alone than with me? Which was worse?

For six weeks, these were the questions that haunted me as I plummeted into a cavern of self-pity. In six short

weeks, I'd mutated from a normal individual pursuing a
Ph.D. and a reasonable future to a wild-haired social pho-
bic, rationalizing my obsession with *Pride and Prejudice*
by linking it with my dissertation topic, "The Retelling of
Austen in Post-Feminist Women's Literature." Forget that
I hadn't written a word since the day Peter left. Forget that
I'd left the house only to teach my classes and to grab
Cheetos and chardonnay at Wegmans. Forget that I had
just earlier that very day briefly considered getting a cat.
If nothing else, I should have been tipped off by the fact
that when Peter and I were together, I'd more than once
caught myself fantasizing about coming home one day to
an empty apartment, leaving me blameless and beatified.
And free. Now that my dream had come true, it begged
the question: What, exactly, was I mourning?

Continue action.

I carried the bottle of wine and the glass with me to the
living room, kicking a path through the notebooks and
pens on the floor as I settled back on the futon. The tape
had stopped, and a blond sitcom star from the seventies
was hawking diet pills. I debated internally whether the
energy would be better spent getting up and hitting the
PLAY button or continuing my futile search for the remote
when the phone rang.

Again.

Two calls in the span of fifteen minutes greatly in-
creased the probability that whatever she was calling
about was actually urgent. I pulled myself up off the futon
and headed into the kitchen, flicking on the light and
grabbing the receiver off its crooked base. "Yeah?"

"Portia, darlin', I knew you were home."

"In the shower." I took a sip of my wine. "I heard the phone ring. Was that you?"

"Yes, baby," she said. Her voice sounded tired. I wondered why I hadn't noticed it before. I rifled through the junk drawer in the kitchen. Remotes have turned up in stranger places.

"Baby, I need your help. My back has gone out on me, and every moment is acute pain and torture. Doctor Bobby says I need to stay in bed for a few months."

Only in Truly, Georgia, would a grown man who'd earned a doctorate in medicine allow himself to be referred to as "Doctor Bobby." I stood up straight and slammed the drawer shut with my hip. "A few months? Jesus, Mags. What did you do?"

"I don't know," she said, distress raising her voice an easy octave. "But Doctor Bobby has given me strict orders. Which puts us in a bit of a spot. Vera can't run the store alone, and Bev needs to be slowing down at this time in her life. So, I've been thinking . . ."

I raised my glass of wine to my lips, knowing exactly what was coming. "Thinking? What about?"

"Well, we had a family meeting, and we thought you might come home for a while. To help out."

I knew it. "How long a while?"

"Oh, not too long, I'm sure. If you could come home for the summer, that should be fine."

I choked on a sharp gulp of wine. *"The summer?"*

"I'm sure I'll be up and around by August. September at the latest."

"The *whole* summer?" I glanced around the apartment, my mind whirling in a desperate search for reasons why I could not leave. My dissertation. My shot at getting the assistant professor position opening up next spring. My life . . .

My eyes grazed over the window, then zoomed back. A chunk of ice formed in my throat. I squinted at my reflection in the glass.

Epiphany.

"Oh my God," I said, and walked closer to the window, touching my face, straightening my glasses, running my hand over the bird's nest ponytail hanging off my head at a tilt.

"Portia?" I heard Mags's voice come through the line, tinged with concern. I walked over to the mirror by the front door and took a good look. Pale skin. Bags under the eyes. I practically had a neon sign over my head, flashing the same empty message over and over.

Alone.

I swallowed, and the ice shifted to the back of my neck. I blinked and looked around my apartment, seeing fresh the mass of empty junk-food wrappers and dirty coffee mugs. My chest tightened.

"Darlin'?" Mags's voice was muffled; I'd let the phone drop against my chest, where it vibrated to the beat of my frantic heart as the neon sign flashed in my imagination.

Alone. Afraid.

Oh my God, I thought. *I'm four cats and a* Reader's Digest *subscription away from being totally irredeemable.*

"Portia? You still there, baby?"

I shook my head, got control of my breathing. The ice receded. I pulled the phone up to my ear. "Yeah. I'm here."

"Oh, good," she said, apparently missing the panic in my voice. "I thought I'd lost you there for a minute. So, when can we expect you here? You know our busy season starts around mid-May . . ."

"Hold on for a minute, okay, Mags?" I put the phone to my chest again. I breathed deep, turning my back to the mirror, raising my eyes to the ceiling, which was the only place in my apartment showing no evidence of the fact that I'd driven my life into one hell of a ditch.

Use logic. Make a choice. Stay here and recite Austen movies with the actors and never write another word of your dissertation and morph insidiously into the Crazy Cat Lady in the attic apartment . . .

My heart started to pump erratically again. I took another deep breath.

. . . or, spend a summer in the clutches of the Mizzes. Lesser of two evils. Make a choice, Portia.

"Portia?"

"Just a minute, Mags." I grabbed a quarter off the floor and flipped it in the air. Heads—Syracuse. Tails—Truly.

I caught the quarter in the air and slapped it on the back of my hand. Tails.

Best two out of three.

"Portia? Honey?"

I flipped again, then sighed and tossed the quarter back on the floor. I rolled my head on my shoulders. My breathing stabilized. My heart fell into a reasonable rhythm. I squinted at the calendar.

"My last class is May nineteenth," I said, feeling the words stick in my throat as I croaked them out. "I can settle things here and be there by the twenty-second or so. Assuming I can find a sublettor. If I can't find a sublettor . . ."

Mags squealed and giggled. I'd have pictured her

jumping up and down if it weren't for the acute pain and torture in her back. "Oh, darlin', that's just perfect! I knew you'd come through for us. I just knew it!"

I grabbed a red marker, took the cap off with my teeth, and spit it onto the kitchen counter as I flipped up the pages to August. The panic subsided as resignation flowed in. "I'll have to be back by . . ." I ran a finger over the days. "August twenty-second."

I circled it in red, then put two stars on either side. August twenty-second. Three months. Twelve weeks. Was it really going to kill me?

Chances were fair to middlin' that it would. But the dismal state of my life had been recognized, and it had to be dealt with. Even though my response was to run far, far away, at least I was doing *something*. At least I wasn't floating around town with open cans of Fancy Feast, trolling for strays. That was good. Wasn't it?

I muddled through a few more niceties and finally shrugged Mags off the phone. I scuffed through the living room, reaching down to flick off the television set as I headed toward the closet, grabbing the last clean towel and revealing the remote, sitting there on the naked shelf.

I stared. All this time, it had been sitting there, waiting for me to hit rock bottom, to get to the place where I'd whittled the laundry down to the last pair of clean underwear, the last clean towel. I raised my fingers to its bumpy, worn surface, then rolled my eyes at myself as my vision started to blur under the tears.

Peter would not be coming back.

I tossed the stupid thing down the hallway, where it skidded to a stop on the living-room rug. I longed for a warm, furry kitten snuggling up against my ankles, justifying my existence by needing me. Maybe if I got just one, it would be okay. You have to have more than one to be the Crazy Cat Lady. I tossed the towel over my shoulder and decided to think about it on August 23.

I drove the fourteen hours home for two reasons. One, it allowed for the possibility of changing my mind and turning back, something that's much harder to do on a plane. Two, it gave me a fourteen-hour reprieve from my immersion into the collective bosom of my mother, aunt, and grandmother, known throughout Truly as the Miz Fallons. The nickname stems from the fact that our family has been suspiciously lacking Mr. Fallons. None of us has ever been married, and when we get knocked up, we have girls.

"Men just don't stick to Miz Fallons," Mags had often said throughout my childhood, as though it was simply a fact of life to be accepted and moved past, like having freckles or being color-blind. I hadn't accepted it as fact, but so far, I had to admit the phenomenon was consistent. I've termed it the Penis Teflon Effect. Patent pending.

When I pulled my rattling Mazda sedan past the town limits of Truly, Georgia, population 6,618, I had fourteen hours of self-talk under my belt. I would be gracious. I would be pleasant. I would ignore any quirks, insensitivities, and unintentional offenses. I would enjoy my time with the Mizzes. I might even wear makeup and dresses if it made them happy. After all, how much did it really matter? It was one summer, and I'd be going back to Syracuse at the end of it. I could be gracious for one summer.

I rolled down my window and drew in the clean air,

watching the sun set behind the purpling northwest Georgia mountains. I was overwhelmed by contentment, even a little nostalgia, as I traded Battlefield Parkway for Truly's Main Street. As I drove past, my eyes clung to the old-fashioned wooden sign that hung over the family bookstore, The Printed Page. I was surprised by the ache I felt, the longing to see once again the shelves of books and random knickknacks, drink the brew from our little coffee bar, inhale the musty wood and pulp.

"God," I said to myself as I waited at Truly's only stoplight and stared at the Page's storefront. "I had no idea how much I missed you."

"Why, Portia Fallon!"

I turned my head to see a large woman in a blue dress waving from the front stoop outside of Whitfield's Pharmacy. I fluttered my fingers at her and laughed.

"Hi, Marge!" I called through the open window, surprised at how quickly she'd recognized me. With the exception of the occasional low-profile holiday visit, I'd been gone twelve years. I didn't know whether to be glad or disturbed that I'd changed so little.

"Good to have you home, baby!" she called, as the light turned green and I moved on. It was a short six blocks from the center of town to our old two-story colonial, but I took it slow, remembering every oak tree I'd ever fallen out of, every friend's house I'd ever ducked behind to try on lipstick or smoke a cigarette. They were all there, every last one. How is it possible that a place could be exactly the same after twelve years? Had I been raised in Brigadoon and never even noticed?

By the time I pulled into our driveway, I was feeling pretty good. I chuckled to myself as I stepped out of the car, wondering what all my dread had been about. It was just Truly, and Truly wasn't so bad. It was a place where kids played safely in the streets and neighbors all knew each other, and there were definitely worse things than spending a summer drinking iced tea in pine-scented mountain breezes. The Mizzes would behave themselves, certainly. Hell, Mags would be in bed most of the time. Everything was going to be just fine.

Maybe even fun.

I popped my trunk open and looked up with a smile as I heard the creaky porch door swing open, followed by squeals of excitement.

I heard a pounding on the steps and looked up to see Mags bounding down the steps toward me like a Great Dane released from a small pen. My smile froze. She was all energy and verve, and there wasn't even the tiniest evidence of acute pain and torture on her face.

"Good to see you, Mags," I said, when she released me from her exuberant hug. "How's your back?"

She gave a dismissive wave as though there was a small fly rather than a huge deception between us. "Oh, my back's fine. That was just to get you here. And now you're here!"

Mags flashed her sparkling white smile at me, and her blue eyes shone under her perfectly lined lids. Not a hint of guilt or shame or anything that anyone with a moral center might show. Either she didn't think it was wrong, or she didn't think I'd be mad.

Or, and this was my vote, she just didn't think.

I pushed my indignant gaze up to the porch. My aunt Vera waved and held up a glass full of clear liquid and clinking ice cubes. I didn't have to taste it to know it was a gin and tonic, the signature drink of the Miz Fallons.

God bless Vera.

"Come on up, darlin'!" she called. "We're fixin' to celebrate!"

Mags easily lifted my heavy duffel bag out of the passenger seat of my car, and I felt my irritation flare up again.

"I don't know why you can't get some proper luggage, Portia. Something with corners, maybe. And wheels. You know they make 'em with wheels nowadays. Isn't that smart?"

I slung my laptop bag over my shoulder and snatched the duffel from her, slamming the car door shut and hearing a small, fading voice in my head calling, *Gracious!* as though from a great distance.

"Acute pain and torture," I said. "I seem to recall those exact words."

Mags sighed and turned to me, grabbing the duffel bag back. "Oh, baby, you're dwelling. It's not attractive. Now come see Vera and Bev; they've missed you so."

About the Author

Lani Diane Rich's first job was at the age of eleven, when she combined her love of books with an overdeveloped sense of ambition and volunteered at her local library. She has been writing stories and screenplays since she could pick up a pen, but never pursued writing because—well, really, who ever makes it as an author? She graduated from Syracuse University's Newhouse School in 1998 with a degree in television production, and has been, in no particular order, a pyrotechnician, a nanny, a convenience store clerk, a theater critic, and an associate producer of an Alaska newsmagazine. She wrote the original draft of her first novel, *Time Off for Good Behavior,* in twenty-five days while participating in National Novel Writing Month 2002 (www.nanowrimo.org) and decided on December 31 of that year to start dedicating herself to seriously pursuing her writing. Now she works in her pajamas, and she really, really likes it.

Visit her website at www.lanidianerich.com.

THE EDITOR'S DIARY

Dear Reader,

When desire flares up, who can help but succumb? Whether it's a sexy ex or a roguish stranger, life is full of delicious surprises in our two Warner Forever titles this June.

Who would ever have thought that a smelly, featherless and flightless parrot could be so valuable? Dana Wiley in Lani Diane Rich's MAYBE BABY certainly never did. But when her mother is held by kidnappers who are demanding it for ransom, Dana has to get her hands on that bird. The only problem: Nick Maybe, the man she left at the altar six years ago, is the only person who knows where the parrot is. With kissable lips and unforgettable eyes, Nick hasn't changed a bit. And Dana can't deny he's stirring up that old black magic. But as the bird is worth a cool quarter million, they aren't the only ones on the hunt. With two thieves on their tail, Dana can't help but think: could Nick be her hero...again? *New York Times* bestselling author Jennifer Crusie calls Ms. Rich "a great voice," so grab a copy and find out why.

New York Times bestselling author Lisa Jackson raves that Marliss Melton's first book is "filled with romance, suspense and characters that will pull you in and never let you go." Well, hold on tight because her latest book, IN THE DARK, is even better. DIA Agent Hannah Geary was wrongfully thrown in a Cuban prison and left for dead. Now she wants revenge. Not just for herself, but for her partner who was killed too. All of the evidence points to a rogue SEAL commander. But to catch a bad SEAL, she needs a good one. Lt. Luther Lindstrom needs Hannah's help too, but he's used to calling the shots. And the last thing he needs in his life is a sexy, strong willed woman. But as the danger mounts and Hannah and Luther are steps away from one of the FBI's most wanted criminals, Luther's defenses break down as his desire for Hannah grows. But will it be too late for them both?

To find out more about Warner Forever, these titles and the authors, visit us at www.warnerforever.com.

With warmest wishes,

Karen Kosztolnyik

Karen Kosztolnyik, Senior Editor

P.S. Get ready for a cold shower-next month's titles couldn't be hotter! Sue-Ellen Welfonder weaves the sensual tale of a betrothed knight who's tempted by a stunning and mysterious stranger who cannot remember her identity in ONLY FOR A KNIGHT; and Toni Blake delivers IN YOUR WILDEST DREAM, the irresistibly erotic story of a woman who must infiltrate the world of high-priced escorts to find her sister-and the sexy bartender who helped her.